THE DYERVILLE TALES

THE
DYERVILLE
TALES

M. P. KOZLOWSKY

Drawings by Brian Thompson

WALDEN POND PRESS
An Imprint of HarperCollinsPublishers

Walden Pond Press is an imprint of HarperCollins Publishers.
Walden Pond Press and the skipping stone logo are trademarks and registered
trademarks of Walden Media, LLC.

The Dyerville Tales
Text copyright © 2014 by M. P. Kozlowsky
Illustrations copyright © 2014 by Brian Thompson
All rights reserved. Printed in the United States of America.

Library of Congress Cataloging-in-Publication Data
Kozlowsky, M. P.
 The Dyerville tales / M. P. Kozlowsky ; illustrations by Brian Thompson. — First
edition.
  pages cm
 Summary: "A young orphan named Vince takes a journey to reunite with his
missing father and learn about his grandfather's mysterious, magical life"
— Provided by publisher.
 ISBN 978-0-06-199871-3 (hardback)
 [1. Supernatural—Fiction. 2. Magic—Fiction. 3. Books and reading—Fiction.
4. Family life—Fiction. 5. Blessing and cursing—Fiction.] I. Title.
PZ7.K8567Dye 2014   2013037286
[Fic]—dc23   CIP
                                                                              AC

Typography by Alison Klapthor
14 15 16 17 18 CG/RRDH 10 9 8 7 6 5 4 3 2 1

First Edition

For my grandfather
Mario V. Marone
1912–1994

CHAPTER 1

Some tales are worth telling. Of all the children living in the Obern House Orphanage, none knew this more than young Vincent Elgin, he of the fair skin and the sad eyes, the disheveled hair and the honest smile. The poor boy arrived at his new home knowing full well what could be found in a tale. He was sure of it, as sure as the sun's rise each morning, as definite as the delicate fall of leaves onto the crisp grass every autumn. In the lonely days of his life spent within these aged walls, of which the mice had uncontested rule, it was what kept him looking out the filthy attic window for hours at a time, day or night, out at the vast sprawl of colorful land stretching and sloping for miles on end, out at the distant houses and buildings and people populating almost every inch in sight, at the cars zooming by, tearing up asphalt and ripping through deep puddles reflecting the cloud-cluttered sky, at life in full swing under the steady and sweltering sun or the cool gaze of a pale moon. It was what kept him peering out past the rusting orphanage gates while the other children played in the yard behind him, the house up on its steep hill looming menacingly over them all. It was what kept his dreams from becoming nightmares. It was what kept the despair out.

The other children, who Vince believed should thrive on hope as well—in a place such as this, what else was there?—seemed to do anything but that. From day one, it appeared to him that they were content with where they were, with no real expectations of ever leaving the orphanage. Here dreams were like the dust on the floorboards; they went trampled and unnoticed. For most, this was their home, and there would never be another, so why hope otherwise? Instead, they orchestrated their games, completed their lessons, groaned through their chores, and ate their bland meals, all without ever gazing into the distance, as Vince always did. No, these children had given up long ago.

He found it all quite sad really. Didn't they want out? Didn't they want families of their own? Adventure, love, life? There had to be more than this. Then again, maybe that was because he was the only one who had ever known a life beyond the orphanage. Unlike the other children, he hadn't lived under its dilapidated and oppressive roof his whole life. He'd arrived later, just two years ago, when he was ten years old.

"Tell us again, Vince," the children would say each night just before bed, the second their newest "brother" slipped under his thin, moth-eaten covers. "Tell us how you got here."

And for the first six months or so of his stay, he would do just that. He would sit up in bed, scrunch the pillow behind him as a cushion against the metal headboard, clear his throat, and begin his tale for all the eager children in the room.

"It was a cold night. A very, very cold night." He always began in his best storytelling voice, which was rather hushed and enigmatic and also soothing; it had been his mother's bedside voice. "There was already a foot of snow on the ground with another foot yet to come. It was heavy snow, the kind you can't lift with a shovel without straining your back, but absolutely perfect for packing snowballs. I sat in the living room by the fire while my parents were talking in the kitchen; they had been conducting secret conversations for a while now, going back weeks, maybe months. They always kept it to a whisper, but I still tried to hear as much as possible. However, on this night more than ever, I was listening as hard as I could, blocking out everything else so that it was almost as if I were in the room with them. I knew something wasn't right. I could hear it in their voices.

"'We shouldn't have come here,' Mother said. Her panic was clear; it was in every word she spoke, tiny vibrations that buzzed my ears. 'We're putting him in danger. What kind of parents are we?' Meanwhile, all this time, I could hear Father pacing back and forth, back and forth, the wood creaking beneath his feet. He was a small man, but he had big footsteps. 'I need time,' he said somewhat desperately. 'I have to think. I'll figure this all out. Don't worry. I will never let you down.'"

This was actually how Vince remembered it, every action, every word. There wasn't a single truth he had to stretch. Of course it wasn't much of a tale yet either—the other children never really cared much for this part, not when they knew what came next—but he felt it needed to be said, for the impact of what followed as well as for selfish reasons: these were his final moments with them, the final moments before everything changed. It was the very last time he was part of a real family.

"I just sat there playing with the fire," Vince would go on, imitating his actions with the poker by thrusting his arm and waving his hand. He used only one hand while telling the tale because with the other he always kept his fingers crossed, as if this might change some aspect of the story. By crossing his fingers, he believed he had some kind of advantage, as if he could manipulate fate and change history, perhaps will something into being. It was like a wish or prayer. "I poked the logs over and over, watching the sparks fly and the wood crumble. Every now and then I threw another log in so that the flames wouldn't die. I crumpled newspaper just as my father had taught me and tossed that in too. I liked the way it burned; it seemed like those colors didn't belong—blues and greens. There is something mesmerizing about a fire." He usually paused here, his thoughts momentarily carrying him away until another child coughed or shifted in bed, causing the stiff mattress to creak. "Still"—he went on—"my parents continued to talk. It seemed like hours, their words growing louder and more desperate. 'I can't do this any longer. I'm taking him,' Mother finally said. 'Where? Where else can we go? We have no one,' Father pointed out. 'Vincent can stay with his grandfather.' For almost a full minute after this comment, no one spoke. Then, finally, Father said, 'I . . . it's been too long. You know that.'"

"Come on, get to the good part," the impatient children would interrupt. Usually it was Anthony, the only other boy his age, shy by seven months, and the closest thing Vince had to a best friend in this place. He was the chubby troublemaker of the Obern House, sneaking out of the room at night to steal some food or place some booby traps for the adults who worked there or rummage through their

5

belongings. The children in the orphanage loved him to pieces. Besides Vince's stories, Anthony's antics and humor were the only distractions in the house.

Still, the comment always bothered Vince. *The good part,* he thought. *They think it's the good part.*

Regardless, he went on.

"Mother and Father kept glancing out the windows, pulling the blinds and curtains aside, checking for something. It was nonstop throughout the night. They couldn't stop looking even though there was absolutely nothing in sight. Just snow, constant snow. Every now and then Father would freeze and bring his finger to his lips. 'Shhh. Do you hear something?' But we didn't. Not yet. What were we listening for? At one point Mother came over and sat beside me. She looked very sad. She put her arm around me and pulled me close. 'I love you,' she said, giving me a kiss atop my head. 'You have a long and great life ahead of you. There's nothing you can't do. I want you to know that. Never forget it.'"

Every time Vince got to this part he nearly cried. He could feel the lump in his throat growing by the second until it felt like a baseball with nowhere to roll. His eyes watered, his voice cracked as if his words were being sliced by the syllable, but still, he had to say it. He said it for them; he said it for himself. And when his father came over, it was even worse.

"Father picked me up and brought me to the window. I

remember his arm wrapped tightly around me. I was focused on his hand, the gold band glistening on his ring finger. I loved that ring. He told me he would one day give it to me like his father gave it to him. He caught me staring at it. 'I wore this ring a long time before I understood what it really meant. One day I just might explain it all to you, and when I'm done, it will be yours because you will be ready. You will understand.' He lifted my head with a finger beneath my chin. 'Look out there,' he said, guiding my eyes. I listened to him, looking out at the falling snow, how hard it came down, how fast. It seemed to freeze absolutely everything, even time. 'Out there is a world where anything's possible. Anything. If you think it, it can happen. There are places on this globe so amazing that the sun refuses to set. There are people who've seen things that no one else on earth has. There are worlds within worlds. I know this now. I just believed too late. Your grandfather—' He shook his head slowly, sadly. 'Don't be like me, Vincent. Don't ever let anybody tell you otherwise. Okay? Don't just see the world; see through it. That's where you'll find the answers.'" Vincent repeated this emphatically. He wanted the other children to believe this too. Deep down, he felt he was reaching them, just as his father had reached him on that sorrowful night.

"Then he sent me off to bed."

The children of the orphanage were waiting for this cue. They sat up, eyes wide. They knew what came next.

"I woke up when I heard the noise. *Whump, whump, whump.* It wasn't morning yet, far from it, but everything was so bright. I felt incredibly warm, as if the sun had fallen atop the house and rolled across the roof. What was going on? I jumped out of bed and ran out of the room. It was like running headfirst into a nightmare. Fire was every-where, climbing up the walls, stretching across the ceiling. Everything was crackling, collapsing. There was so much smoke, clouds and clouds of it. And still the noise. *Whump, whump, whump.* I couldn't move. I was trapped, once more mesmerized by the fire. But this one was different from the one I poked. This one raged. It carried fear with it, menace. The fire closed in. It was coming for me. Like it was alive and hungry. I should have done something, I should have been smarter, but I was so scared, so utterly scared I couldn't move. I felt the hairs on my body begin to singe. My eyes watered; my throat burned. I was sure I was going to die. Then, out of the flames, came Mother. I couldn't believe it. Her clothes, her hair were on fire. She was coughing horribly. But still, she grabbed me and shoved me out the bedroom window and into the snow. 'Run!' she screamed as she stumbled through the opening after me. 'Where's Dad?' I called, but again, she just told me to run. The snow was deep; I had trouble lifting my legs. Outside, the noise was even louder. *Whump, whump, whump.* What was it? Where was it coming from? Then I looked up and saw it."

This was what the children wanted. They didn't want reality, although reality was the foundation from which the tale grew. Indeed there was a fire to Vince's family's home. And indeed his mother, already badly burned, saved his life. But what he said next, he said because he knew it was what the children wanted. And in turn, that was what Vince wanted too. He wanted a reason to tell this story over and over again. All his hope depended on it.

"I looked up," Vince told the children, "I looked up, and I saw something unbelievable. I saw the most hideous thing I had ever seen. Flying through the air, just above my head and home, was a dragon. It was bloodred and had not one, not two, but seven fire-breathing heads."

"Wow!" one of the boys called out.

"Crazy!" said another.

Anthony jumped out of bed. "Awesome! So awesome!"

"Quiet," came a chorus.

"Its tail was longer than some streets, and it was spiked on the end. It thrashed wildly, like an unmanned fire hose, knocking down the thickest of trees with one swipe. As the dragon circled the house, I realized it was its wings that I heard, the constant beating of them. The span must have been a hundred feet long. Maybe more. Probably way more. I couldn't believe it. I stood there dumbstruck, the fire behind me forgotten. My mother crawled to me in the snow, her skin smoking. I thought she was going to make it. I could've sworn she would. 'Where's Dad?' I said again, almost in a trance. But there was no need, for at that moment I saw him. He was on the crumbling roof. He had a sword in his hand, its steel reflecting the flames. He was going to save us." Vince paused for effect, taking in the absolute silence of the room. "But then the dragon spotted him. Its yellow eyes grew wide. One of the heads opened its mouth, ready to breathe a fatal flame. Father didn't have much time. The mouth opened wider, then wider still. A light erupted from deep down its throat. It had to be now. In a flash, Father swung his weapon and sliced off its tongue. *Zwoom!*"

"*Eww!*" a child from the end of the room yelled.

"Nasty!"

Anthony, still out of bed, enraptured and clutching his blanket, again yelled, "Awesome!"

"He did this three more times before the dragon finally fled in pain. And as it did, Father looked back to me, nodded, and took off after the beast."

"Did he catch it?" Vince was always asked.

"I don't know. I never saw him again."

And this was true. In the hospital later that night Vince's mother passed away. She was one room over from him, and he could swear that when she died, he knew it, the exact moment, because it felt as if his own heart had stopped.

Vince's father, however, wasn't found. Vince never did see him emerge from the house, as he told in his tale, and the authorities never discovered a single trace of him in the ashes of their home. No bones, no teeth, not even the gold ring Vince had been promised. And for Vince, this changed everything. This was where he found his hope. This was where his tale grew.

But this next part he always kept private. Mostly because it remained fluid and elusive. As hard as he tried, he just couldn't find a way to make it stick. He knew his father had survived the fire; he just knew it: there was no other explanation. But where did he go? Why was he on the run? Why didn't he ever come back for him? Not even a card or letter. Did he know Mother died? Did he know Vince lived?

Because of these unknowns, the tale always veered wildly from here. He considered his father's being a government spy or a man wrongfully accused, impossible to open up any form of communication lest he be caught. Maybe he was taken hostage by some fanatical group. Or what if he witnessed a horrendous crime and had to go into hiding? It could be anything; why not a dragon? All that really mattered, all he really needed to believe, was that his father was still alive and that he would one day come for him.

"Wow, do you really think there are dragons?" a boy asked, falling back onto his pillow, a look of deep satisfaction on his face.

"Maybe in caves or volcanoes," someone answered.

"I bet there are. There has to be."

"Could you imagine? I'd try to keep one as a pet."

"Are you crazy?" Anthony said. "You can't do that. It'd swallow you whole. No chewing or anything. Just— gulp!—right down."

"Okay, okay, enough talk. We should get to bed," Vince told them.

"But wait, tell us another one."

They were always so eager to hear more. With each telling, the children seemed happier and happier. And Vince knew exactly why. They were taken away. Through his tales, they escaped, as if through a hatch. In those tantalizing minutes the orphanage was left far behind them. It made the tale worth telling. But as more time passed, wearing away at him and everything he hoped for, Vince wished someone would tell him a story, if only once, so that he too could get away.

"How about one of you?" he said hopefully. "Let's hear a tale from someone else for once."

But no one ever volunteered, and Vince knew it was because they had nothing from which to draw. This life was all they knew. And worst of all, because of it, they had nothing left to believe in.

"No one?" He looked around the room. "No one?"

They all shook their heads, eyes drifting anywhere but toward Vince.

"Anthony?"

He too looked away. "I can't tell stories, Vince. You know that."

Unfortunately, Vince did. "Well, like I said, it's late. Maybe I'll tell you another tomorrow."

CHAPTER 2

The screen door of the orphanage creaked closed, and the outdoor air was somewhat of a reprieve from the house's claustrophobic nature. Outside, the world opened up.

Beyond the orphanage gates, Vince could see the town spread out at the bottom of the hill, all the activities of daily life, all the possibility. Every day he didn't try to just see it all; he tried to see through it all, as his father had said to him. He tried to see all the hidden lives, all the secrets and adventures that everyone kept locked away. There were mysteries, he knew, around every corner, inside every glove box, or behind every closet and steering wheel. Out there beyond those gates something was waiting for him: the answers he so desperately needed.

Vince jumped down from the rotting front porch, clearing the three steps in a single bound. On most days, first thing in the morning, he chose to walk the grounds of the orphanage, Anthony usually tagging along, prattling away as if everything were fine and normal, like two kids trekking through their neighborhood on the way to the park.

". . . and I clogged all the sinks and the water was overflowing everywhere and everyone was going nuts trying to clean it up and they had no idea it was me and I was trying so hard not to laugh, Vince, but it was so hard. I almost peed. I'll admit that to you. I almost did."

Vince laughed where he was supposed to laugh, responded where a response was called for, but what he was really doing on these walks along the perimeter of the property was watching the men outside the gates—anyone in the street passing by or doing roadwork or sitting in an idling car. Without being obvious, he would steal glances at these men, looking for his father in their faces. If he could, he would try to see through their eyes and at the men within. He did this often, wherever he was, at times almost convincing himself that he finally spotted him. Like today. As Anthony informed him about his latest prank, Vince eyed a man descending from a telephone pole, a man who, from behind, looked like he could be a dead ringer for his father. Maybe his father was scoping out the orphanage, planning to bust Vince out. Maybe he was rigging the phone lines or the electricity in preparation for a break-in. Shaking with nerves, Vince followed the man along the gates of the property and back to his truck. He made sure to cough and hum for attention, a certain look, a knowing nod perhaps. Anything.

"You okay?" Anthony asked, patting his friend's back. "You getting sick?"

It was useless; the man outside the gates was utterly oblivious. Frustrated, Vince let out a tortured scream, a howl of great anguish that could shred the ears and chill the skin of anyone within two miles of the source. Finally, the utility worker turned around, taking notice. But sadly, there was no recognition behind the man's eyes, just confusion at the sight of a troubled boy.

This was how it always happened, and every time it felt as if a little piece of Vince's soul had escaped from his mouth, drifting away like a balloon in a breeze, never to return.

Still, for as long as he could remember, he never quit looking inside every car that passed the orphanage, staring at the drivers and passengers alike; every time the doorbell rang or the phone went off, it was Vince who answered; each delivery was closely monitored; the mailman was scrutinized. His tales told him his father was somewhere out there, and if he was, Vince was sure his father would be watching him. It was just a matter of time before he finally revealed himself.

But one could do this for only so long before despair sets in and takes over. The scream Vince screamed this day was one of deep disappointment and grief. He knew the man wasn't his father; he just needed to let something out. All the pain and sadness, all his uncertainty and fears, yes; but more important, he wanted to be rid of all the foolish hopes and dreams he had relied upon for so long. He wanted to be empty, completely drained, a boy who no longer believed his own tales anymore. His eleventh and twelfth birthdays came and went, and there he still was at the orphanage. No sign of Father, no word.

"I think maybe my father's really gone," he told Anthony as they walked back toward the orphanage. He looked up at the cracked walls of the Victorian house. "Maybe this is my home for good. No one is ever going to adopt me. It's like you said, nobody wants a full-grown boy." Saying these words aloud made it a sort of reality. Vince made a vow to himself right then and there. He would stop searching for his father in the faces of strangers; he would leave the door and phone unanswered, the attic window abandoned. There was nothing to see through; the world was what it was and nothing more. He believed he no longer had any right to hold out hope. He had become like the rest of them.

"Don't listen to me. I just say things sometimes. Half

the time I don't even know what comes out of my mouth."

"No, it's true. I need to wake up, Anthony. I need to stop fooling myself."

"Sometimes, if you fool yourself about something long enough, you start to believe it, and if you believe it long enough, sometimes it comes true. Like some kind of circle or something."

"Yeah, well, I've been doing that a long time, and not a thing has changed. Here I still am in this orphanage, my dad somewhere out there, my mom . . . No. I'm done. That's it. I can't do this the rest of my life. I can't." He glanced back at the utility worker loading up his truck. How had he believed it might be his father for even a second? There was nothing even remotely similar between the two men. It was a crushing blow. It always was. Every time he searched for his father and didn't find him, the pain was far too great, a giant chip out of his heart. He refused to do that to himself anymore. He had to preserve whatever was left. He said it again: "I'm done." Then he said it again and again and again: "I'm done. I'm done. I'm done."

That night, when the children asked for one of his tales, Vince said he would no longer tell them. They begged, but he couldn't bring himself to ever cross his fingers again and tell his stories as he had done last night and every night before. Over the next few weeks, the children continued to plead for the tales, and at first, Vince broke them up into pieces, warping the plots, treating each story recklessly until they amounted to nothing but empty words. They became worse and worse with each telling, shorter and shorter, without any flair for the dramatic, and eventually the children stopped asking for them and Vince truly had trouble even remembering them. When it came time to sleep, everyone went to bed silently, his thoughts barren of hope.

It was a Monday, the weather a bit brisker, and Vince and Anthony walked the grounds again, Vince with his head down the whole time. He didn't want to look at anyone or anything, not the men changing a flat tire on the side of the road, not the man Rollerblading by, not the mailman walking up the drive. What was the point?

They passed an old man on a ladder, painting the house. He went by M. Nobody knew what the initial stood for, and every time someone inquired, a different name was given. The story was that M was once an orphan here like all the rest and that he never left. He just grew up and got his own room, staying on as a sort of handyman. He did everything from taking out the trash to plumbing to carpentry to gardening. A fixture of the house, he was aware of everything within its walls; the two would forever be connected.

Seeing M always bothered Vince. He wondered if he would share a similar fate, losing everything in the process, even his name. Anthony, however, reacted in a different manner—he had pronounced M his archnemesis—but Vince wondered if it was for the same reasons. Seeing M now, Anthony jutted Vince in the side with his elbow. "Check this out.

"Earthquake," he screamed, shaking the handyman's ladder. "Don't fall!"

"Anthony!" M yelled in a strange accent nobody could ever place, holding on for dear life. "You quit it! I've had enough of you! I mean it!"

Anthony was bowled over in hysterics, but Vince continued walking on with his head down.

"What's with you?" Anthony asked, catching up to him, wiping away tears of laughter. "You didn't think that was funny?"

Vince spun around, his face full of frustration. "When are you going to stop joking around all the time? Don't you see where you are? We've been abandoned. Nobody wants us. What's so funny about that?"

"You weren't abandoned, Vince. Like in your story, you said your father—"

"It's a tale, Anthony. A made-up story. I have no one. You understand? No one! Get that through your head!"

"Vincent! Vincent, come here!" A voice from the house.

"Mrs. West. Shoot," Anthony said, spotting the woman who ran the orphanage standing at the front door, glaring in their direction. "Don't worry. Whatever it is, tell her it was me, Vince. I'll take the blame."

Upset with himself for blowing up at his friend, Vince looked at him fondly. Finally he smiled. "It probably *was* you."

"Get in here, Vincent," Mrs. West said. "I have something for you." In her hand she held up a package.

Vince hesitated, unsure if his eyes were deceiving him. A package? That couldn't be right. It had to be a mistake. Was it? Could it be . . . The closer he came to the package, the more his heart began to race, and he immediately regretted the feeling. *Don't get your hopes up*, he told himself. *Don't be a fool.*

But when one wants something so very desperately, when one has wished for so very long that those dreams could still be heard somewhere out in the ether, floating on wisps of wind or in the vacuum of space, hope can never be suppressed for good. It can always be found; it can always be renewed. And it turned out Vince's hope came in the form of a letter, the only one he ever received at the Obern House Orphanage.

Once they reached her private office, Mrs. West slapped the package down on her desk, across from Vince. It landed with a thud, fluttering some loose papers that were strewn about. "You forgot to shut the door behind you," she said.

"Sorry, Mrs. West." Vince jumped up and closed the

door and promptly returned to his seat.

Mrs. West was a very thin, very fragile woman, but the tone of her voice alone managed to put in line the children of the orphanage, even Anthony, in a matter of seconds. This valuable tool of the trade was usually preceded by a death stare no one ever hoped to see twice. She had a difficult time warming up to anyone, including Vince.

At her desk, she adjusted her glasses. "The return address is a very small town many hours north from here. The middle of nowhere. I never even heard of the place before today. Dyerville. Does it mean anything to you?"

Vince raced through his memories, searching for something, anything, that might link him to this town. He tried to pull clues from every corner of his brain, but nothing came. Then a tiny spark.

"I—I think my grandfather was born there."

"It was sent from a nursing home. I did the research, checked your files." She pulled Vince's file from a drawer and plopped it down on the desk. It was thicker than any of the other orphans' that Vince could see from the drawer, and he wondered what exactly was written in there. "I didn't know your grandfather was still alive when you came here. That or I had forgotten. I suppose you didn't go to live under his care because he couldn't care for himself. It seems he began experiencing the symptoms of senility sometime ago, is that right?"

Vince nodded. "I think so. I—I don't remember much about him. But I do remember everyone said he was crazy. Especially my dad. I remember he really got fed up with him and told him he wasn't allowed to visit anymore."

"His own father." She said this with a disapproving scowl. Then again, she always scowled.

"Yes, ma'am. I remember feeling sad about that because even if there was a screw or two loose, I loved him. He babysat for me since I was little. He was fun to be around." Nostalgic, Vince smiled. "He would sing to me in foreign languages, chase me through the apple orchards near the house, teach me games that no one else had ever heard of. He was always correcting people about his age. He'd say, 'I'm not ninety-eight. I'm one hundred and ninety-eight.' He'd say it in this really shaggy, time-worn voice too. And there was this big scar on his face, as if a giant chunk of his cheek had been carved out long ago. No one knew for sure how he got it, and everyone shared their hunches, but my grandfather always denied them all. Then he would tell us how it happened, the scar, and the story always changed. And not slightly either. They were completely different and preposterous scenarios. Every time."

"So, he was losing his mind."

"I guess. I mean, most of what he said didn't make much sense, and my parents didn't really give what he said much consideration." It got worse as time went on too, he remembered. Almost every utterance was part of some mad rambling or strange tangent. There was a phrase he always shouted: "Umbia Rah." Every time he saw Vince, it was, "Umbia Rah! Umbia Rah! Umbia Rah!" And he'd raise his arms like a ghost or zombie. Just a whole lot of nonsense. Vince was surprised at how much he actually did remember, but he felt there was more, so much more and that every crazy thing his grandfather said actually made some sense somewhere in this world. And that made him want to find out even more.

"You were named after him. Is that right?"

Vince nodded. "My parents said I looked just like him too. Almost identical. I don't know. I didn't see it."

"Well, this is for you." She slid the package across her desk.

Vince just stared at it, too frightened to pick it up. It was a severely weather-beaten envelope. It was dirty, ripped, discolored; the edges were battered. It looked like it had traveled years to find him, traveling across distant lands, but according to the postmark date, it had been sent only a few days earlier.

He just continued to stare.

"Well," Mrs. West said, "open it up."

As he placed his hands on the package, Vince's mind began to race. There was nothing he could do to fight it. Maybe his grandfather had gotten better. Maybe he wanted to reunite, to take Vince from this place for good. It was possible, wasn't it? But the best suspicion of all was, maybe his grandfather knew where Vince's father was and inside this package was how to find him. A sort of treasure map perhaps.

Excitedly, Vince ripped the package open. Inside, folded very carefully, was a letter, a single page. It was frayed as well, just like the envelope, except not as harshly. The paper was thick with a texture almost like skin, with grooves and indentations throughout. It was like nothing he had ever seen. And the writing, the writing was in script, but it was a perfect script, fanciful and from another place and time. Trembling, and with his mind already racing, he began to read the letter aloud.

Dear Master Elgin,

I regret to inform you that your grandfather, Vincent Michael Elgin, has passed away. His funeral will be in a week's time, Saturday the 28th at noon, here in Dyerville, and it is hoped that you will attend. Enclosed you will find a book, his only true possession, the only one of any real value to him. He emphatically informed me that upon his death it be sent directly to you. This is your grandfather's story, young Vincent. I had the pleasure of sitting

*down with him every day, listening to his tales,
writing them down for you. I did not question
him. I did not interrupt or interfere in any way.
I did not ask why he spoke of himself in the
third person or why he waited so long to reveal
all this. Your grandfather simply told me his
life story, and I listened. And what a story it
is. I hope you find some comfort in it. Perhaps
you can see through this world of tales and
straight to the heart of the man who told them.*

    My sincerest apologies,

    Andrew J. Ennis

He was dead? Vince didn't know what to feel. Should he be crying? He couldn't even remember the last time he had seen his grandfather.

He glanced down at the book. It was leather bound, old. Inside were pages without lines and the same beautiful script as was in the accompanying letter. There was no title on the cover, but on the first page it read: *The Dyerville Tales: A History of Vincent Elgin.*

"These tales," Mrs. West said, "do they mean anything to you?"

"I—I don't know. I remember him telling me stories, stories from when he was a young boy, but I don't quite remember the stories themselves. Is that weird? I remember my father getting angry at him, yelling about filling my head with nonsense. That's when he started telling me my grandfather was losing his mind, to ignore everything he said. I guess that makes sense, you know, when someone nears one hundred."

Mrs. West grew wildly uncomfortable in her plush chair. Irritated, she kept shifting and fidgeting. She grabbed at her throat, trying to massage the words free. "It is quite difficult to lose someone, even if you didn't know them very well—"

Here she went on and on in a very cold and detached manner, like a textbook come to life, speaking to him of all the difficulties of the world, teaching Vince about loss and sadness and grief, all of which he was much too aware of, and so instead, his mind wandered off to where he needed it to go: the letter. Something about it, some small detail that he couldn't put his finger on, struck him. What was it? He reread it once, and then again.

"—it breaks the heart a million times over. If you want to cry, cry. But try not to let the other children—" Mrs. West stopped herself, looking closely at Vince's perplexed face as he scanned the letter. "Now, I know you'll want to be there at the funeral, but . . . you must understand . . . we don't have the means to get you there."

"Wait, what? Are you saying I can't go?"

"Vincent, I . . . you . . . I didn't think—"

"What?" he snapped. "Mrs. West, you didn't think what?"

Mrs. West looked as if she had been punched in the face. She shifted in her chair again. "Vincent, I'm sorry. Like I said, we don't have the means to get you there. It's a long ways away, and we don't have an extra car with which to take you. And even if we did, we don't have anyone who can spare a few days escorting you to and fro, and we certainly can't let you go unsupervised. I'm sorry, but you'll have to grieve your grandfather from here."

Vince's head dropped, and he stared down into his lap, the details of the letter momentarily forgotten. All he could think of was his grandfather and how he was gone. Of course he wanted to be at the funeral. It was the least he could do. He wished he could have seen him one more time; after all, he was family, the last family he had. And now he was being told that he couldn't go? It was beyond unfair.

Mrs. West went rambling on again, pointing out all her responsibilities and repeating her long and ever-growing list of reasons why Vince would not be able to travel to Dyerville in time for the funeral. But through all this, something hit him, and it hit him hard, like a comet to the chest, his body disintegrating into a million pieces and then suddenly being pulled back together again by a force stronger than gravity. His father, he realized. There

28

was that line in the letter, the line about seeing through the world of tales. That was the detail that had sent his mind reeling. How had he missed it? Surely this was a message from his father. In fact, this Andrew person probably *was* his father. Vince glanced down at the letter again. He couldn't believe it. Andrew J. Ennis—AJE, the same initials as his father's. Now his mind really began to roll. His father must have been there in Dyerville those last days. How could he not? Like Vince, he was an only son. Wherever he was, whatever he was doing, he had to have heard about his father's impending death. Vince's heart skipped a beat; it leaped right over it. *A letter must have found him,* he thought, *just as his found me. A carrier pigeon dropped it into his hands in the middle of a dense rain forest somewhere in Southeast Asia. After fighting off giant snakes and frenzied panthers and raging apes, he opened it, read it, and immediately began hacking his way out of the jungle. Although he was tired, weak, sickly, there was no way he wouldn't be there. He would make it to Dyerville no matter what.*

And like that, Vincent had a new tale. And renewed hope. "No. No, you don't understand," he said, interrupting Mrs. West yet again. "I have to go. I have to. My father . . . he'll be there. He'll be there, and once he sees me, he'll want me back, and then I can stay with him for good. I won't have to come back here. It'll be one less kid you have to care for. I don't need an escort, Mrs. West. I can manage on my own. Please."

"Vincent, I can't. I'm sorry. You are a child of the state. And that makes you my responsibility. I can't allow it. I'm sorry."

"Please . . ."

She nodded toward the book he held so tightly in his hands. "You want to see your family? You will find them in there." Then she got up and stiffly exited the room.

Vince's head dropped into his hands. Tears began to fall between his fingers, splashing upon the leather of the book. The pain was almost unbearable. This couldn't be happening. He pulled his grandfather's tales close to his chest, stood, and headed upstairs.

Anthony kept checking on him, trying to comfort his friend, although it was clearly no use. "I was outside, at the window. I had to know if the hammer was going to come down on me. Vince, I heard everything. I'm so sorry, man. Anything you need. Anything."

But what Vince needed Anthony could never give him. He needed to get out of this orphanage. He needed to get to his grandfather's funeral. He needed to find his father.

Vince remained in his bed all day, crying, inconsolable.

Then, at night, as was the ritual, the children asked Vince for a story. He tried to ignore them, he tried to keep quiet, but they kept asking over and over.

"I don't have any stories," he said, finally snapping. "You keep asking. Night after night after night! I don't have any stories anymore. Do you understand? None! They're stupid! Grow up! All of you!"

Then he turned over in bed, pulling the covers over his tear-streaked face. He could hear the other children, the younger ones beginning to cry too. Their pain hurt him. He knew how they felt, but there was nothing he could do to help them. All he could offer were some stories he didn't believe in anymore.

The blanket dropped from his face, and Vince opened his eyes. He saw his grandfather's book sitting on his night-stand, illuminated by the moonlight. He reached out and grabbed it. Then he turned over to face the other children.

Sitting up, opening the book, he said, "Maybe I do have a tale to tell."

The Curse

Vincent Elgin was born on the side of the road, in the middle of nowhere, two months too early. His mother, Anna, empty basket cradled in one arm, was on her way into town to buy some food—fruit, vegetables, meat from the butcher, and other assorted goods—which was part of her weekly routine. It was a long walk, several miles on a dirt road, nothing on either side but deep and dark woods, but she thought such exercise was good for the baby. She had done it for months now. In all this time, she never expected he would want to arrive so soon.

Almost halfway into her walk, with the excruciating heat of the sun shining directly on her head, she felt a bolt of pain streak through her swollen body. She collapsed straight to the ground, scraping her hands and knees on the rock-strewn earth. She knew something was wrong. Deeply and horribly wrong. She waited for a short while, hoping and praying the pain would cease, but it only intensified, and rapidly. Anna screamed out. But no one heard her cries.

The minutes dragged on, as such minutes do. The sun continued to pound relentlessly, not a cloud in sight, not a stretch of shade in which to hide. Anna was trying to control her breathing. Inhale, exhale. Inhale, exhale. In and out. Her face was flushed, dust and dirt clinging to her teeth. She was drenched in sweat. She felt feverish, sick. If she didn't get help soon, she knew it was likely that neither she nor her unborn child would survive. And so she called out again. Still nothing. She looked down the road in one direction, then the other. Not a thing in sight. It was always deserted, she remembered.

On either side of the road the woods were silent. Nothing beyond them for miles. She looked deep into the treacherous wilderness and cried, "Please, somebody! I need help!" She screamed until her throat was hoarse.

Finally Anna's head dropped in desperation. She closed her eyes and clutched at the earth, dirt lodging under her fingernails. "Please," she whispered. "I'll do anything. Just save my baby. Save my baby."

An abrupt noise erupted from within the woods, slicing

through the silence: a high-pitched squawk that echoed several times before fading.

Anna's head shot up. She had never heard such a sound before. She peered back into the woods, focusing on a thick and twisted tree stump about thirty feet into the forest. She believed the sound might have come from this area. She cast her eyes about the forest, and when she looked back toward the tree stump, she saw something sitting upon it.

No, not something. Someone.

Could it be? Anna wiped at her eyes, a mix of sweat and tears and dust. Yes, someone was there all right, someone just as gnarled as the dead tree was: an old woman dressed in rags, hunched over, leaning on a staff of wood.

Without further hesitation, Anna cried out to her, "Help me! Please!" The pain increased with each scream, and she clenched her teeth and closed her eyes again. In the darkness behind them, she felt as if she could see her pain take shape in odd forms of light. It was as if the sun were peeking through. Seconds later, when she opened her eyes again, the old woman was beside her. Anna wondered, only briefly, how she could have traversed the distance so quickly, before her body was racked with another bout of pain.

"Please, you've got to help me," she begged the old woman, "the baby's coming now!"

"The pain, it overwhelms you, yes?"

"Yes!" Anna screamed through gritted teeth. "Help me!"

The old woman hobbled closer. "All in due time. All in due time. I've been waiting for you. I've known this day would come for almost my entire life. Now, here we are."

Anna gazed up at her, getting a good look for the first time. The old woman was hunchbacked so devastatingly that her chest was nearly parallel to the ground; the bump on her back matched that of Anna's stomach. All her weight fell on her warped staff, an extra limb. Long, ratty gray hair was hanging from outside her tattered hood. It framed a hideous face, excessively wrinkled and laden with open sores. She was missing teeth while the rest were browned and crooked; her nose was so long it nearly sloped down past her mouth, sealing it closed. One eye was bigger than the other, and neither was the same color.

"What? What are you talking about?" Anna said. "Just help me. You've got to help me. The baby is coming!"

"I'm sorry. The child will not make it, dearie."

"What do you mean?" Anna cried.

"He won't survive, and neither will you." With this the old woman howled with laughter. It was a disturbing, chaotic cackle.

Anna's eyes widened with fear; the woman was insane. "Help!" she screamed into the dead air. "Help!"

"No one will hear you," the old woman said calmly. "No one will help. There is only me."

"What do you want from me?"

"There is always something, isn't there? Always . . . an exchange."

"Exchange? What do you want, you hag? I have nothing to give you."

The old woman cackled again, her body pulsing with pleasure. "Is it not clear? I want the child."

"Get away. You're mad."

"Perhaps slightly"—but here she didn't laugh. Instead, she watched as a snake slithered their way. Slowly she raised her staff a few inches in the air. Then, like lightning, she dropped it, crushing the serpent's head. She twisted her staff back and forth, grinding the snake into the ground as its tail twitched. Ever so casually, she turned back to Anna. "You may raise him, of course. I'll allow you that much. He's yours until he reaches the age of twelve. Then he belongs to me."

She kept calling the baby a he. How did she know? She couldn't possibly. But suddenly it was as if Anna knew as well. It was a boy growing inside her. "Be gone! You can't have him."

"If you don't agree, no one will have him. And you will be no one's mother, no one's wife, no one's daughter."

"I don't believe you." But her voice wavered. The old woman smiled a broken grin, and Anna was crushed with tremendous pain.

"Believe your pain, my dear Anna. Believe that. It doesn't lie."

"How do you—" The pain overwhelmed her. She doubled over. "Ahhhh!"

"Just give me your word, and all will be well," the old woman shouted over the cries. "Agree that the boy is mine."

"I can't!" Anna wailed.

More pain. Unbelievable pain. There wasn't much time left.

"Do it! Agree!"

"He's my baby, he's my baby," she sobbed.

Anna couldn't see anymore. Her vision was blocked out with a white light. She felt like she was on both a pyre and a block of ice.

"Last chance, Anna! Agree, and you both will be saved!"

Death was so near, just above her; she could feel it hovering. It came for her and her son. In a moment it would reach out for her.

Anna screamed. "I agree! I agree! Help us!"

"Say the words! Say, 'At twelve years of age my son is yours.' Say it!"

Anna could hardly speak. "At twelve . . . at twelve years of age . . . my . . . my son . . . my son is . . . yours."

The old woman's hand sprang forward and grasped at the air, as if she were snatching the words right out of it. Then she slammed her hand to her mouth and swallowed. With yet another cackle, she dropped her staff and knelt beside Anna. She placed her hands on the distended stomach. The pain ceased immediately.

"You did a wise thing. This boy shall live," the old woman said. "You both shall live."

Anna cried. For which reason she did not know.

Minutes later Vincent was delivered. A healthy baby boy. Anna, cradling him in her arms, looked up at the hideous old woman. She wasn't sure if she should thank her or not.

"There is but one more thing to do," the old woman said.

"And what is that?"

The old woman reached out her hand. Her fingers were closed in a fist, all except a lone crooked thumb with a long, jagged nail. She brought it toward the baby.

Anna quickly pulled Vincent away. "What are you doing?"

"A deal's a deal."

Suddenly Anna found that she couldn't move. The old woman's thumb came closer. Closer. Soon the thumb was an inch away from Vincent's face. The old woman pressed her thumb against his cheek, and the skin sizzled. Vincent cried out in pain. When she pulled her thumb away, his cheek was blazing red, and in the center of it was a large wound. And that was how Vincent came to bear the scar he was to carry for the rest of his life.

"What did you do?" Anna squealed, suddenly free to move again. "What did you do to him?"

"The mark has been made. The pact has been sealed. I will see you both again on his twelfth birthday."

There were sounds coming from up the road. Anna turned to look. It was a carriage pulled by horses.

"Here!" she screamed. "Over here!"

When she turned back, the old woman was gone. Anna looked toward the woods, toward the stump, but saw no sign of her. Nor would she for a dozen years.

CHAPTER 3

"Wait, why'd you stop?" one of the children asked.

Vince had closed the book. He now held it in his slightly shaking hands, silently staring at the cover long enough for it to blur, as most of the other children chimed in with similar queries to the first's.

Why had he stopped? He wasn't exactly sure. The story had made him feel uneasy; that much he knew. The part about the curse especially: that hit too close to home. Maybe his grandfather truly was cursed, he began to wonder, and maybe that curse was passed down to Vince's father and from Vince's father finally down to him. Cursed. It certainly felt that way.

"That's it for tonight," he said, tossing the book back onto the nightstand.

The children moaned and complained, but it was clear that they were happy to have their storyteller back.

A few minutes later, when most of the children were beginning to drift off and thunderclaps boomed just overhead, Anthony walked over and sat at the end of Vince's bed. "That's how your grandfather was born? The one who just died?"

"It's not real, Anthony."

"How do you know it's not real? You don't know. You said you barely knew him."

"A witch? Curses? Come on. You believe in curses? You believe in any of these stories?" Even as he said it, though, there was a certain fear beginning to overwhelm Vince's consciousness, a paralyzing fear that he would never be able to shake this single thought from his mind: he was cursed.

Anthony thought about this and shrugged his round shoulders. "Why not?"

It wasn't the answer Vince wanted to hear, and so he turned away and faced the wall.

"Vince," Anthony said, with all seriousness, "you really think your father will be there?"

Still facing the wall, Vince shrugged his shoulders. "I don't know."

"Tell me a story about him. A real story. Nothing made up, no fantasy, no dragons. Tell me a story about your father."

Vince turned around and moved closer to his friend. "He was always busy, my dad, traveling a lot for work and everything. He kept jumping from one company to another. He said he was helping them learn to walk again, like they were hurt or something. I didn't really get it. All he said was that people make mistakes and he tried to correct them so their lives could get better. So one day, when he was leaving again for who knew how many days, I stopped him at the door and said, 'Well, what about the mistake you're making right now?' I told him he should be home with me and Mom. I said we were the ones hurting. I saw the look on his face. He was stunned. Pained. He dropped his suitcases at his side and sat with me on the couch. 'I am trying to help you,' he said. 'Why do you think I'm doing all this? You think I like leaving you guys? It kills me. It tears me apart. But I want you to have everything I never had growing up. I want you in good clothes and in good schools. I don't want you to ever worry about where your next meal is coming from or if they're going to turn the power off on us. I don't ever want you to suffer like I did.' I told him I didn't want him to leave, but he said he had to. I begged; I cried. He told me he would be letting a lot of people down if he stayed; some might even get angry. And with everything he said, I just turned it around on him. I said he'd be letting me down. I was getting really upset now, and whenever I did that, I used to slip his ring off his finger and play with it. I tried to slip it on each of my fingers, but it would always slide off, even on my thumb. I think I just wanted it so bad because if he did have to leave all the time, at least I would have a part of him with me, and I think, watching me, he knew that too. 'You know what we're going to do?' he finally said, pulling me close. 'We're going to spend the entire weekend outdoors, and we're going to finish that tree house we started. We're not coming in until it's done. I'm serious.' 'What about your job?' I said. 'So they get mad. What can I do? You're my boy. You're my reason for living. I want you to know this, to remember it: there's no trip, no matter how far, that can keep me from you. The next time you tell me you need me here, I don't care if I'm halfway around the world, I'll walk to you if I have to. I'll fight through anything to get to you.'"

"Vince, you need to go to that funeral."

Vince shook his head and sighed. "It's impossible. I'm not allowed. I'm never getting out of here. Not now, not ever. I'm going to be the next M, just you watch. I'll take over when he's gone."

"No way, man. Not you. Listen to me," Anthony said,

licking his lips. "I know I'm not the brightest, but I can get us out of here. I've been dreaming of busting loose for years. I think we can do it."

"You would," Vince said with a roll of his eyes.

"I'm serious. One hundred percent."

Vince stared long and hard at his friend. Anthony really was serious; it wasn't just another prank. It was written all across his face and deep within his eyes. "There's a guard at the gate."

"So what? It's not like he's armed or anything. He's just there to let visitors in and out. Forget the guard."

"Forget the guard? There's no other way out."

"You're leaving tomorrow, and that's the end of it. All you have to do is pack a little bag and sleep in your clothes. Leave everything else to me."

Anthony was probably being ridiculous; most likely it was just another one of his hare-brained schemes. But even so, Vince got dressed and packed a bag, just in case. It was important for him to pack clothes that were somewhat formal, an outfit that would be appropriate and respectful for a funeral and something his father would be proud to see him in. Unfortunately, he didn't own much that fell in that category, and so he had to put something together by waking up a few of the other boys in the house and asking them to borrow some pieces that might fit. The result wouldn't be what he hoped for, but it would have to do.

The outfit was all he packed. That and his grandfather's book.

It took hours for Vince to finally fall asleep, and it wasn't because he was wearing jeans and a sweatshirt or because the rain battered the roof like an army of wraiths. It was because his mind wouldn't rest. His thoughts went from the curse to his father to fairy tales to escape to the funeral and back again. When he finally did drift off, it was a restless sleep filled with troubled dreams and wild images and repressed fears.

He was asleep just short of two hours when Anthony woke him up. It was still early, still way before anyone else was awake, the sun just about to rise and cut through the darkness like a stained guillotine.

"Are you ready?" Anthony asked.

He was.

"Good. Take this." Anthony handed him a piece of paper he had folded up. "I had to sneak into Mrs. West's office to print it up. It's directions. Dyerville is pretty far. Once you're out of here, you're going to have to get to the train station. Then it's a straight shot all the way up. When you reach your stop, it's just a mile or two. Vince, you can totally do this."

Vince took the paper and shoved it in his back pocket. "Thanks."

"Don't mention it. Now, let's go," Anthony said.

They walked through the silent house, Vince wearing his backpack, Anthony carrying a lock and chain over his shoulder. Vince wanted to ask his friend about it, as well as a dozen other things, but he decided it would be best not to speak until they got outside.

They opened the front door as quietly as possible and stepped out onto the damp lawn, the temperatures near freezing and the skies overhead threatening a storm.

"There's the guard," Vince said, looking down the driveway, past the gate and inside the phone booth type of box. "He's not going to open it for us. No way."

"I know. You're going to have to scale it while I distract him. Hop over and start running."

"Me? What about you? Aren't you coming?"

Anthony looked away, kicking at the dirt. "Nah. I'll get out another day. Besides, where am I gonna go?"

A voice came from high above them. "You shouldn't discuss your plans so loudly. Don't you know anything about secrecy?"

Startled, the two boys turned around. On their way out of the house they had failed to see M up on the ladder, and now it seemed their plan had been blown. The old man stepped down and stood before the two boys. He had gray hair parted neatly to one side and a trim matching mustache along with day-old stubble that looked so sharp it could

47

grate cheese. His blue eyes ran deep, as did the lines on his weathered face. Although he had never left the orphanage all his life, his shoes looked as if they had walked a million miles. The old man, short and lean, held a cap in his slightly quivering hands, dangling it gently before him.

"I heard you last night, and I heard you just now. These walls are thin. Like sheets of ghosts. The wind blows straight through them."

"What are you talking about, old man? What plans? You're losing it," Anthony said, failing to convince anyone.

"I hear everything. I know everything. Haven't you learned that by now? Escape. *Humph*. Let's say you make it out of here," M said, turning to Vince. "How are you going to make it to the train? You're going to walk? That's pretty far. People will be looking for you soon enough. You'll be scooped up in no time. And what about money? Even if you do make it to the train, they won't let you ride for free. Have you not considered this? Either of you?"

Vince looked to Anthony. "He's right. We don't know what the heck we're doing."

Anthony slapped his hand against his head. "I—I didn't think that far. . . . I—I thought . . . Ah, what am I doing? I have a stupid brain."

M placed a hand on each boy's shoulder. "You are dreamers, and dreams are just wishes without a plan. Anyone can dream, but the ones who achieve theirs don't just wish it.

48

They don't just rely on luck."

"We're trying," Vince said. "It's not easy." He was angry with himself again. Angry for believing that he might escape, that he might actually find his father. He was angry for dreaming. He turned to his friend. "Anthony, thank you for trying, but I don't think we have this figured out."

M waved a finger at him. "Ah, ah, ah. Don't quit now; you're just gaining momentum. You can get out of here. Passion will carry you that far. As for the next part . . ." M pulled something from his back pocket and placed it in Vince's hand. It was one hundred dollars. "For the train. And whatever else might pop up."

Vince looked up at him, disbelief shadowing his face.

"Don't ask. Don't say thank you. You have five minutes before Mrs. West is awake and patrolling the grounds. Get moving."

Anthony grabbed Vince's arm and pulled him down the driveway. "Vince, he's right. Let's go."

Vince had to be dragged. He couldn't take his eyes off M. "Thank you," he said.

"If you want to thank me, Vincent, get to where you need to go. Find your father."

Vince nodded, and M called out again: "And don't think this means I'm done with you, Anthony!"

Anthony, grinning like mad, didn't turn around. "You're my archnemesis, M. I would expect no less!"

They reached the bottom of the driveway. On the other side of the gate the guard sat within his glass partition, reading a magazine.

Vince stared up at the gate. It was massive. It looked like a giant mouth, all teeth, black and rotten. A mouth that wished to do nothing more than swallow him whole. He had no idea how he would climb such a thing, and, if he did, what would be awaiting him on the other side.

Anthony turned to Vince. "Are you ready?"

"Anthony, thank you. You didn't have to do this."

"I know . . . I . . . Look, I know that you don't like telling your tales anymore, but you know, I've memorized all of them. If you don't mind, I can—I can tell your stories while you're gone."

"They're not my stories," Vince said, smiling. "They're everyone's."

Anthony nodded, swallowing hard. "Okay. Okay then. Here we go." He handed Vince the lock and chain. "Use this when I get the guard away from the gate. It'll buy you some time." Then he gripped the bars of the gate and took a deep breath. A moment later he began to scream as if his life or someone else's were depending on it. "Help! You have to help! Mrs. West, she—she won't wake up! Oh, God, help!"

The guard jumped out of the box, nearly toppling over. The magazine flew from his hands, falling into a large puddle. "What? What's going on?"

"You have to hurry!" Anthony continued screaming. "I don't know what to do!"

The guard looked confused, unsure whether he should abandon his post or not.

"You have to come quick!"

Vince felt terrible for all involved. This man was being horribly duped, and Anthony was going to pay severely when all was said and done.

"Back away," the guard said to the two boys. "Back away!" He opened the gate and closed it again right behind him, the exit automatically locking. Then he ran inside the house with Anthony in the lead.

Alone, Vince tried to open the gate, but it was no use; he would have to climb. Before doing so, he looked at the lock and chain in his hands. He was beginning to understand Anthony's plan. The kid was much smarter than he let on. He would miss him.

Vince wrapped the chain around the bars of the gate and closed the lock. With the guard on a wild-goose chase that could end at any moment, he quickly began to climb.

The bars were slippery from the overnight rain, and there wasn't much to grip. Every time he climbed three feet, he fell two, his palms dragging the rust from the metal. His muscles immediately began to ache. And worst of all, he wasn't halfway up when he heard yelling in the house. The jig was up.

Frantic, Vince picked up his pace. If he were caught, he would never get another chance.

Moments later Anthony came running out of the house, waving his arms. "Hurry!" he screamed. "Hurry, Vince! They're coming! They're coming for you!"

The guard ran right past Anthony, shoving him hard to the ground. But as he passed M, the old man's foot somehow invaded his path. The guard went flying head over heels.

Vince heard the commotion but told himself not to look back. He had to concentrate on climbing. He thought of what would be waiting for him at the end of this journey. In Dyerville he would find his father. A new life would be waiting; all he had to do was make it to the other side of the gate. Suddenly it didn't seem so impossible.

Behind him, the guard was back on his feet. Vince, however, had picked up speed. He was nearly at the top now.

After failing to break Anthony's lock, the guard started shaking the gate, rattling it with a harrowing frenzy. Vince nearly fell. He slid down some, and the guard shook it again. Still Vince slid. Now the guard saw his opportunity. He began to climb. He was quick, much quicker than Vince. But Vince climbed with far greater purpose, and he reached the top in no time. As he threw one leg over the side, the guard desperately reached up and grabbed hold of Vince's back pocket. With three fingers, the guard yanked down hard, trying to bring Vince back to earth. Vince couldn't move. His grip was loosening. The guard pulled even harder. Something had to give.

And something did. The pocket ripped, the directions to Dyerville falling to the ground along with the guard. Vince, however, made it cleanly over to the other side. Halfway down, he jumped and landed on his butt in the same puddle as the guard's magazine. Spinning around, he pulled the hair out of his eyes and glanced back at the orphanage. Every window was filled with a face.

Suddenly Vince found himself crossing his fingers once again. Somewhere deep within his mind there was now a spark glowing. It was small, but it wanted to grow.

As Vince stood, he saw Anthony standing beside M several feet from the gate. They both seemed to have tears in their eyes, and Vince did too. He waved good-bye. Then he turned away from the orphanage and ran into the gaping mouth of the world.

CHAPTER 4

V ince picked a direction and went with it. He knew
      he didn't have very long before the chain would be
off the gate. Soon enough everyone, led by the unrelenting
Mrs. West, would be out looking for him. It was best to be
as far as possible by then.

He ran for over three miles, but as agonizing as it was,
he didn't want to stop. He sprinted straight through the
residential area he had called home these past few years and
into the busier part of town, filled with fast-food restaurants, supermarkets, department stores, banks, and coffee
shops, among other places he would never set foot in. Right
now he just hoped he had memorized the map correctly in

the few moments he'd been in possession of it before the guard ripped it from his pocket. The train had to be in this direction, he told himself. But he couldn't recall its being this far. Nothing looked familiar. What if he made a wrong turn somewhere?

Finally, after nearly two hours, he couldn't run anymore. Wheezing and cramping, he found a back alley behind a small shopping center and settled down beside a Dumpster. His pants were ripped and soaking wet, and the weather was getting cooler by the minute. He would have to change before he got sick. He had only the one outfit in his pack— his so-called nice clothes for the funeral—but they were all he had.

Once changed, he knew he would have to make a decision: either head back out there and wander the streets in search of the train, risking capture, or wait it out here for some time, letting his pursuers believe he had already made it clear out of town. Settling on the latter, he remembered there was one other thing in his backpack: his grandfather's book. Exhausted, he settled back down against the Dumpster, took it out, and began to read.

The Cave

It was the day before Vincent's twelfth birthday. He was outside, up on a ladder, painting the small shed he had just built with his own two hands over the previous weeks to store his mother's gardening tools. His mother, Anna, was in the back doorway of her home, leaning against the frame, watching her son, a terrible sadness in her eyes. After some time she called out to him: "Vincent! Vincent, enough of that. You've been at it nonstop for hours. Come inside. Let me make you something to eat."

Vincent turned and smiled, the sun illuminating his silhouette. He had grown into a fine-looking boy. Dark tousled hair, fair skin reddened from his constant work and play outdoors. His hands were large and calloused; his chin was square and strong. He was a mature boy, older and wiser than his years, as suggested by his deep-set blue eyes. "Thanks. I sure could use something in my stomach," he told his mother.

"I have all fresh foods from the market. I'll make you whatever you'd like."

Unable to take his eyes off the work he had just completed, he descended the ladder at a casual pace; he had to see if anything wasn't to his satisfaction. So far so good. At the bottom he placed his brush across the rim of the paint can and walked serenely back to the house, wiping the sweat from his brow. "It's coming along nicely, don't you think?" he asked, pointing over his shoulder.

Anna took in the shed once again. It sat to the east of the house, right beside the abundant garden Vincent cared for so passionately, and each time she glanced at it, it reminded her of her son: sturdy, charming, and . . . "Beautiful," Anna said. "I'll treasure it always. Now, what would you like to eat? If I could make you anything, what would it be?"

"Just a sandwich. That's all," he said, removing his gloves.

"A sandwich? Nothing more elaborate?" Anna asked as she walked inside.

"You can put as much as you would like on it. How about that? Stack it high."

Anna turned around. "That's a deal." She hadn't meant

to say these words. She shouldn't have. They'd just slipped out. But it was as if someone had struck her in the chest. She couldn't move. Her face drained of color.

"Are you okay?" Vincent asked.

Anna spun around and hurried over to the kitchen counter. "No. No, I'm not," she muttered. She began preparing the sandwich in a frenzied fashion. She picked up a package of meat and dropped it; instead of unwrapping the cheese, she tore through the wrapping; she forgot to add the pickle—her sandwich staple. Cutting the bread, she fumbled with the knife, nearly slicing her hand open. With her head down in an attempt to hide her face, her chin trembled. Tears began to fall, the bread absorbing each one.

"What is it?" Vincent said. "What's wrong?"

Anna looked to the ceiling and took a deep breath. When she spoke again, she didn't dare look at him. "You have to leave tonight," she said.

"Go into town? What for?"

"No, not into town." She lowered her head and turned around, looking directly into his eyes. She needed all her strength to say what came next. "You have to leave home. You have to go far away and never come back."

"Leave home? What do you mean?"

"This isn't easy for me, Vincent. I have long dreaded this day."

"Mother, what's going on?"

"I never told you the truth about your birth. Not exactly."

Vincent stared at her, his throat tightening, his jaw clenching.

Anna couldn't bear such a look and covered her face with her hands, crying into them. "I was all alone. It was my only chance. I had to agree."

"What are you talking about? Agree to what?"

Anna pulled her hands away. Her tears, for the moment, ceased, and she returned Vincent's gaze. "You remember that I said you were born on the side of the road into town? Before you were born, an old woman emerged from the woods. It was she, not Dr. Nicholl, who delivered you. I was in so much pain, and it was clear to me that you were going to die if I didn't do something. I couldn't take the chance. . . . I didn't know she was a witch. I should have, but I was so scared."

"A witch?"

Solemnly, Anna nodded. "As of tomorrow, you belong to her."

Vincent took a step backward. "You made a pact with her?"

"I had to! Please understand. Please forgive me."

"What does she want with me?"

"I don't know."

"Well, I won't leave. I'm not going with her. We don't

60

have to honor the deal."

"And I agree. But you don't know what she's capable of. If we disobey her, she might hurt us or use her magic to force you to go with her. And that's why you must run. It is time to start your own life far from here."

Shaking his head, Vincent felt his own tears beginning to fall. "Mother, no. What will she do to you?"

"I don't care, my darling. You must leave. I know it will be difficult, but you have to be strong."

"And where do I run to?"

"I don't know. Head to the mountains. Reach the other side. The witch cannot cross them."

"I can't, Mother, I can't," he cried.

"I'm sorry, Vincent. I'm so sorry I have done this to you."

They embraced and wept in each other's arms. They didn't let go for some time.

That night, however, he did leave, but only after he had completed the shed—his final gift. Then, when it came time, he carried a small bag of provisions, kissed his mother, and walked toward the mountains. Anna knew to not watch him walk away, just as Vincent knew to not look back. Sometimes this is the only way.

The next morning Anna heard a knock at the door. It was an odd knock, as if it weren't a hand that was rapping. Immediately she knew who it was—there wasn't a doubt in her mind—and for having the courage to even open the door she must be commended.

Sure enough, standing there in her crumpled stance was the witch.

"It has been twelve years," she croaked. "I have come for the boy."

Anna stood straighter, head held high, refusing to show a shred of fear. "He isn't here. Nor will he be again."

Quizzically, the witch turned her head. She spit on the ground; it was an ugly yellow phlegm that sizzled like acid. "No?" She wiped her mouth with the back of her hand.

"And you will never find him either."

"Oh, but we had a deal. He is my boy now."

"I have broken the deal."

The witch cackled, her tongue lashing wildly with each ululation. "Did you now? Not without consequences, my dear."

The witch reached out and touched Anna with her fingertips directly in the center of her chest. Instantly, painfully, Anna crumpled to her knees. She felt as if her insides were on fire, a ferocious, untamable blaze, her blood like burning gasoline. It started in her veins and coursed throughout her body in a matter of seconds. To her, it was the burning of her soul, and growing in its place was charred blackness. She could feel every inch of her insides being consumed by this evil. Still, through it all she stared hard at the witch, betraying her agony. "I may die, but my boy will live, and live free."

"I have no desire to kill you just yet, but you are wrong about your boy. He is another story. He is cursed. The longer he avoids his fate, the greater he will suffer. Over time his ordeals, his trials, will eventually break him, and then he will be mine."

The witch bent down and touched Anna again, and the pain became unbearable. Her body stiffened; her joints locked; her fingers and toes curled.

"I will find the boy," the witch said into her ear. "Our paths are destined to cross. Make no mistake, he will be mine." She turned to leave but looked back over her shoulder at Anna. "Let's go. You haven't outlived your usefulness just yet."

Anna had no intention of going with the witch, but she discovered she had no control over her body. She moved involuntarily, following in the footsteps of the witch, unable to even voice her refusal and dissent. In her mind, she ordered her legs to stop moving; she commanded her arms to reach out and grab the witch; she wanted nothing more than to scream. But none of this happened. Her body was no longer hers. As she unwillingly tailed the witch toward the woods, she passed the shed Vincent had built for her. And the final act that was within her control was displayed in the tear that fell from her eye.

At the moment of his mother's abduction, Vincent heard thunder. He had just reached the mountain base when he looked at the sky and saw terrible storm clouds rushing in. The wind picked up. The sun all but vanished. He had to find shelter.

Scanning the mountain, he spotted the mouth of a cave not very far up the cliff face. It would serve perfectly. With the rain beginning to fall, he began his ascent.

It was a difficult climb, what with the slick surfaces, fierce wind, and spiking rain, not to mention his lack of experience and equipment. His feet had trouble finding hold, and his fingers strained to maintain a constant grip. At one point, as he tried to pull himself higher atop the mountain, some rocks gave way, and Vincent slipped. He tumbled several feet down and crashed against the rough surface, his cheek pierced clean through by a jutting rock. And that was how Vincent came to bear the scar he was to carry for the rest of his life.

When he settled on a flat landing, he could feel the throbbing of the open wound. But the storm was nearly atop him now. He had to keep moving or the gash on his face would be only the beginning of his problems. Through the pain Vincent maintained his focus on where he was trying to go. If he didn't make it to the cave, what his mother had done to protect him would have been for naught.

As he got closer, he couldn't believe how large the cave's entrance was. He was but an insect in comparison, insignificant, nothing. It made him realize how very big the world was and how utterly alone he was in it. By now, however, he was soaked from head to toe, and such troubling thoughts had to be shoved far aside. Freezing, he wanted nothing more than to be under the cave's protective roof, a fire at his feet.

Body aching, he finally reached the massive black opening, the top of the entryway towering at least seventy feet above him. It was as if the earth had been torn open and the darkness of space were peeking through. It was pitch black and cold. He wished he had a weapon of some sort; who knew what animals made this their home?

"Hello?" he called. He waited a minute or two, heard nothing, then slowly stepped inside. It was like being swallowed by a whale.

He knew he didn't have to venture in too deep, just enough that the rain couldn't reach him in its windblown recklessness, but after a few steps, he noticed something, the faintest of lights coming from deep within the cave, like a distant star flickering in the night. It was so small it seemed like a pinprick, a slight puncture in the darkness. Curious, Vincent decided to walk toward it. He crept forward for what seemed like hours, the light growing but slowly. How deep was this cave?

He couldn't see much—he walked with his arms groping the dark air before him, tracing the wall at his side—nor did he hear many sounds, just the repetition of his hesitant footsteps. As he wondered why exactly the mountain's tremendous weight didn't collapse atop him, he kicked a rock that tumbled and ricocheted off the wall, creating a loud echo that traveled throughout the cave.

Vincent froze. He had awoken something. He heard a peculiar sound, one he couldn't place, growing in pitch and number. *What did I do?* Then something else began to stir, something very large.

"Who goes there?" a booming voice questioned, the words echoing off the towering walls of the cave, searching him out.

Vincent considered turning and running, but instead, he just stood there in the darkness, hoping not to be seen.

"Who goes there?" the voice asked again. It was a very deep and intimidating voice. "Answer me! I know someone's there!"

"V-Vincent. My name is Vincent," he croaked. "I was only seeking shelter. I didn't mean to—"

"Come closer!"

Frightened, Vincent did as he was told, not realizing how much farther he actually had to walk; he could have sworn the voice came from so near.

For several minutes he walked closer and closer to the

light. It wasn't a small flicker after all. No, what guided his path was a candle that stood over ten feet tall and more than four feet around. It was like a pillar or column from some ancient structure and must have been burning for quite some time, for wax spilled all down its sides in massive white gobs. The flame, Vincent noticed, was nearly as tall as he was.

However, beyond it was something even more amazing. Illuminated in the candle's glow was an entire home built within the cave. It looked timeworn, as if it had formed along with the mountain millions of years ago. Vincent was awestruck. The space was larger than anything he had ever seen, as if a gigantic asteroid had crashed straight through the mountain. There was a long hall that tunneled farther into the cave, eventually opening up into a wide circle with a dozen doors along the perimeter. Yet for some reason, these doors were even larger than the candle, most unnecessary and awkward for any human. Just outside this hall was a chain that must have been over a mile in length, wound up in a large pile. Off to the side was a pen. Confined in it were scores of sheep, the source of the odd noise he had heard, now unbearably loud. In the cave their sounds became something else, something otherworldly.

What is this? Vincent wondered. *Who called me?* "Hello?" he said, meekly, barely audible over the mad bleating of the sheep.

He was answered by the heavy footsteps heading his way. Immediately he knew why the candle was so huge, why the doors were so very big. In his haste to find shelter, he had imprudently entered the home of a giant.

CHAPTER 5

A door was kicked open with great violence, and Vince, heart jumping as if loaded onto a springboard, snapped the book closed. Two teens dressed in khakis and collared shirts stumbled out of the building and into the alley like bewildered beasts without any regard for their surroundings. They were messing around with each other in the way many teen boys do, cursing, throwing playful punches, and making jokes, many of which hit well below the belt, as did their fists. They were loud and rambunctious and oblivious of the boy cautiously watching them beside the Dumpster, hoping not to be seen. One of them, tall and lean, with long, flowing black hair and a narrow face, finally called a time-out to the unruly activities and, exhausted, collapsed against the wall of the building, face to the sky. The other, breathing heavily, the more aggressive of the two, followed suit and pulled out a cigarette for each of them. Where the other teen was tall, this one was wide and burly and had a large stomach and a full orange beard. They were about to light their cigarettes when they finally noticed Vince huddled up beside the Dumpster.

"Hey, kid, what are you doing back here?" the tall one asked.

"You Dumpster diving? You homeless?" The wide one was hunched over and severely out of breath but still managed to get these questions out with only minimal interference from his overworked lungs.

Vince stood up as quickly as he could, shoving his grandfather's book deep into his backpack. "Sorry. I'll get going."

"Now, hold on a minute, we're not going to bust you," the tall one said. "Are you hungry or something? We can get you some eats. Whatever's in the break room."

"No, I'm okay. I was just resting."

"Back here?" The tall one didn't seem to be buying it. He cocked his head. "Where are you supposed to be really?"

"Nowhere," Vince answered.

"Everyone's supposed to be somewhere," the wide one

70

said. "Like us. We're supposed to be working right now." Apparently, he found this to be very funny, although the laughter quickly gave way to more hacking and phlegm.

"School," the tall one said, pointing a finger. "You should be in school right now, shouldn't you?"

"No, I'm excused. I—I have to get to a funeral."

"Oh, sorry, man. Sorry to hear it."

"Yeah, bummer," the wide one said. "Is it around here?"

"No, I have to get to the train station."

"The train?" the tall one asked. "Where is this funeral?"

"Dyerville."

"Dyerville? Way upstate? Shoot. Don't you know a crazy storm's heading that way? A blizzard for the ages. They're shutting down the trains soon, little man."

"They are?" Vince said, slipping his backpack on in a panic. "Please, how do I get there?"

The tall one pointed to his left. "Let's see . . . What you wanna do is go two blocks this way, then, uh, make a right, and then, uh, head three blocks down. Then you take a left. Can't miss it."

"No, no, no," the wide one said, shaking his head. "What's with you? You have it all wrong. You go this way," he said, pointing to his right. "You go this way for one block, then make a left and go for four. It's right there on your left."

Vince knew he should have been running by now, but

he wasn't sure which way to go. Both of them could have been right, he had no real way of knowing, and if he picked the wrong direction, he could miss the train.

"You can't find your way to the bathroom with the lights off. You have no idea what you're talking about."

"I'm not the one who was driving to the concert downtown and ended up in another state."

"I wasn't paying attention. You can't hold that against me. We were having a good time."

Three stories up, a window slid open, and a body leaned out. With the way the sun was situated in the sky, Vince couldn't make out the figure. It was nothing but an outline of a person.

"What are you two doing? Did I say you could take a break?" came a high-pitched voice.

"Boss!" the tall one shouted. "Boss, if you want to go to the train, don't you go left for two blocks, then—"

"It's right for one," the wide one muttered, taking a drag from his cigarette.

"Is not!"

"Is too!"

"Will you two be quiet!" the boss screamed. "You drive me crazy. I can see the dang train station from here. You go left. Now get back inside and get to work."

"Ha!" said the tall one, poking his friend but immediately

recoiling in case of swift retaliation. As it turned out, there was only a bluff, a fake punch to the gut.

"Don't laugh," the boss said. "I heard you baboons from my office. You weren't exactly correct either. You go left for only one block, not two. Then make a right and go up three. It's right there on the left."

"I was closer," said the tall one.

"You can get there my way too," said the wide one. "Just might be a little longer, I guess. The scenic route."

"Scenic? Around here? Please. You'd get lost your way. Lost or mugged."

They began arguing again, the boss included, but Vince didn't hang around to hear how it all turned out, and they didn't notice his disappearance or hear his thank-you. Not that it mattered; he had already wasted too much time. He had to make that train.

Repeating the directions over and over in his head, he ran as hard as he could, running through whatever pain and cramps and weariness he might have had. As he got closer to his destination, he could hear the train pulling into the station, and that just added even more urgency to an already pressing situation. He sprinted down another block, then another. How many minutes had it been?

Finally the train station was in sight. As he turned the corner, Vince could hear announcements being made, although he couldn't make out exactly what they were saying. He crossed the street, a car nearly plowing right through him. It honked repeatedly, the rubber from its tires burning after the sudden stop. Vince waved a hand in apology to the fuming driver and ran up the stairs and onto the platform and nearly straight into Mrs. West.

Terrified, he stared up at the back of her head. She hadn't seen him. A small miracle. Quickly, he ducked back behind a column, his heart beating at near-impossible speeds. This was trouble—big, huge, terrible trouble—and he was so close too. Carefully, very slowly, he peered out from behind the column. Mrs. West, arms folded, was standing there with the guard and a policeman, informing them to keep an eye out for a runaway boy. They knew he would be coming here.

Moments later there was another announcement echoing across the platform. This one he could hear clearly. Final call. The train, the last one of the day, would be leaving in one minute. There might not even be another one tomorrow. Vince had to get on. It was now or never.

He had a plan. It wasn't much, but it was all he had. He would wait there behind the column until the very last second, until he was absolutely sure that none of them would have time to grab him when he darted past because they wouldn't even realize what was happening. Mrs. West and her cohorts would never react quickly enough, he hoped, and he would be well past them before they did, hopping onto the train just as the doors were closing, sealing him off from their clutches for good.

But he would have to time this perfectly. He knew that much. If he went too soon, they could jump on the train with him; if he went too late, he'd miss his ride completely. How much time since the last announcement? Thirty seconds? Forty? It was going to be pure luck.

The wait seemed eternal, and with each second that passed, more and more doubt crept into his plan. He was going to have to run right past the very people looking to stop him, including a cop. Ludicrous.

Twenty seconds left, he decided.

He tightened the straps of his backpack. Ten seconds.

At five, he would begin to run.

Nine . . . eight . . . seven . . .

He crossed his fingers.

Six . . . five . . .

He took off, blowing right by Mrs. West, so close that he even felt his arm brush up against hers. She spotted him and shrieked, but she was too late. Vince was already steps from the train doors. He was going to make it. The doors started closing. Perfect. He was nearly there. Just squeeze through and wave good-bye. One more step, and that would be it.

Then . . . smack! He ran face-first into the closed doors.

He spun around on impact, holding his smashed nose. Not that he felt the pain. All he could think of was how he just missed the train. One second too slow.

"Let's go, Mr. Elgin," Mrs. West said, approaching carefully. "You have reached the end of your line."

Vince's head was bowed in crushing defeat. He couldn't believe—

He heard a sound. Behind him the doors were opening. Something obstructed them.

Fingers still crossed, Vince turned around. A man had kept his hand in the doors' path. "Getting on?" the stranger asked.

Vince jumped on, and the doors immediately closed behind him; he barely even got his backpack through in time.

Looking back through the glass, he could see Mrs. West and the others racing toward him, arms outstretched, but it was too late. The train had left the platform.

CHAPTER 6

Passengers seated in the car shot him odd looks, perhaps wondering why people were chasing after a young boy, but Vince found a row of unoccupied seats and settled in beside the window, away from these glares.

Placing his bag on the seat beside him, he kept staring out the window, waiting to see and hear police sirens chasing down the train. He kept waiting for the brakes to hit, for the doors to open, every finger pointing at him. But none of this happened. The train continued to pick up speed, and the orphanage was moving farther and farther away.

He couldn't believe it. He'd made it. He was on his

way to Dyerville. The idea of seeing his father again was suddenly an overwhelming likelihood, and he pulled out Andrew's letter again so that he could compare handwritings. The script was impressive indeed: dramatic, elegiac, stirring. It almost defined his father in every way. He tried to think back to lunchtime in school, when he would open the brown bag that his father had filled for him and inside, along with his well-balanced meal, would be a napkin with a note, something simple yet also charming and loving, but the image in his mind was blank. He couldn't easily recall his father's penmanship, but in the end he figured it probably didn't matter because even if they didn't match up, it was most likely due to his father's having studied calligraphy sometime in the past few years just for such occasions. He was a smart man; he had to cover his every step.

How Vince wished he had one of those napkins now. Instead, he placed his palm against the letter, trying to absorb its warmth. He felt like bursting into tears, but he told himself if he did so, they would be tears of joy. He was on his way to his father. It was really happening. This realization was both terribly exciting and incredibly nerve-racking, and so, to help calm his thoughts, he opened his backpack, grabbed his grandfather's book, and began reading once again.

The Giant

The booming steps echoed from down the hall. The giant walked carefully toward Vincent, his colossal body hunched over as if he might hit his head. Although there was light, his gargantuan hands traced the walls just as Vincent's had when he entered the cave.

Something's not right with him, Vincent quickly realized. Then he saw it. There was a blindfold over his eyes. The giant couldn't see a thing.

"Please, do not run," the giant said in a desperate tone. "There is nothing to fear. I will not hurt you."

Vincent found his head tilting farther and farther back the closer the giant approached. He must have stood close to thirty feet tall. Absolutely massive. His head was the size of a boulder and just as peculiarly shaped. The dark hairs falling over his face were longer than Vincent was, and his boots could have served as a small apartment for someone Vincent's size. Each tooth was like a tombstone; each arm, the size of a coffin. Curiously, the giant was covered in gruesome cuts and bruises, his nose apparently having been broken several times over. His clothes were in tatters; his body was filthy.

When the monstrosity reached the end of the hall, he slowly dropped to one knee as if bowing.

"Step forward," he said. "Do not worry. No harm will come to you. I just want to meet my guest. Please." He stuck out his hand.

Approaching the giant sounded like the worst idea in the world. A flick of a finger could nearly kill Vincent, crush his chest and ribs, shatter some bones. Still, he didn't run. Instead, he bravely moved closer.

The giant reached out for him, his fingers writhing in the damp air. "Where are you?"

"A little closer," Vincent said.

The giant brought his hand back for a moment, a perplexed look on his face. "You—you are not frightened of me."

Vincent most definitely was, but he also felt sorry for him. "If I were, I would have run far away by now." And this sounded true enough to him.

The giant smiled and reached out again. Soon he found his uninvited guest. He picked Vincent up gingerly in one hand, brought him close to his face, then traced his features with the tip of a single finger.

"You are quite small, Vincent. And I take it you are very young. Yes, you are, aren't you?" he said, nodding to himself.

"I am old enough. But age doesn't really matter, does it? One's actions can betray any number."

"Wise words," the giant said as he reached out his free hand to search the ground behind him for something. "You sound like a pleasant boy, Vincent. I am sorry I have to do this."

Vincent eyed the wandering hand, and then he watched the giant's expression change. "Sorry for what?" he cried, suddenly becoming extremely frightened. "What are you going to do?" Wrapped tightly in a coarse palm, he struggled to squirm free.

"Don't fight," the giant said. "I can squeeze the life out of you in but a mere second. I can pop that little head right off and drain you of your blood as if you were nothing but a bottle of ale."

Vincent opened his mouth and bit the humongous hand that held him captive, bit it with all he had.

The giant merely laughed and gave him a slight squeeze that almost caused Vincent to lose consciousness. "Don't tempt me, boy." Finally his hand settled on the lengthy chain coiled up outside the hall. Having located the end, he yanked it closer and, with some difficulty, shackled it to Vincent's leg. Once it was secured, he placed his prisoner down.

Vincent dropped to the ground and groped at the chain, trying to pull his leg free. "Why are you doing this?" he asked, panic nearly consuming him. "What do you want from me?"

The giant answered his questions with one of his own: "Why have you entered my cave?"

"I was retreating from the rain. That is all. I promise you, I had no corrupt intentions."

"What I mean is, what are you doing in these mountains all alone? Don't you know how dangerous they are? Are you brave or merely foolish?"

Vincent continued to struggle with the thick chain, slamming it with a rock. "I . . . Well, I was running away."

"Running from what?"

"A witch."

"A witch?" The giant's hands reached up to his face, his blindfolded eyes. "The witch of the woods?" He sounded truly horrified. Under his breath, he began to mumble. "Perhaps this is no mere coincidence. This is the way of the world, is it not? This is how it was meant to be." The giant reached out for Vincent and picked him up once again. "The witch, she is why you are chained, Vincent. Just as she is the reason I am blind. Yes. She did this to me. And for no reason other than my trespassing in her woods. But I am a shepherd, and I must tend to my flock. I meant her no harm. And yet this is my punishment." He removed the blindfold and revealed the white eyes behind it. The irises were gone, the corners oozing not tears but yellow pus. "Tell me, why do you run from her? What has she done to you?"

"She wants me for her own," Vincent said. "She cursed me at birth."

"No doubt she is a vile hag. She must be stopped. She must be killed." He rubbed his eyes. "Sadly, I am in no condition to do so. But you, Vincent, you can change that. You can return my vision. You see, the witch spoke of a cure, an antidote consisting of six ingredients, three of which I already possess. You find me the other three, and I will reward you greatly."

"And how am I supposed to find them when I am chained?"

"As a cruel taunt, the witch hid them within my home. Of course I can't find them all, although I've tried my best, searching desperately through every room on my hands and knees. My body, as I am sure is clear to you, has taken a toll."

As Vincent was lowered yet again, he noticed that even the giant's fingers were badly damaged, the tips almost rubbed raw, the nails cracked and jagged and black as if the curse had spread from his eyes, deadening the rest of his body as well.

"And if I find the rest of the ingredients, you will let me go?"

"Yes, you find them and I will not kill you," the giant said. "That is your reward."

Vincent stared at the chain and gave it one last tug. It was incredibly heavy and most likely impenetrable. He had no choice. The only way to be free was to help the giant regain his sight.

"You didn't have to chain me," Vincent said. "I would have found them for you without the promise of any prize."

"I am sorry; I couldn't take the chance of your running off. It is not often that someone enters my cave. You must understand, my sight is at stake. You cannot imagine a fate such as this, to have the light of the world snuffed out. I can barely recall the beauty of our land."

Vincent looked from the chain to the giant to the hall with its many doors. "What are the three ingredients I am looking for?"

"First, you must find a crab so that I may take its claw. Second, you must snatch me a ladybug so that I may rip its wings from off its body. And finally, you must capture me a snake so that I may cut out its forked tongue."

"Very well," Vincent said. "I will begin immediately."

"First, my friend, there are two things you must know. One is the most important rule of my home." He stood up and walked down the hall, farther into the cave. "Follow me," he said.

Vincent obeyed, dragging the heavy chain behind him.

Ahead, the giant extended his arms. "You may go anywhere you like, search every inch of my home, open every door." He stopped and turned around in the middle of the circle with the twelve doors. "Every door but one." He pointed to a door the farthest from the cave's entrance. It was painted a dark red, as if sprayed with blood, the only door that was this color. "No matter what, you are not to enter this room, under any circumstances whatsoever. It is forbidden. Disobey me, and it will cost you your life."

"But what if one of the ingredients is in there?"

"None of them are. I know this. Do you understand? You are not to enter this room."

Vincent eyed the door closely, wondering what was so very important. "I understand," he said. "What is the other thing I should know?"

"This will make your task even more difficult than you already thought it to be. The snake I seek has become the pet of a gnome living somewhere within my home. He is a quite mad gnome, hell-bent on entering this very room." The giant rubbed his palm against the red door. "But the red paint keeps him out; he cannot ever cross the threshold.

However, he believes he has found his own path in, a way to circumvent these ancient laws. You see, the gnome carries with him a mirror. But this is no ordinary mirror. Every so often it begins to glow, and when it does, this gnome stares into it, and the glow becomes so bright it is almost as if he had captured the sun itself. There is a tremendous flash; nothing can be seen; the world around him is eliminated. Then, just like that, the glow is gone, and the gnome finds himself transported to another room in my home. Unfortunately for you and me, in the process, the magic mirror shuffles everything around. The dozen rooms are ever changing, you understand. Because of the mirror, they become hundreds, thousands, no two ever alike. All but the room beyond the red door: this one will always remain as it is. The gnome, however, hopes to one day find himself transported inside. He will not stop until he succeeds. We must stop him before this happens. Vincent, I want you to take from him this snake and destroy his mirror. Find my ingredients and return order to this cave. Then I will free you. But be careful. The gnome is of a warped mind. He is pure evil, and he knows I seek the snake. He will do anything to keep it from me, for if my sight was to return, he is well aware his days are numbered."

Vincent took in every word and nodded. "With the rooms forever changing, you understand there is a chance I will never find any of these."

"I am aware of the circumstances, boy. Are you?"

"I am," Vincent said, nodding solemnly. "You will have your sight back."

"Confident. Very good. Then off you go."

But before he began his search, with the giant unable to see, Vincent reached out and touched the red door. It chilled his spine.

Later, after lighting all the wall torches, for which the giant no longer had any use, Vincent explored the hall from end to end, inspecting every crevice, every crack in which a ladybug might hide. This alone consumed almost two hours, although he spent a good amount of time trying to peek under the red door, all to no avail. He found that just being near it revved his heart, quickened his pulse. Something tugged at him from the other side. *What is behind this door?* he wondered, placing his ear against it, hearing nothing. It had to be something immensely powerful. Perhaps more riches than he could ever dream of. Perhaps something that could reunite him with his mother. If it weren't something special and powerful, why would the giant need to protect it so?

When he completed his search of the hall, he moved on to the first room to the right of the red one. Looking up at the humongous door, he couldn't imagine having the strength to open it, but as he pushed against the thick wood, he found that it swung open rather easily.

Inside, he couldn't see a thing. The room was hidden in the densest fog. Vincent raised his hand just an inch from his face and couldn't see it in the slightest. He imagined this was how the giant must feel all the time. Maybe he didn't see darkness at all, but rather a thick haze of white. To be blinded in such a way was a horrible thing, and a part of him had great sympathy for the giant. But then a terrifying thought entered his head: *What if the gnome is in this room at this very moment? What if he can somehow see me through this haze?* Vincent spun around, arms extended. His heart raced yet again, but for much different reasons. Was that a sound? Footsteps? No, he had to be calm. If he wasn't, he might never find what he needed. But how could he find anything in here? It was almost as if there were no "here" to even speak of. He decided that his best bet was to crawl about the room, feeling every inch in his path for a snake or a ladybug or a crab. He didn't believe the room was very big, but at such a crawl, as he searched for such small prizes, it took him over four hours to cover every inch. It was madness. Of course in the end he came away with nothing.

Once he had exited the room, he closed the door and, as he was about to walk away, suddenly stopped. He turned back. "What if . . ." Slowly he pushed the door open again, and to his wonder, he found himself in a completely different room from the one he had just left. In the time he spent searching through the fog, the gnome must have used the mirror. This way, when Vincent's chain was finally clear of the door and it was able to close, it shuffled into its new state, however temporarily. It was a brutally disheartening experience. How would he ever search every possible room? Was there an infinite amount? And how was he supposed to complete this task all before the gnome somehow entered the forbidden room?

Vincent hung his head in defeat. The new room before him looked like another cave. It was just more dank and empty space with walls of rock and dripping water. He gave a quick scan of the room and noticed nothing that might aid him on his quest—no immediate signs of any gnomes, snakes, crabs, or ladybugs. But then, coming from the far wall, he heard a quiet scratching sound. As Vincent approached, he noticed cave drawings. But they weren't ancient. They were active. Lines of dark chalk or charcoal or hematite began creating images upon the wall like a canvas, only there was no guiding hand, nor was there any chalk either. Just the art and its miraculous creation. Vincent reached out and placed his fingers over the magically shifting lines and felt a slight vibration against his skin. How was this possible? What was being drawn? He stepped back and saw a massive forest and the outline of a solitary house. There was a window, and inside, he could see some people, but he couldn't tell how many or who they might be. A cloud emerged overhead, and two figures exited the house and headed for the edge of the woods. Suddenly flames engulfed the house, and in seconds it was gone. The image lasted only a few seconds more before everything was erased and the chalk lines began to take on a new drawing. Whatever invisible hand was at work here appeared to be creating the entire night sky now, every star, every planet and comet and moon and galaxy. The drawing, like the universe itself, seemed like it would never end, and Vincent decided to move on with his search, scouring the floor and walls yet again for the elusive ladybug that might be hiding anywhere. When he didn't find it, he left through the same door a second time, the chalk still creating the cosmos.

For the remainder of the day Vincent went in and out of rooms without finding anything but oddities, one after another. In one room were hundreds of tiny pyramids made up of rocks and pebbles. Every time Vincent toppled them over to check for one of his three pursuits, the rocks would roll about as if alive and rebuild the pyramid in a matter of moments. Another room was filled with an abundance of chairs, each one a different ornate design. Every time Vincent had a seat in one, he heard a unique sound and the chair would vanish, practically evaporating into the ground. Later, when he asked the giant about the room, the giant laughed and said, "Too bad you don't have a necklace of alligator teeth." Vincent had no idea what this meant.

There were rooms that were so big he almost believed he was no longer inside the cave, and there were other rooms in which he could fit without crouching and crawling. Some rooms had their own weather patterns while others gave him reason to believe they were haunted.

Every now and then, as the giant sat with his sheep, consuming barrels of wine, as he so often did, he would call out to him, "Have you found anything yet?" and Vincent would wearily respond, "Not yet," to which the giant would belch and laugh. It was such an arduous and long process. On average, he searched each room for over three hours. There were moments when he lost his patience, there were times when he thought he might lose his mind, all the while wishing he could just return home and see his mother once more. His hatred of the witch grew by the minute, and he vowed that if he ever escaped the cave, he would find a way to destroy her before he made a life for himself.

At night the giant served him lamb that he cooked over an open fire, neither one talking to the other. Then, chained, Vincent slept on the ground. Every morning he had to help the giant tend to his sheep. The giant said that before Vincent's arrival, the giant had used the chain to keep himself tethered to the cave, so that when he ventured out, he could always find his way back. But he was losing too many sheep in the process. Now, as they grazed in the grass at the bottom of the mountain—near the woods but not too near—Vincent served as his eyes. Then, when they returned to the cave and as the giant drank, Vincent began his search again. And every time he passed the red door, he felt its pull. Why not just risk a peek, what did he have to lose? *No*, he had to convince himself daily, almost hourly, *you still have a chance to be free; you still have a chance to live the life your mother wanted for you. Don't ruin that.* What he needed to do, and soon, was heal the giant and get away from that door for good, lest temptation overwhelm him completely.

Two long and arduous weeks into his stay, he opened yet one more of the ever-changing doors—this one previously being the room of fog and a closet of skulls shortly after that—and found himself falling face-first into water. After the initial shock, Vincent quickly stood up and collected himself. He was hip deep in the clearest of cool water. The room was either a lake or a pond or a pool, maybe a bath, however the giant preferred to use it, he supposed. How deep did it go? Vincent took another two steps in, gathered his breath, and then dived under.

He swam toward the center, noticing the land dropped off ten feet, then twenty, then thirty. *There has to be a crab somewhere in this water*, he told himself. Fish swam in their schools around him. They were bright and beautiful colors, more likely to be found in tropical waters than within a mountain cave, not that this surprised him; behind these doors it seemed anything was possible. The floor was covered in thick sand and peculiar plants and critters. Desperately, he looked for a crab scuttling about but found nothing.

Every few minutes he had to return to the surface, get some air, and dive back down again, the chain making his swim incredibly difficult. Each time he hoped he could hold his breath just a bit longer, swim just a bit farther. Then, when he was farther and deeper than he had yet been, he saw huge mounds of sand, one after another, protruding from the ground. It was as if there were waves on the seabed or as if somehow, an ocean had submerged the dunes of a desert. Thinking that this might be something to inspect, he swam closer and soon noticed that at the end of each dune was a piece of stone with words written on them, and immediately, even without understanding the language in which they were written, he knew what lay beneath the mounds of sand. This was a giant burial ground.

Vincent kicked wildly for the surface. He didn't want to search such a sacred site; it didn't feel right to him. But he also knew there was a great possibility that a crab would dwell in just a spot. And so, with renewed breath, he returned to the burial ground.

There were six mounds in all. Were these relatives of the giant? Parents, siblings? Vincent hovered over each one, searching for a sign, a disturbance of some sort. But everything was still. Then, just as he was about to give up and get some much needed air, he saw bits of sand cascading down like an avalanche. He moved in closer. *Please. Please.*

Yes, there it was. A claw. The crab was half under the sand and unaware of Vincent's approach. Vincent had been underwater for far too long already, but he didn't want to risk losing this opportunity. Without further hesitation, he lunged for the crustacean. But it was as if he were moving in slow motion. The crab began to skitter away. Vincent, taking in water, his head pounding from the pressure, reached out. He almost had it. The crab tried to dive back under the sand. Vincent's finger just traced its back, scratched it with his nail. A little closer. A little more.

He snatched it up.

As he swam to the surface, nearly blacking out from the lack of oxygen, the crab, clearly agitated, snapped at him. Its huge claw gnashed his cheek, removing a large chunk. And that was how Vincent came to bear the scar he was to carry for the rest of his life.

Finally, after he had returned to the surface, bleeding and gasping for air, he ran out of the room and found the giant.

"Here," he said, hunched over and panting. "A crab."

The giant extended his hand, and Vincent placed it in. Feeling his prize wriggle in his palm, the giant grinned.

"Yes. I was beginning to lose hope. But it seems all is not yet lost. You have done well. Only two more left, and then you will be free."

With such monotonous work, the days felt more like years, and Vincent, without ever fully realizing it, grew stronger and wiser. He was disciplined, keeping his mind active, telling himself stories as he searched, repeating poems and philosophies over and over in his head. He created entire worlds in which to lose himself, beautiful songs that rang between his ears. The only times he felt like a child again were whenever he walked by the red door. Only then did he yearn to give in to his impulsiveness.

Every now and then, as he ventured from door to door, Vincent would hear a scream, a terrible, hideous shriek, and he knew it was the gnome, angry again at not appearing where he so desperately wanted to be. But as hard as he tried to locate the gnome and his snake, they never encountered each other. Somehow, Vincent always chose the incorrect door to enter.

After nearly another six weeks of searching, upon hearing such a scream, Vincent, thinking he had found the gnome at last, stumbled, instead, upon a room filled with tall grass and flowers, an entire field of them stretching for what seemed like miles. The ladybug was in this room; there was no doubt in his mind. He would have to search every blade of grass, every flower stem and petal and the soil in between. He quickly realized he could be in here forever.

And indeed it felt that way, for he painstakingly inspected every inch of that field, never once stopping to rest, forgoing all meals, forgoing all sleep. However, in all this time, he never came across anything even resembling a ladybug. How long had he been in this room? He wanted to cry; he wanted to just give up and open the red door—be done with it all. He would never escape the cave. Disillusioned, he left the field behind, pushing the door open to walk back into the hall and start again in yet another room. But as he did so, he happened to glance at his arm. And there, crawling across his sleeve, was a ladybug.

CHAPTER 7

V ince turned away from the book and glanced out
the window, catching a reflection of himself in the
smudged glass. It was an odd image there, staring coldly
back at him. For a moment he couldn't even recognize his
own face. There was something different about it, especially
in the elliptical darkness surrounding his weary eyes. It
was a lost boy trapped in a sheet of glass, a two-dimensional
being going nowhere.

As the train continued to run along its tracks, he tried
to look past this distorted reflection and out at the trees
and roads streaming by. But beyond the glass, the scenery

seemed to be repeating over and over again as if the outside world were running in one long, depressing loop. It didn't look nearly as exciting and thrilling as Vince had always imagined it to be and certainly not like the world his grandfather had grown up in.

But his grandfather's stories weren't real. This was the real world. In a strained whisper, he said to his estranged image, "What are you doing, Vince?"

The next stop approached, and the train began to slow. Vince tossed the book on the seat beside him. *Why are you even reading these tales?* the Vince in the glass wondered. *Your grandfather was crazy. I mean, he can't even get his own story straight. First he got the scar from the witch when he was born, and now he gets it from a crab? That makes no sense. Which is it? It's all fantasy. Just like reuniting with dear old Dad.*

"You're wrong," he said. "He'll be there. Dad will be there."

The train came to a full and screeching stop, and still glancing out the window and through his warped self-image, Vince saw a man waiting on the platform, bundled up in the cold, the collar of his jacket covering half his face. The first thought to pop into Vince's head was that of his father: he was on his way to the funeral, no doubt. Fingers crossed, Vince couldn't help rising in his seat and scrutinizing the stranger as he stepped onto the train.

Peeking over the headrest, Vince felt his nerves start to take over, the same feelings he had nearly every day at the orphanage. *And how did that always work out for you?* the voice within the glass said. *What are you doing? Stop this. It's not him. You know this.*

But still, he looked, waiting for the man to turn his way.

And then he finally did. The man walked right past Vince and chose a seat two rows ahead of him. He looked nothing like his father.

Vince glanced down at his hands and quickly uncrossed his fingers. He leaned his head against the window, meshing with his reflection, and glanced up at the gray sky, as if he might find some explanation for his naïveté there. The sun's appearance was brief today, and the sky was darkening by the second. The clouds were moving in fast, and the snow had begun to fall lightly across the dreary landscape. Looking up, Vince wished he could take flight, rise above the dense clouds and just keep going, watch the world from far overhead. Why not?

Like a rock, his head fell into his hands with an audible smack. He sat there for some time, like this, unmoving— however long it took for the tears to go away. What was he doing? What was this whole trip really about? He had a sudden yearning, a strange desire he never believed he would have: he just wanted to go back to the orphanage.

Minutes later he had nearly fallen asleep in that comforting darkness when bits of conversation from the other passengers began to penetrate his thoughts. They were at first like the cloudy comments of a dream state but became more like short spikes of intruding information. "Look real close . . ." "Have you seen . . ." "On the run . . ." "Police are searching for . . ."

Groggy, Vince looked up, and immediately his stomach sank. It was the ticket collector, shuffling from one passenger to another. As she went through the car of the train, checking and punching tickets, she was holding up a piece of paper and asking each passenger if he or she recognized the person in the picture. "Take a good look. This is important."

He didn't know what to do. Clearly, they were on to him. Should he run? Pretend to sleep? He stood up, his legs heavy with fear.

Backpack in hand, he shuffled over to the aisle. *Do it. Run. Now.*

Too late. The ticket collector saw him. "Excuse me, young man. Wait right there. I need to see your ticket."

Vince kept his back to her. He didn't want to turn around. "I—I don't have one."

"You can buy one now. I just have to add a three-dollar surcharge to the price."

Still, Vince didn't budge. His eyes were closed, as he wished for everything around him to vanish.

"All right, so, where are you going?"

"D-Dyerville."

"Dyerville. That'll be twenty-four dollars and fifty cents."

Vince turned around, making sure to keep his head down. He took out the money he had received from M and meekly handed it over.

After sifting through a wad of bills, the ticket collector gave him his change and shoved a piece of paper inches from his face. "Look familiar to you?"

Slowly, and with intense dread, Vince raised his eyes to the paper. As he took in the images, a sudden wave of calm washed over his body. There wasn't a picture of him. He was safe; she was looking for someone else.

There were three photos on the paper in all. The first was a middle-aged man, pale and skeletal with a scar like a worm traversing across his scalp. The second was of a young woman with a faraway look and no eyebrows, with a nose so slight it might just be nostrils. The third image was a blur, a woman hidden in shadows. Nobody would ever mistake Vince for any of them. Relieved, he shook his head. "No. I've never seen them before."

"Are you sure?"

Vince nodded. "Positive."

As the ticket collector walked away, Vince slumped back into his seat and asked, "What did they do?"

But he wasn't heard. Not by her; she was already on to the next passenger. Instead, Vince was heard by the man sitting across the aisle from him, the same man, it turned out, who had prevented the doors from closing.

"Bad people," the man said. He was looking down, sketching on a large pad. "Very bad. Haven't you seen the news?"

Vince said he hadn't.

The man stopped sketching and edged closer. "It's been all over. They're wanted for knocking over banks. A whole slew of them."

"Really?"

"They call themselves the Byron Clan. They even grabbed a rich kid from his home and held him for ransom for days, asking for millions of dollars. Huge news. Police were able to track them down, but the situation got out of control pretty quickly. They were able to save the kid, but the Byrons escaped. Now authorities are checking this train because they think this demented family is heading upstate to hide in the blizzard. Probably think they'll be safe with everything shut down. Hide out in the snow. Buy some time. Not a bad plan. I just hope they find the sickos. And fast. Before anyone gets hurt."

He studied Vince through narrowed eyes and went back to sketching, his hand moving incredibly fast. The man appeared to be about the same age as Vince's father. He was a tall man with perfect posture, pale skin. His hair was long and pin straight, drifting down over his boyish face so that he constantly had to flick it aside with a snap of his thick neck. Each muscular arm was covered with dried paint, but almost purposely so, like temporary tattoos.

Finished, the man tore the page free from his book and handed it across the aisle to Vince. "For you."

Vince grabbed the paper and found a sketch of himself leaning against the train window, reading his grandfather's book. It was a beautiful image, very well done, and the style reminded him of the drawings on the cave he read about; there was a brutal simplicity to it, a certain timelessness.

"Habit I have," the man said. "I'm always sketching people I see. Places. Still lifes. You name it. I can't glimpse anything without wanting to capture it on paper." He extended his hand. "Name's Eric."

"Vince. Thanks . . . for before. For holding the train."

"Oh, no problem. Saw you running. Figured you had somewhere important to be."

"I do. I'm going to see my father." He was disappointed for saying this aloud, as if it were a fact, when really it might end up being a wild-goose chase.

"Been awhile since you seen him?"

Vince nodded and with great sadness said, "Years."

A twitch crept across Eric's face as if his skin were ripping open from within. He held up a finger. "One minute." Frantically he flipped through the pages of his pad, one sheet falling back upon another. "Oneminuteoneminuteoneminuteoneminute—" Then he stopped and, without taking his eyes from the drawing, picked up his pencil. His rambling ceased. A look of concentration fell upon his face. His chestnut eyes didn't blink, and his tongue protruded from the corner of his mouth. He was ready to create.

But the pencil never had a chance to leave a mark. Like a weak spell, the trance was abruptly broken, and Eric shook his head in frustration. "Ah! For a second there, I thought I had it." He snapped the pencil in half between his two fingers.

"Had what?"

With slight hesitance and perhaps some embarrassment, Eric handed the pad over to Vince. "I don't know how to finish it."

For a moment Vince believed the drawing to be complete. It looked perfect, in fact. A drawing of a man, an old but intriguing face with many lines and grooves and marks, a face of great history. But then Vince noticed the eyes. They weren't filled in. They were empty, having been erased many times over, the paper thinning.

"I can't get it right," Eric said. "I've been working on this portrait for years now, but I don't know why I can't finish those damn eyes." He sighed, running his hand through his hair. "Art is such a precarious pursuit. I tell this to all my students. We lose a part of ourselves with everything we create. Sometimes I can feel that loss; I can somehow feel myself becoming a little bit smaller. I shrink. Is that possible?

"I haven't seen my dad in years either. But a part of me believes he never died, not really. I think that maybe after the hundreds, thousands of pieces he created, he just became so small he vanished. Popped out of existence. I don't know. Maybe he's just so high above me I can't see him anymore. I've tried to follow in his footsteps, but—" He gestured at the piece Vince was holding.

Vince took another glance at the drawing and shook his head in confusion. "Your work is amazing."

"Thank you for saying so." Eric continued to study Vince as if he were not yet finished with his sketch either. He even pulled free a new pencil. "You know, I started this drawing when he was still alive. But I never got around to finishing it. I always thought there would be more time. We always do, don't we? He guided me on most of the work, telling me where I could improve, where my strengths were, where I was lacking. Even though he was arthritic and couldn't paint or draw anymore himself, he could still give advice. That never left. Every day he would come to my studio for a visit and tell me how proud he was of me, my work. That meant a lot. In the end I suppose he wasn't meant to see this finished. It wouldn't have been right. I have to finish it myself. Only I don't know if I can."

"Maybe it doesn't matter. Maybe he doesn't need the eyes. Maybe he can already see you and everyone else."

"It's lovely to think so, isn't it? You could be right."

Eric looked away, and Vince peered closer at the drawing. The strokes popped like gray tides, giving the work a greater depth, another layer, another world. *Funny*, he thought, inspecting the blank eyes, *it looks like there's already life in there*. A shadow of existence maybe, but life nonetheless. Maybe, for Eric, there was nothing to fear. Regardless how much he erased or how much he filled in, it didn't matter. He could never erase his father's life. It would always be there in everything he ever did.

"Tell me," Eric continued. "Why haven't you seen your father in so long?"

Vince wasn't sure how to answer. "I—I couldn't find him."

"Until now."

Vince nodded. "Right. Until now."

"What do you remember best about him?"

"I—" Vince shifted in his seat. He wasn't sure anyone had ever asked him something like that. "I remember how much he loved the house we grew up in. It was this cozy little house in Eastbrook. Out in the woods. He built it himself years before I was born. Only it was kind of like your drawing; it was never really finished. He kept working and working on it, adding something here and there, and I would watch him all the time, help out wherever I could. One day he showed me the spot on the foundation where he had carved his initials, and I don't know, those letters seemed so lonely to me. It seemed like he was all alone down there on the cold cement. And so he laid down some new cement, and I added my initials right beside his. It looked better that way. We were always together."

"Will you be stopping there? Eastbrook?"

"No. I mean, I'd like to. I'd give anything to see the house again, what's left of it. But I don't know how to get there."

"But Eastbrook is a stop on this line. Just one before Dyerville. That is where you're going, isn't it? Dyerville?"

"Eastbrook is near Dyerville?" How had he not known this? He supposed that made sense; it was just that the

109

world seemed so much bigger back then. A town over was a universe away.

"Ten miles or so, I guess. You could get off at Eastbrook, and then it's only a short ride to where you have to go. Won't take much time out of your day. Not if you can beat the majority of the snow."

Smiling, Vince sat up straight. "Yeah. Maybe I'll do that." And why not? It was only Tuesday, and the funeral wasn't until Saturday. He had plenty of time. It would just be a short detour.

"Something to tell your father before you reconnect with him, right? I bet he'd like to hear about the house he so cared for. It was his art, you know; his story. Yours too. Maybe take a picture of that foundation with your initials."

"I wish I could go back there and lift up that foundation and carry it on my back; I don't care how heavy it is."

Eric stared at Vince. The artist's mouth stood agape. He dived across the aisle and hugged Vince very tightly. When he finally let go, he grabbed his pad and feverishly began to draw. "I can finish it!" he yelled. "Thank you, Vince! I can finish it now!"

As Eric got to work, Vince slid back across his seat and leaned his head against the glass. His reflection was gone, and outside, the snow began to come down even harder. It made the world look beautiful. Stunning and peaceful. Yes, he would return to his home today. He couldn't explain why exactly. It just felt like something he had to do. It wouldn't be long now. Another few stops.

As Eric feverishly penciled away, Vince turned from the window, reached into his backpack, and again opened his grandfather's book

The Gnome

V incent had been in the giant's cave for over five months. He had searched the dozen rooms hundreds of times, rarely ever stumbling through the same door twice. Not once had he ever come across a snake. This, however, also meant the gnome had not found what he was looking for either. For both of them, there was still a chance for success, however slim.

One morning Vincent entered a room that was empty except for a large painting hanging on the far wall in an elaborate gold frame—not that such art mattered to him at this point in his life. Most important, there was no snake to be seen, no sign whatsoever of the gnome. Another dead end.

As he turned to leave, disappointed yet again, he heard a voice.

"Congratulations on the crab and ladybug. You're almost there. Don't give up now," the sad and distant voice said. "At least you have something to live for."

Vincent's eyes scanned the room, looking for where the gnome might be hiding, playing his games, waiting to strike. "Where are you?"

"Up here."

Vincent backed against the wall, hands balled into fists. He looked around the room but could see no one. Was this not the gnome? "Show yourself," he said, in as brave a voice he could muster.

"You can't see me? Yes, of course. I'm practically invisible, aren't I? Even with nobody else in the room I'm just nothing but background. A pitiful existence. Ah, well. Have a look in the tower window, why don't you, Vincent?"

The voice was coming from the painting. Hesitantly Vincent approached the canvas, an oil painting of a tower, a tower that, surrounded by clouds, stretched into the heavens; at the top was a sole window, and sure enough, inside this window was the silhouette of a person.

"Who are you?" Vincent asked, his fingers brushing the artwork.

"A man without a face. The failed creation of a master."

The voice groaned. "He painted me a millennium ago, was unhappy with the result, and thus stuck me on this wall ever since, to be viewed by no one. It is quite lonely, as you can imagine. One could go crazy. The thoughts that begin to form . . ." He paused. "I look out this window, all the way down, all the way . . . Would it hurt? I'm up so very high."

"How'd you know my name? How'd you know about the crab and the ladybug?"

The silhouette sighed. "From my tower I can see all that goes on in this cave, my dear boy. It is all I have, my view. But oh, what a view it is. Even if it taunts me in how unattainable it all is. I suppose all the best things are practically unattainable."

"You can really see everything from up there? The entire cave? All the rooms? Even as they change?" This gave Vincent an idea. "Have you seen a gnome? A gnome with a snake?"

"Ah, yes, the gnome. He is a maniacal pest. Unpredictable. But from up here, I suppose he is an amusing sort. Keeps my attention. What else do I have? I quite enjoy his antics from time to time. As long as I don't ever encounter him again. Once was enough. I thought he was going to tear a hole right through me. Or worse, carry me off with him. Luckily that mirror of his began to glow; he doesn't know how to control it, you know, not really."

"Please, can you tell me where I may find him?"

"Ah, yes, yes, yes. You need to find him, don't you? Well, I'm sorry. I can't help you there. Even if I do know, I can't tell you where he is. I can't tell you any such thing. Nope. Not possible."

"But why not?"

"I'm not allowed. You see, the witch's powers are far more reaching than you would like to believe. Her knowledge of this land goes very far back, farther even than mine does. She is very much aware of my presence along with my abilities, and when she decided to spite the giant and hide those things in this cave, she placed a spell on me, tying my tongue if I ever wished to disclose their whereabouts. Watch, I will now attempt to tell you where the gnome is." The silhouette began to speak, but all that came out were peculiar moans and a mangling of syllables. Gibberish.

"Oh, I see." Vincent's disappointment was palpable.

The man in the tower groaned. "Well, don't despair. It's not like you've been locked up here for thousands of years. That's not the case, is it? Have you any idea what something like this does to one's mind? You may have a chain shackled to your leg, but at least you're not stuck in a tiny room for all eternity. I can hardly even stretch out in here. And it's quite chilly."

"I'm sorry. I don't mean to think only of myself."

"Of course you don't. Of course you don't. And of course things aren't much easier from your position. Listen, Vincent. I suppose I can help you in a different way. I can tell you about the watch."

"A watch?"

"Oh, yes. It is tied quite closely to the gnome; it used to tick with the beat of his heart. He dismantled it himself, however. But as much as he would like to, he could never destroy it. It sits in pieces in one of these very rooms. Now, if you can manage to put it together again, you will find it to be a terrific tracking device of sorts. When it is working properly, wherever the minute hand rests, upon whichever number, that is in which room you will find the gnome and his snake, which you so desperately covet. For example, this is the fifth room you are currently in. The count begins with the red door and, quite appropriately, runs clockwise— twelve rooms in all."

"And you can tell me where I can find this watch?"

"Well, what's left of it, yes, of course. The witch's curse doesn't cover everything. There are always loopholes. To everything. Let me have a look." There was a brief silence. "Yes. Yes, I see it now. If you hurry, before the gnome uses his mirror yet again, you will find the watch in the tenth room."

"Thank you," Vincent cried. "Thank you so much."

"I pray you succeed. It would be nice to see somebody get what he wants around here. I will be watching with great anticipation." His sad, wistful voice began to drift. "It truly is a wonderful view, seeing the world this way. Just wonderful. But oh, so far. So very, very far . . ."

Vincent thanked the man in the tower once more but received no response. After turning around, he hurried out the room and crossed the circle of doors to the door located at the ten o'clock position before everything changed.

He was in time. Within these heretofore-unseen four walls, he found the watch, as he had been told he would. Dauntingly, it lay in twinkling pieces, scattered about the room as if it had exploded at some point. He had never seen a bigger mess.

Without another wasted second, Vincent fell to his knees and set to work. And yet he had no idea what he was doing or where to even begin. What piece to grab first, and what to follow? It was lunacy. There was the regulator and the winding click, the barrel arbor and the barrel drum, pinions, jewels, weights and coils; there were springs and wheels and screws; there were bridges and balances and studs—not that Vincent could tell one from the other. Every time he thought he was getting somewhere a piece wouldn't fit or something would be left out or the gears wouldn't budge. It was so confounding he wanted to throw it against the wall, break it into even more pieces, and just continue to try his luck by randomly opening doors, even if it took him the rest of his life.

But however frustrated he became, he didn't give in to such desperate whims. Without rest, fiercely determined, he kept at it. And in doing so, he eventually found the process to be more and more interesting. He began to see how the pieces fitted, how precisely they worked together, the intricate beauty of the gears, of the design. The craftsmanship was astounding. Every bit of construction felt exactly right. This watch in its own right was a work of art.

In the end the task took him almost a month to complete. He couldn't risk leaving the room and not finding it again and so was forced to subsist on what little water and bugs and crumbs he could find collected in the corners. But finally he was down to the very last piece.

With a trembling hand, he locked the copper cover in place and, unable to look, brought the watch to his ear.

Tick, tick, tick. "It's working. It's working!" he yelled as he jumped to his feet. He was beaming with pride, tears welling in his eyes, as all the frustration escaped from his body. But there was no time to celebrate. There was more work to be done.

Quickly he turned the watch over. The minute hand went around once, then twice, then so quickly that the revolutions couldn't be counted. Finally it fell still, settling on a number. And that number was nine. The gnome was right next door.

Vincent didn't have a plan. It had never occurred to him that he would actually get to this point. He left the room with the watch and walked to door nine, heart pounding, without a clue to how he would come away with the snake. But what he was absolutely sure of was that he had spent far too long in this cave. It was time for him to leave, and somehow, he would find a way.

With that, he pushed the door open.

Inside, along with the creak of the age-old door's rusted hinges, something squealed, as if frightened by the torchlight suddenly invading the room. Grunting, a small blur scrambled across the floor, dived behind a group of large boulders, and landed with a grunt. Vincent watched as a two-foot snake slithered to the very same spot and disappeared inside a crack.

Bubbling rivers of oil flowed through the room, from one wall to another. The heat emanating from these dark rivers was tremendous. Sweat dripped off Vincent's brow like rain in a thunderstorm. A drop from a bursting oil bubble landed on his clothes and burned straight through. He didn't know what to do or what to say. He stood there dumbfounded.

Eventually, a small hand appeared over one of the rocks. It had long, uneven nails that scratched away at the surface— a chilling sound. Its knuckles were cut and bleeding, a finger or two were broken, bent in grotesque positions, bones practically popping through the yellowed skin. The hand jerked back, and soon something reflective inched out from behind the rocks in its place: the magic mirror. The gnome was watching Vincent through it.

Suddenly the ground rumbled and shifted, and Vincent nearly toppled over into the flowing oil. He fell on his back, rolled toward the stream, and stopped just short of a quick death. It was moments before he allowed himself to even breathe again, let alone stand up.

Once the room settled, a maniacal laugh erupted, and the mirror, scratching along the ground, was pulled back behind the boulder.

"Just a boy. Nothing but a boy, you are. A weak, scared boy."

To Vincent, the voice sounded demented, crazed. The three fragmented sentences almost seemed as if they had spilled from three separate tongues. One voice was deep, another high-pitched, while the third was almost growled, early animalistic in tone. The words were punctuated with heavy and strained breaths, while some syllables were cut short, and others stretched. All this created an odd and disturbing song. He wondered if this was what happened when one pursued something for so very long without ever succeeding. *If I fail here*, Vincent thought, *is this my fate?*

"Boy come for my prize. Can't have prize. No, no, no. My destiny."

"I don't want your prize," Vincent said. "I've come for the snake."

"Never!" The gnome hissed as if attacked by such a statement. "Out, before I have you for dinner!"

A rock flew at Vincent and just missed his head. It bounced off the wall and rolled back to his feet. With his eyes locked on where the gnome hid, he bent down and picked it up. It was heavy in his hand, the only weapon he had.

"I don't want to hurt you," Vincent said.

The gnome could only laugh at this. "But I want to hurt you. I want to hurt you so bad."

The mirror came out again, and this time Vincent finally got a look at the gnome through it. He was a ghastly creature, something like a diseased goblin, his features perfectly befitting his cracked voice. He looked frail, wasted away as if consumed by his quest—nothing but a yellowed, gaunt face with wild eyes. *He sees things differently.* His beard was discolored and haggard, long enough to trip over, and insects crawled throughout it. He was filthy from head to toe, and indeed some toes peeked through the holes in his ragged boots. His hat was in shambles; it too laden with several holes, which, Vincent noticed, the snake slinked in and out of. *How long has he been down here?*

The gnome's feral eyes met Vincent's. He hissed, revealing rotten teeth, and threw another rock in response.

Vincent darted out of the way, and the rock landed behind him, disappearing into the oil that flowed from wall to wall like a serpent. "There's nothing behind the red door," he said. "I've opened it. The room is empty. Your quest has been in vain. You can give up."

"Lies," the gnome cried. "Prize is behind door. Everything you dream is behind door. Life eternal is behind door."

Eternal life? The power to fulfill dreams? Vincent wondered if this was true. Was there a way to break the witch's curse behind that door? A way to reunite him with his mother?

From where the gnome hid, something began to glow. "Must go. Must go now."

It was the mirror. It was beginning to transport him to another room, maybe this time to the exact room the gnome wanted to be in. In a moment he would be gone, along with the snake. There was no time to waste. Vincent ran to the light. As the glow intensified, he jumped behind the boulder, throwing the rock in midair, but the room was so bright by now he couldn't track its trajectory; it was lost in a blinding light.

However, there was the sound. With great force, the rock somehow connected with the mirror and shattered it into hundreds of pieces. It was music, a chimed symphony.

The gnome shrieked, a wail of incredible despair, one that was to haunt Vincent for years to come. With a damaged hand, the sobbing gnome picked up a large shard of glass and came charging at Vincent. His gait was awkward, as if one leg were shorter than the other, but this did not hinder his speed in the slightest. In his mad dash, his mouth hung open, drool dripping from an abnormally long and black tongue. He gripped the glass so tightly blood dripped from his palm, although he showed no pain. When he was only feet away, he jumped at Vincent, jumped higher than one would have believed possible. His arm was arched far back, and when he was close enough to his prey, he brought it flying forward to slash Vincent's face with the jagged shard. And that was how Vincent came to bear the scar he was to carry for the rest of his life.

The two of them crashed to the ground, the gnome on top, continuing to slash away. Defensively, Vincent brought his arms to his face, only to have them hacked and bloodied. The gnome was stronger than he appeared, and through it all he let loose an ungodly wail. Drooling, seething, he writhed and squirmed, his hat falling by his side.

The snake was only feet away from Vincent now. He could almost reach it, his sure path to freedom. With all his strength, he swiped at the gnome, knocking him aside, and in a single motion, Vincent rolled over and scooped up the hat with the snake still inside.

"Give snake back!" the gnome yelled from his hands and knees. "Broke mirror. Prize lost. Give . . . snake . . . back!"

"I can't," Vincent said, one hand clutching his throbbing cheek, dark blood gushing from between his fingers. "I'm sorry."

"Kill you! Carve out eyes! Eat them! *Eat them!*"

The room quaked yet again, the ground shifting violently beneath their feet. Vincent watched as the gnome lost his balance, teetering on the edge of the flowing oil. His body wobbled, his arms flailed, and still, he kept his eyes on his quarry. "Kill you! Kill you! Eat you up!" He raised the bloody shard of glass high over his head, prepared to strike a fatal blow.

But there was another tremor, this one more powerful than all the rest, and the earth split right beneath the gnome's feet. The crack grew drastically wide in seconds, sending him reeling backward.

"Watch out!" Vincent yelled, but it was too late.

The gnome had fallen into the boiling river. He didn't even have a chance to scream as he slowly sank and burned. It wasn't long before there wasn't a trace of him left.

Vincent looked away, clutching the hat close to his chest.

The snake emerged from within the hat and slithered around his fingers. He had them; he had found all three. His quest was over. It was all over.

The giant combined his six ingredients as the witch had informed him to do, and he came away with a liquid most vile. Vincent's eyes watered at the pungent smell.

"If this works," the giant said as he set his trembling hands into the thick liquid, "I shall set you free."

Vincent watched closely as the giant's fingers, covered in what looked like blue paste, rubbed against his white eyes. He rubbed and rubbed and rubbed for several minutes.

"Is it working?" Vincent finally asked.

Like a mask, the giant's massive hands hid his face, his eyes. "I don't want to pull my hands away," he said with great trepidation in his voice.

"You'll be able to see. I know it."

"And if I can't?"

"You will. Trust me."

And slowly the giant uncovered his eyes. The dark irises had somehow returned to the sclera, and immediately they focused on Vincent.

"I can see you. Vincent, I can see you!" The giant leaped to his feet, fresh tears in his fresh eyes. "You did it, my boy! I can see again!" Laughing, he picked Vincent up and swung him around, the chain rattling in a glorious melody. Hearing this, he looked at the shackle around Vincent's leg. "I have my sight. I will keep my promise." After setting Vincent down, he reached into his pocket and grabbed a black key with red teeth. With it, he undid the lock and tossed the chain far into the cave.

Vincent clutched his leg in disbelief. He had almost come to believe the chain was an extension of himself, a fifth limb. He wasn't sorry, however, to see it go.

"But please, stay one more night," the giant begged him. "I will prepare us the greatest feast you will ever witness. A celebration, with you as my guest of honor."

Vincent knew he should just leave the cave. Although the giant's vision had returned, although he was kinder than ever, something wasn't right with him. Those eyes revealed something Vincent didn't trust. Those eyes told him there was another side to the giant, an even darker one, of which he must beware.

But there was something else, something disturbing, in the back of Vincent's mind. He couldn't stop looking at the door through which he was forbidden to enter. It was that room, more than anything else, that kept him from leaving. Over the past months its hidden contents had plagued his mind. And now after what the gnome had said . . . If he was ever going to find out what was inside, it had to be now. He agreed to stay for dinner.

As the giant left to gather food for the feast, Vincent hovered outside the room, feeling the wood of the red door, listening for whatever sounds might come from beyond it. He shouldn't go in, but it was now or never.

It wouldn't hurt if I just took a quick peek, he thought after some time. *The giant would never have to know. I'll go in and out before he even suspects a thing.* And so, as he watched the giant, basket in hand, disappear farther into the distance, the trees swaying in his wake, Vincent made his decision. *Now, now, now*, he thought. *For your mother! Hurry!* He ran to the red door and pushed against it with all his might. It was heavier than all the rest, opening just enough for him to squeeze through. But squeeze through he did. Finally he was on the other side.

The room was more like a barn than anything else. Straw was everywhere, wood beams were overhead, and behind a gate a horse was sleeping. Even more shockingly, it shared its pen with a pacing lion. Yet as odd as this was, the animals didn't capture Vincent's attention quite like the fountain in the center of the room did, for this fountain did not contain water—well, not water as Vincent knew it, but something far more precious. There was definitely liquid pooled at the base and pouring from the mouths of stone gargoyles, but it wasn't blue or clear. It was gold. And in the center of the fountain, set upon a pedestal, was a thick book, and it too was made of gold.

Vincent approached slowly. From behind the gate, pacing even more quickly now, the lion watched him closely.

Vincent reached the fountain and peered into it. His reflection could be seen in the gold liquid. He liked the way he looked; the image mesmerized him. He leaned even closer. The liquid was so inviting, so intoxicating. Was this what had been pulling him all this time? Was this what the gnome had sought?

He reached out with a hand, finger extended. He brought it closer . . . closer—

"Don't!" someone screamed, but it was too late, Vincent had already dipped his finger in.

He pulled it out quickly, surveying the room, looking for who it was that had yelled. But there was no one, only the animals. He turned back to his finger, inspecting it closely. The liquid was warm, beautiful. He attempted to wipe it on the straw but realized his finger didn't come clean. He tried again. Nothing. He had a gold finger. Vincent shook his hand violently as if to throw the liquid off. He sucked on it, he tried scraping it with his teeth, all to no avail.

"The giant . . . ," he fearfully whispered to himself.

"You must conceal it," said the voice. "Hurry."

Vincent's head snapped up. It had come from the

direction of the pen; he was almost sure of it. He walked a step closer. "Conceal it how?" he asked.

Now there was no denying whom he was speaking to. The lion looked directly at him and said, "Wrap it in cloth. Pretend that it is a wound. The giant will never know. Do this, and you will be safe."

Vincent couldn't believe it. How could it speak? Why didn't it ravage the sleeping horse?

"Over there," the lion said, nodding toward a supply shelf. "There is cloth there the giant uses to wrap the horse's legs."

Hesitantly, Vincent approached the shelf on which countless supplies were stocked; it looked like there was everything one could ever need. But there was no time to inspect such contents. Quickly he grabbed the cloth as the lion had said.

"Oh, no, no, no."

Vincent turned around. The horse was up, head sticking out between the bars.

"Best not to hide it," the horse said. "The giant detests liars most of all. Just be honest, and because you healed him, he may grant you a reprieve."

"Like he did us?" the lion roared. "He will kill the boy. Or worse."

The horse ignored the lion. "Boy, you have to trust me. I've been here a long time, far too long; I know everything there is to know about this place, about the giant. Admit your mistake. It is your best chance of leaving this cave alive."

"But the giant warned me already," Vincent said. "I was forbidden to enter this room."

"That's right. That is why you must hide the finger," the lion said. "Hide it. Lie to him, and then, the very first chance you get, when the giant is at his most vulnerable, kill him. It is the only way."

"Don't be foolish," said the horse. "You must not listen to the lion. He is brash and proud. It is what got him locked away in here in the first place. Take my advice. Inform him of what you did. If you don't, you will discover that the giant is wiser than you imagined. He'll know of your deceit immediately, and he'll never let you go."

The lion laughed. "The horse is weak and naïve. Pitiful. His fear bests him, and that is why he has been trapped here for so long now. I tell you the truth. The giant shows no mercy. For touching his fountain, for being so close to the gold book, for even setting foot into this room, he will have your head. Believe me. Hide the finger and kill the giant in his sleep."

Outside the door there were footsteps, loud footsteps. The giant was returning home. Vincent had to hurry. Panicking, he began wrapping his finger. "I'll get away," he said. "I'll figure it out. I just need some time."

"I said the same thing," the horse said, staring down at the hay.

Vincent turned to run out, but the lion called out to him.

"Boy, if you happen to find a key, a black key with bloodstained teeth, would you grab it and come release us before you leave? Would you do that for us? We can escape together."

Vincent thought back to the giant's reaching into his pocket for just such a key. It had freed him, so it stood to reason it could also free them. "I will," he said.

"Do not risk your life any more than you have to," the horse said. "By lying you have already risked too much. If you are able to, save yourself."

Vincent looked at his wrapped finger, then at the lion. "Thank you," he said to the beast. "I will come back for you."

He crept out the door and pulled it closed, and just in time too, for the giant had returned.

"Where were you?" the giant asked, emerging from the darkness. He eyed Vincent suspiciously.

"Nowhere," Vincent said, unable to raise his head and lock eyes.

"Nowhere. I've been there before," the giant said. "It is a dangerous place to be. Especially for a small young boy like you. Tell me, what have you done to your finger?"

Like a guilty child, Vincent pulled his hand behind his

back. There was no way he could tell him where he had been. "Nothing. I cut it."

"Is it serious? I will treat it for you."

"No need. I have already done so."

"I see." The giant was quiet for some time. "Come here," he said finally. "Come here so that I may thank you for healing my eyes."

"You have already thanked me. In fact, I should leave."

"But I wish to thank you again. I have brought you a gift."

"I can receive it from here."

"And what about the feast? I have gathered us a magnificent assortment."

"I am not hungry."

"Why do you play games with me, Vincent? Come. Come to your friend."

Quivering, Vincent walked a few feet closer, his eyes darting around the cave.

"Closer," the giant said.

Vincent, desperately searching his mind for a way out, took another step. "I have done what you asked, and now I wish to leave."

"Closer," the giant sang.

He would have to run, right between the giant's legs. Vincent placed his foot forward and was about to flee when the giant, with uncanny speed, reached down and snatched him up. In a flash, he grabbed Vincent's hand and unwrapped the cloth, revealing the gold finger underneath.

"Aha! What have we here?" he growled.

"It was an accident!"

"Betrayal! You have betrayed me!"

Vincent could feel the giant squeezing the life out of him.

"The book! Did you open it?"

"N-no." He could hear his bones cracking.

"I have warned you the price you would pay for entering that room."

"I didn't mean to— Please. I made a mistake."

"Indeed you did. And now you shall pay for it."

"But—But . . . I healed you. Why is it that you were even able to see the cloth?"

The giant hesitated, his grip loosening. "Yes. Yes, you did heal me. But you have also lied, something unforgivable. I will spare your life, Vincent." Vincent exhaled but then saw the giant's eyes go dark. "But you must still be punished. You like gold, do you?"

The giant rushed down the hall with Vincent still clutched in his hands. The giant kicked open the red door and stepped inside. The horse neighed, the lion roared, and the giant stripped Vincent of his clothes and tossed him face-first into the fountain.

"There," the giant said as he removed him moments later. He brought Vincent back out of the room and locked the chain around his leg once more. "You are now my golden boy."

CHAPTER 8

An announcement crackled and buzzed through the overhead speakers and vibrated straight into Vince's ears: "Next stop: Eastbrook."

Already? Vince tucked his grandfather's book into his backpack and glanced to his left. Across the aisle the seat was empty. Eric was gone, and in his place was a single piece of paper with the words "Thank you" written on it. It seemed Vince had been so absorbed in the book he hadn't even noticed the artist departing the train. When he read, it was almost as if he were connecting with his grandfather, as if the stories were the real history of his family. But these, he had to remind himself, were fairy tales and nothing more.

It was the same as it was with the stories he had told at the orphanage. His father wasn't a spy or world traveler, and there was no truth in his grandfather's book. His grandfather certainly wasn't gold when he last saw him. And what about the horse and the lion? How were they able to talk? Where was that tower painting now? Had anybody gone back into that cave to look? Was everybody just ignoring that there was a fountain of gold somewhere in it?

Vince laughed and shook his head. It was funny when he thought it through like that, especially after finding himself hanging on every single word of that last tale, even going so far as to envision himself in his grandfather's place; he could almost feel the chain locked around his own leg. He saw it all so clearly—the painting of the tower, the volcanic room, the fountain of gold—and for the entire length of the tale all his doubt was gone. In those moments, as far as he was concerned, it was all true, every word. He believed. And that scared him.

Maybe it was safer to think his father wouldn't show, not now, not ever. Maybe Vince really was abandoned for good. Maybe his father had found a new life, a happier one with a new family, and everything in Andrew's letter was just a coincidence. Or maybe it was just safer to think that back in the fire his father . . .

His stop came, and Vince stepped off the train and into the steadily falling snow. There weren't many people around, and the few shops in the station that were still open wouldn't be for much longer. Vince stopped in a few and, with the money he had received from M, bought two slices of pizza to fill his stomach and a map to guide him to the place where his home once stood. Then, somewhat warmed and rested, he set back out on his journey.

The snow was persistent in its dense accumulation, falling with a sort of permanence. There was nearly a half foot piled on the ground, and to judge by the sky and repeated news reports, there was plenty more to come. Temperatures were nearing zero, and there was no evidence that the mercury in the thermometers would halt its rapid descent any time soon. The wind picked up in the direction Vince needed to venture, severely slowing his stride. It was so sharp it practically had teeth, tiny teeth that pricked Vince's face and blurred his eyes and pierced his threadbare clothes, scratching away at his skin and bones beneath. His clothes were ill suited for such weather, his shoes much too thin. But still, he pushed on, tucking his head to his chest and shoving his hands into his pockets as he marched through the deep snow.

For a while nothing looked familiar to him, especially with all the snow blanketing everything, whitewashing the entire town. But as he turned a corner, that all changed. He saw a huge oak tree that he used to climb with his father on their walks to the local park. It was beautiful, the snow clinging to the bare branches like white moss, the trunk twisted and gnarled as if uncomfortable from the cold. In deep reflection, he walked up to the tree and placed a trembling hand against it. His head lowered and his eyes closed as he recalled those happier times.

"Grab my hand," his father said, dangling from a thick branch high above him. "I'll pull you up."

Vince remembered how scared he was that first time, scared but excited. As fun as the climb might be, the ground felt safe; he wasn't sure he should ever leave it.

His father extended his arm even farther. "Don't be scared. I won't let you fall. I'll hold on. I promise."

"Dad . . ."

"You have to see the view up here. It's magical."

Without another thought, Vince reached up and clasped the outreached hand. It was his father's eyes that compelled him. It was as if they had truly seen that magic and were filled with the splendor of it. In that moment, Vince so badly wanted to share such an experience his fear was wiped clean.

Without time to even close his eyes, he was off the ground and hanging from the same branch as his father.

"Okay, that was the hard part. The rest is just fun. Come on."

From there they climbed higher and higher, his father guiding him carefully up every branch until they reached the top.

"We're high up," Vince said, looking out over the town, all the trees and wilderness to the south, the mountains far to the north, the river to the east, his house to the west. It was a stunning sight, one of undeniable beauty sprawling as far as the eye could see. There truly was magic up here, the strongest kind.

"Top of the world. It's all yours. Go ahead, shout something. Anything you want. It's your kingdom. Let them hear you."

And how does one come to reign over such a land? Vince wondered. *What does one say?* He looked over at his father and shouted the very first words that popped into his head. "Umbia Rah!" His voice echoed for miles like a slight thunderclap.

Laughing, his father shook his head. "Umbia Rah. I can't believe you remember that. That's what your grandfather always used to say to you when you were a baby. It was like your own language, just the two of you. You shared a terrific bond."

After that the mood changed, and Vince and his father climbed down, not saying a word, and went straight home instead of to the park.

The memory ended when Vince's eyes snapped open.

Chills, colder than the air around him, were running up his spine. He wanted so badly to see his father spring out from that tree once again. He wanted to see him dangle from that last branch, swinging back and forth, picking up speed. He wanted to watch him let go and spin and flip and land right in front of Vincent. A young boy and his father once again. They would play together; they would run all through Eastbrook—their town, their kingdom—sprinting down every street, slapping stop signs, and tossing snowballs, never once saying what needed to be said, never once acknowledging their relationship, never once saying how terribly they missed each other, because it would all be felt, it would all be understood. Vince saw this and smiled.

With his head down, without really knowing why, he began to run. Feet crunching the fallen snow, he ran and ran and ran, eyes closed. And when he opened them again, he saw his father beside him. They were perfectly in stride, a father racing his little boy. Vince saw it as clearly as any-thing.

Facedown, he ran as hard as he could, trying to run straight into this new reality. He ran for what felt like hours, completely unaware that his fingers were crossed in hope once again. He ran dozens of blocks, creating hundreds of footprints in the snow leading to a place he called home but wasn't. He ran until he couldn't run anymore, until he nearly collapsed from exhaustion.

His eyes closed. And when they opened again, his father was gone.

There in the snow, bent over and gasping, his breath escaping like his soul, Vince stared ahead into the blizzard, waiting desperately for his father to reappear.

Instead, on this barren road, squeezed shut by trees on either side, not a house in sight, he saw a dark car idling along the shoulder, stuck in a bank of snow, black smoke spiraling from the exhaust as the tires spun in place, kicking up filthy flurries. A man and a woman—the only people for miles—were trying to push the vehicle free but were getting nowhere. As Vince walked closer, he called out to them, "Need any help?"

Nobody turned around or acknowledged him in any way. Vince figured they must not have heard him through the howling wind. He waited until he got closer, and then he asked again.

"Need a hand?"

The man and woman pushing against the rear of the car froze like much of the town and the trees surrounding it. Although it was clear they heard Vince's query this second time, they didn't move or say a thing.

Vince looked past them and saw behind the wheel an old woman glaring at him through the rearview mirror. The gas was hit again, and the tires rotated, but the car went nowhere.

Vince placed his frozen hands against the trunk of the car. Beside him, the man watched from the corners of his eyes. Together the three of them pushed, and soon the car was free from the snow.

"Now get in here," the old woman in the driver's seat yelled to her companions. "Let's go, you imbeciles!"

The man turned to Vince. It was peculiar; his body didn't move in the same manner as everyone else's. It was like he was stiff, locked at the joints, a dead man just learning to walk. He was a tall specimen, towering over Vince by nearly two feet. The man's face was that horrifying. Oddly shaped and emaciated, it was all popping bone, the skin pale and immensely tight against it. His nose was severely broken, almost knocked flat on his face, a fresh wound, dripping bright red blood. He didn't wear a hat, and his hair was stubbly. This made the jagged scar that ran inches across his scalp so easy to see. And it was this more than anything that gave him away. Vince swallowed hard. He had seen this brutal face before. Without even getting a decent look at the other two, he knew he was standing before a family of criminals. He was face-to-face with the Byron Clan.

"What do we do with this one, Lonnie? Do we take him for a ride?" The voice was like the wind if it carried nails in it, cutting up the inside of Vince's ears.

He looked at the crazed woman, who now knelt down before him. She sat in the snow as if it were sand on the beach. She didn't react to the cold; she didn't look uncomfortable in the least. Her black hair was knotted and ragged and wild, like Medusa's serpents, and her equally dark eyes seemed to stare straight through him into some other realm. There was a slight screeching sound, and Vince soon realized it was her hyper and excited breathing.

Lonnie's large hand came to rest on his sister's head. His fingers were so long they nearly engulfed the entire skull. "Ask Mother," he said in a baritone voice, tapping those long fingers against her scalp. "She'll know."

But his sister didn't budge. With her tongue wagging like a dog's, she continued to stare at Vince. "Would you like a ride, little boy? You were such a good, helpful little boy. We'll get you through this snow. Bring you somewhere nice and warm. Toasty." As she spoke, her eyes twitched.

Lonnie lumbered to the front of the car and leaned down and talked to his mother. His sister meanwhile reached out and caressed Vince's face. Her touch was repellent, and he was thankful his face was already numb. She was a petite thing, but there was more to fear in this woman than from a dozen Lonnies. She leaned in and placed her lips against Vince's ear. Her breath was colder than the wind. With her lips touching his skin, and in a childish voice, she began to sing: "Oh, I have the moon in me. And everything beyond. I am a black hole, you see. And I'll eat me some vagabond."

And with a hiss, she opened her mouth really wide

only to have her brother yank her back the second her jaw snapped like a rabid dog's.

"Misty. Not yet. Help me put him in the car."

Pleased, she rubbed her hands together. "Yummy."

As they stepped closer, the old woman in the driver's seat yelled out to the others, "Cover!"

A plow truck was approaching from down the road, steering waves of snow onto the sidewalks, and seeing this, Lonnie and his sister quickly hid their faces. Vince saw his opportunity—most likely the only one he would get—and took off in the snow. Lonnie moaned and Misty hissed, but he was in the clear; chasing him would bring far too much attention. As he escaped, he could hear the driver of the truck stop his plowing and call out to the Byron Clan, "You guys stuck? I can get you out of there; no problem."

"Yummy," he heard Misty say, and then she began to sing, the words lingering in Vince's ear as if her lips were still pressed against them. "Oh, I have the moon in me . . ."

Vince's heart was beating wildly. That poor man, what were they going to do to him? He had to get help. He had to alert the authorities. The area, however, was still deserted, and so he kept running alongside the dense woods, hoping to stumble upon someone he could trust. But the snow grew higher and his pace grew slower and the temperature continued to drop. He walked through the fierce isolation, his teeth clattering like coffins in a quake. He was soaking wet; he couldn't feel a thing anymore. He imagined himself slowly becoming a block of ice. First his feet, then his hands. He'd walk with them encased in cubes of ice until his body succumbed, and, finally, his head. A giant ice cube. If he could have laughed, he would have. This would be the end of his journey, he realized, a frozen boy waiting for spring. What a fool he was.

His vision was blurred, and he wasn't even sure he was going in the right direction anymore. But he couldn't go back. Anywhere but back.

It was clear his body was beginning to give out on him. Everything hurt. How long had he been running now? However long it was, it felt like double because of the snow. Maybe triple. He was close to collapsing, close to blacking out. He could feel it. It would happen at any moment now.

And that was when he saw the house. His house. *But that isn't possible*, he told himself. *It burned down. You're hallucinating.*

A young girl stood outside the house, building a snowman, her dog taking laps in the snow, barking merrily. She saw Vince staring at her. And then she saw him fall face-first into the snow.

Darkness.

CHAPTER 9

Hours later, when Vince woke up again, he was in what should have been his house. He was in what should have been his bed. And around him were a man and woman and the young girl he saw just before passing out.

"Get some rest," the mother said, adjusting one of the many blankets over him. "Warm up. There's some hot chocolate right there. You're safe now. We'll get you all squared away in the morning, when you have more strength."

"Thank . . . thank . . ." He could barely speak.

"Don't," the father said. "Just rest. You've been through a lot."

With that, the parents left, and the young girl, perhaps the same age as Vince, perhaps a year older, sat in a chair beside the bed.

"My name's MJ," she said. "I was the one who found you outside. You know, it's kind of funny. I was so bored and lonely out there by myself, as usual, that it was almost like I wished for you to appear. And then there you were. You face-planted right into the snow. I couldn't believe it. My dog started barking and licking your face. I called for my parents, screaming about a boy fainting in the snow, and I just knew they weren't going to believe me. They always accuse me of making up stories. Anyway, I ran over to you as fast as I could. You were mumbling something. Umbi-something or other."

Vince's throat throbbed with pain. "Umbia Rah."

Features scrunched in confusion, MJ placed her hand on his forehead. "You're going to be okay. You had my parents really worried there for a minute. They wanted to get you to a hospital, but the roads are all closed. I hope you don't mind, but we went through your backpack looking for something that might tell us who you are. We didn't find anything, but we did find this." She held up his grandfather's book. "I've been reading some, and I love it. It's a great story. I love the main character."

"It's my—my grandfather."

"Your grandfather? That's amazing. If you want, I can read some for you right now. Maybe it'll help you feel better. Is that okay?"

Vince nodded his head. "He's—he's gold. . . ."

MJ smiled. "That's right where I left off too."

The Forbidden Room

Vincent sat chained to the wall, his gold body gleaming in the giant's roaring fire. Every day for a week straight now, the giant demanded that his prize pose for his amusement, like a living statue. "Arms up, neck stretched!" or "On your knees, face in the dirt!" or "Stand on one leg with the other straight out behind you!" Then he ordered Vincent to hold such poses for hours. Typically, Vincent collapsed or cried out, and the giant laughed mightily at this, especially while eating his abundance of exotic foods.

This night, however, the night Vincent had been waiting

for, was a different night in one important way. It was the giant's birthday, and as he feasted in celebration of himself, between every bite and explosive burst of laughter, he consumed even more wine than usual, one barrel after the other.

Unfortunately, this of course led to further abuse for Vincent to withstand. Belligerent from the booze, the giant forced him to act out scenes, dramatic and comedic alike, his very own puppet, the only string being the metal leash locked around his leg. When he was satisfied with the performance, and that was rare, the giant tossed food at the golden boy, striking him in the head and chest. Vincent then dropped to his hands and knees and, starving, gobbled everything up. When the giant wasn't satisfied, however, he yanked on the chain, sending Vincent crashing hard to the ground. At one point, he even dragged him around the cave, laughing maniacally as he did so. The jagged rocks cut at Vincent, blood seeping through his gold skin. The giant pulled him all around, looking for especially harsh terrain on which to drag his body. The cave's floor was like teeth; it ate from his flesh, biting at his face, deeper, even, than the gold. One spike cut straight through his cheek. And that was how Vincent came to bear the scar he was to carry for the rest of his life.

As the night wore on, the giant, between deafening belches, drank more and more, much to Vincent's delight, until a dozen empty wine barrels lined the cave. Vincent was willing to withstand a night of ridicule and torture, so long as the giant slept deeply. He didn't care about being toyed with or, pinched between the giant's fingers, sadistically dangled over the flames. He didn't mind being showered with wine when he fell out of his pose or flubbed a line. He didn't mind being laughed at and taunted. *Just keep drinking*, was all he thought. *Drink and sleep well, giant, for tonight I escape.*

Finally, just hours before dawn, the giant began to tire. He quieted down, his eyes appearing heavy, his commands becoming more and more infrequent—almost involuntary and practically indecipherable. He stretched his legs out, yawning repeatedly. Then, sure enough, he fell asleep, with snores like rolling thunder.

Minutes later Vincent decided it was time to act. He knew he had to be very careful as to not wake the giant, even as he searched his pockets for the black key with red teeth. But if he did wake, there must be a plan. And Vincent had one.

As silently as possible he walked in a circle around the giant. When he completed one lap, he simply walked another. Then another. He circled the giant as many times as the length of chain would allow, and when he was finished, Vincent had his very own prisoner.

Next, with the giant bound, Vincent crept over to the pocket in which he had last seen the key. He thrust his hand in, but couldn't reach, and so he stuck almost his entire body into the deep pocket to retrieve it, but retrieve it he did. The iron felt cool in his hands as he pulled the black key free.

The giant shifted in his sleep, and Vincent jumped to the ground. Quickly, yet also quietly, he undid the lock shackled to his leg.

Now, get out of here and don't look back. And yet he did look back. His eyes went down the hall and right to the red door.

He had promised the lion and the horse he would rescue them. But was that really why he hesitated? No. There was something in that room that he needed, that he couldn't leave without. The gold book. Was that the answer to everything? To breaking the curse and defeating the witch? Could the book tell him how to return to his life with his mother?

He glanced up at the giant, whose chest was heaving with each obnoxious snore. He could wake at any moment. The chains would have to hold. *I won't be long. In and out. No time at all.*

He hurried to the red door and, without slowing, pushed it open. Inside, the lion jumped to its feet.

"I have the key," Vincent said, holding it aloft.

"The giant, what about the giant?" the lion asked, pacing anxiously. "Did you finish him?"

154

"No, he's asleep, wrapped in my chains."

"Hurry," the horse said, it too rising from its slumber. "That won't hold him for very long."

Vincent shoved the black key into the lock and opened the gate.

After years of captivity, the animals were finally freed. The lion, however, brushed right past his liberator and ran from the room without looking back.

The horse began to follow but stopped just outside the door. "The giant will come for us," it said. "We must prepare ourselves. Vincent, go to the shelf and grab what I tell you to."

Vincent's eyes, however, were locked on the gold book. "What for? There's no time," he said in a dazed tone. "The lion's right. We have to get out of here."

"Do as I say. You have to trust me."

Vincent struggled to take his eyes off the book and, recalling how the horse had been right before, did as he was told. Standing before all the supplies stacked neatly on shelves, he asked, "What do we need?"

"Take the razors and the needles and that vial of water there on the end. Place them in the leather sack hanging from that nail."

Vincent curiously eyed the horse. What was this all about?

"Go on, grab them."

He collected the items, and the horse appeared pleased.

"Very good. Now we must run. The giant will wake soon."

Vincent turned around. "The book. I can't leave without the book."

He had to have it. Was that what the gnome wanted, not the golden liquid? What was written within those ancient pages? What was so special about it? Did it have all the answers? Would it solve his every problem and so much more?

"Vincent, leave the book. There is great power within it, but it is not to be taken lightly. It is locked away for a reason."

But as if hypnotized, Vincent ignored the horse. He walked closer.

"Vincent, no! If you take it, the giant will surely kill you."

"Maybe I can use it," he said, more to himself than to the horse. "Maybe I can defeat the witch and reverse her spells. Maybe I can set things right."

"It's not that simple!"

To Vincent it was. Hastily, he ran to the fountain and grabbed the gold book from off the pedestal. In his hands, the pages felt like absolute splendor. His body vibrated; his eyes couldn't look away from the shining cover. He couldn't even place it in the sack. It felt as if the book belonged in his hands.

"Quickly," the horse said with a snort. "We've wasted too much time."

This seemed to break Vincent's trance. The book slipped from his fingers and into the sack.

The two ran out of the room and down the hall, only to find that the lion hadn't escaped at all. Rather, it was threateningly circling the sleeping giant.

"Don't," said the horse, anticipating its next move. "Let us leave while we still have a chance."

"No," the lion snarled. "I've suffered far too long. He must pay for what he's done." And the lion leaped at the giant and slashed his face on each side.

The vicious blows awakened the giant, but the lion bravely and stubbornly continued to slash and bite regardless.

Arms pinned to his sides by the chains, the giant stood, unable to defend himself from the relentless attack. But the chain didn't hold him for long. With a roar that far outmatched the lion's, he broke free, metal links flying in every direction like shrapnel. Then he squared off against his opponent.

The lion froze, a look of hesitation and fear on its face.

"Run!" the horse and Vincent yelled. "Run!" But the

lion ignored the pleas.

"Come, little lion," the giant said, waving it on. "I should have done this a long time ago."

"This ends now!" the lion bellowed as it lunged forward, claws extended, teeth bared.

Vincent could only watch in horror as the giant snatched the lion out of midair and held its squirming body in his massive hands. Then, with a disturbing laugh, the giant snapped the beast's back with ease and threw it hard to the ground. The lion lay motionless, eyes rolled back, its tongue hanging limply from its mouth.

"No!" Vincent screamed.

The giant glared ferociously at the golden boy. "You!" He spotted the leather sack hanging over Vincent's shoulder, the gold book shining through from inside. "My book!"

"On my back," the horse yelled to Vincent. "Hurry!"

Vincent ran and jumped on the horse and locked his arms tightly around its neck. Together, they took off toward the mouth of the cave, the giant right behind them.

The horse ran with all its might out of the darkness and into the waxing light of early morning. Vincent was finally free. As he escaped the cave, the world seemed new. Everything was magnificently different somehow.

Sadly, there was no time to take in such pleasures, for behind them the giant's feet could be heard rapidly pounding the ground.

The horse wove and hurdled its way down the mountainside, stumbling and sliding atop loose rocks, while all the giant had to do was execute one large leap and he was at the bottom, waiting for them.

"Come to me!" he yelled, and the horse did just that.

The giant couldn't help grinning at the pair's foolishness. He crouched down, ready to swipe them up and into his powerful arms so that he could slowly crush the life out of their pitiful bodies.

Head down, the horse charged, full gallop. It was only yards away now.

"Yes!" the giant wailed, nearly on top of them. "Yes!"

The horse snorted. Vincent slammed his eyes shut. And the giant lunged forward.

But the horse was anticipating such a move and was far too quick for the lumbering monster. It deftly sidestepped the swipe and took off between the arches of his legs. Off balance and off guard, the giant fell face-first to the earth.

At the sound of the thud, Vincent opened his eyes and looked back. The giant was on all fours, shaking his head in disbelief.

Meanwhile, the horse made its way into the open farmland and, with no obstacles in its path, galloped even harder. It practically flew through those fields, scaring up birds and scattering varmints. But still, they could not lose the giant. Pure determination on his face, he was up and gaining on them. His strides were so long he would surely have them in no time.

The horse yelled back to Vincent, "Throw the needles! Throw them now!"

"What?" Vincent hollered over the thrashing of the horse's hoofs. He didn't think he'd heard right.

"The needles in the sack! Throw them at the giant!"

Vincent dug into the leather sack and pulled out the needles. *What are a handful of these going to do against something like him?* he wondered.

"Throw them! Do it now!" the horse yelled again.

Vincent did as he was told. He tossed the needles far behind them, straight into the giant's path. But they failed to reach him. And yet the needles were never intended to strike their enraged pursuer. They were only meant to hit the ground, for the moment they did, an entire forest sprang up out of nowhere, further separating hunter and prey. Thousands of trees grew in a matter of seconds. Only this forest was no ordinary forest. Each tree was made up of devastatingly sharp needles. Needles for branches, needles for leaves, needles for roots, needles for bark. Millions of needles sitting atop one another, all blocking the path of the giant.

The giant, however, fuming mad and refusing to turn back, ran straight into the forest without slowing one bit. The needles served their purpose, meeting him head-on and puncturing his entire body, every inch of it. They pierced his feet and jabbed his skull; they dug deep into his arms and stabbed his throat. He was speared over and over and over again, losing an eye in the process. The giant howled in pain as he pushed through, knocking trees to the ground left and right in enraged swipes.

Meanwhile, Vincent and the horse kept running, the giant's screams filling their ears. Their lead widened.

But eventually Vincent glanced back, and he saw the giant in pursuit once again. Bleeding from head to toe, he ran faster than ever, as if fueled by his pain and fury. The land trembled beneath his feet.

"I'm coming!" he screamed. "I'm coming for you, Vincent!"

"The razors!" the horse yelled, with fear in his voice. "Throw them!"

And this time Vincent didn't need to be told twice. He threw the razors over his shoulder, and when they hit the ground, a mountain erupted from the earth. It was a towering mountain, wide and steep, and every inch of it was covered with razors. There was not a single place to set one's hand or foot without having it sliced open on ultrasharp steel.

This, however, did not deter the giant either. He ran straight for the mountain, jumping at the very last moment. He jumped so far that he landed almost halfway up. But as his hands and feet came down, they were met with the blazing pain of razors sinking deep into the skin. Still, the giant climbed, up and over the mountain. He lost one finger, then another. Three in all, along with two toes. Veins were cut, as was some bone. His ears were slashed to bits; his tongue was split in two, forked now, like a serpent's.

However, down the mountain the giant came, Vincent and the horse locked in his sights. He wouldn't give up; he would never give up, and again, even more amazingly now, he gained on them.

Finally the horse told Vincent to throw the vial of water.

Vincent removed the clear blue liquid from the sack. It was their last weapon, their final hope. But what was some water going to do? How was that going to stop the giant when a forest of needles and a mountain of razors didn't? Regardless, Vincent tossed the vial.

It hit the ground hard, shattering upon impact. The water seeped slowly into the earth. Seconds passed. The giant gained.

Then, glancing back, Vincent watched as a massive lake appeared, a lake so large that it was impossible for the giant to run around it and still hope to catch them; it seemed to stretch from horizon to horizon. But surely he could swim across? It wouldn't slow him down for very long at all.

"A lake?" Vincent said into the horse's ear.

"Not just a lake," the horse said in return, a gleam in its

162

eye, "but a lake of salt water."

The moment the giant jumped in, he wailed to the heavens. Salt entered every wound, shocking him with tremendous pain. The pain was so great, in fact, so agonizing, that the giant couldn't swim. He tried to make his way back but found he couldn't do so. He could hardly move at all. Within seconds the lake had turned red.

"Help!" the giant cried, waving his arms. "Vincent! My friend, my only friend! Please! Help me!"

Vincent looked back with terrific sympathy for the giant. Maybe he should help him.

Almost reading his thoughts, the horse said, "Don't listen to his cries. He is pure evil; you can count on that. Were you to save him, you would only doom yourself. I too sought shelter in his cave. I was a boy, just like you. My name is Orin. And now look at me. No, that giant deserves what comes to him."

As the horse called Orin galloped on, Vincent glanced back at the flailing giant. He saw him sink lower and lower and lower into the lake until there was no longer any part of him left to see. He was gone.

Vincent, gold body shining in the sun, turned ahead and gazed into the radiant distance.

Where to now?

CHAPTER 10

~ꕥꕥꕥ~

Vince woke up to a wonderful scent filling the air. Cinnamon perhaps. Or maybe vanilla. He was alone in the room that had once been his own and didn't realize he was half naked under the billowy blankets until he saw his ragged clothes hanging over some chairs and the heater. With the covers wrapped around his body, he got up and felt the fabric of his garments. Dry. All of them. As he slipped back into his clothes, he noticed how refreshed he felt, as if he had slept for days.

Fully dressed, he glanced out the window to his right. The snow continued to come down at a steady pace. There must have been well over two feet on the ground. And in that snow he saw his father. He had a football in his hands, and he was casually tossing it into the air, a wide smile on his face. A thick fog of breath drifted from his mouth as he turned and waved Vince outside.

Vince reached out, his hand against the windowpane. "Dad?"

Through the bedroom door trotted the family dog, an old beagle, and Vince's eyes were momentarily pulled from the window. The dog's ears, he noticed, were peculiarly crinkled, and there was a white patch amid all the black and brown fur, as if a chunk of snow had settled permanently behind its neck. The elderly canine didn't pay Vince any mind; it was busy chomping on some food it clearly wasn't supposed to have. Vince turned back to the window, but his father was no longer there.

"Romeo, no!" A redheaded woman ran in and snatched the bread from the dog's mouth. "Oh, I hope he doesn't get sick. It's spiced bread, and he has a very sensitive stomach. You don't think he ate a lot, do you?"

"I don't think he got very much," Vince said. This wasn't completely accurate, but he said it mostly to keep the woman from worrying. She had eyes of constant concern, as if all she had ever done was care too much. It was one of the few things he remembered from the previous night. Sometime in the midnight hours this woman checked in on him, spoke kind words, felt his forehead, adjusted his blankets;

he woke up only briefly during this kindhearted intrusion, noticing her eyes and feeling their deep warmth, and then he fell back to sleep, not stirring again until morning.

Looking at her now, he found her to be a woman of staggering beauty. She had thick bright red hair falling just past her narrow shoulders. Her skin looked like cream, and her eyes like green zinnias. Every feature was just about perfect, as if she were a painting come to life. An apron was tied snugly around her petite frame, and she was wearing a very thin silver necklace with a ladybug charm hanging from it. At the sight of the disappointed dog, she bent over to pet it affectionately.

"Romeo," she said in a voice that could melt the snow outside, "you know you can't eat that stuff. It'll hurt your tummy. Go to the kitchen, and Daddy will give you a healthy treat."

The dog left, as if understanding these words, and the woman looked over at Vince. "I don't know if you remember, but my name's Michele. We didn't get yours yet. You mumbled something, but it wasn't clear."

"Vincent."

"Vincent, yes. We're lucky we found you when we did, Vincent. You could have frozen to death. Any longer out there, and you might have lost some toes. Now, unfortunately, there's no way of driving out of here anytime soon, but is there someone we can call to tell you're okay? Your parents must be worried sick."

Vince shook his head and explained that he was an orphan on the way to his grandfather's funeral in nearby Dyerville.

"I see," Michele said. "Well, come to the kitchen when you're ready and have something to eat. I'm sure you can smell it. MJ and I have been cooking all morning."

"That sounds wonderful," he said. "Thank you so much."

"It's our pleasure. Please, make yourself at home."

She left the room, and Vince looked around one more time. Home. This was what it would have been like, he imagined. If that one tragic day had been ripped from the time line, this would have been his life. He would have woken up on a cold morning in this very room, and his mother would have had breakfast cooking, and he would have sat down to eat it with his father, and maybe eventually he would have had a sister too. And a dog. Home. Yes, it seemed perfect.

And then into the room walked his mother. She was like a ghost, passing right through him. Vince followed her with his eyes and watched as she glided to the bed—his bed, with his blankets and sheets, with his toys tucked away beneath it—gently rousing his younger self awake. "Time to get up," she said with a kiss to his forehead. "Breakfast is ready. You have to beat your father to the best pancakes. Hurry now."

The two of them vanished, and the lovely scent grew stronger all around him. Vince, covered in goose bumps, followed the path of the aroma, his heart warmed by the bountiful generosity offered to him by these strangers. He wished there were more people like this.

The kitchen smelled and looked fantastic. There were pancakes and French toast and bacon on the stove, some gorgeous pastries in the oven, ingredients strewn all around—jellies and jams, nuts and spices, sugars and frostings. Flour coated every surface like the snow outside. There was love here; Vince felt it immediately. At this moment he believed this was exactly where he needed to be. He didn't know why, but he thought that maybe he had come home for a reason.

MJ was placing some pancakes onto a plate when she turned around, beaming a bright smile, her cherubic face flecked with flour. "Glad you're awake. You have to try these," she said, sliding over the plate. "Chocolate chip. They're amazing. My favorite."

Vince, somewhat hesitantly, sat down on a stool at an island; he was stunned by the beneficent turn his life had suddenly made. "Mine too," he said. He took one bite, and then he couldn't stop. They really were amazing, far better than anything he'd ever received at the orphanage.

"We're all very sorry to hear about your grandfather," Michele said.

With his mouth full, Vince lowered his head and nodded. "Thanks."

"Mom, you should read this book Vince has. It's all about his grandfather's life, and you just wouldn't believe the things that happen to him in it." With a curious look, MJ turned to Vince. "Do you think any part of them is real?"

Vince wiped his mouth with a napkin. "They're just stories," he said finally.

"Paul's grandfather had some great stories too," Michele said. "All grandparents do. Right, Paul?"

There was no response from her husband, who was seated at the kitchen table, and so she crumpled up a napkin and tossed it in his direction. "Head out of the paper, Paul. I'm trying to talk to you. You're being rude. We have a guest."

"What? Oh, sorry," he said, folding up the previous day's edition. "I was just reading about that Byron Clan. I think they might actually get away. Can you believe it? In this day and age? The storm might have saved them. Talk about an injustice."

Vince stopped eating, the previous day's events suddenly overwhelming him. For a minute there he'd thought it was all just a horrible dream. "I saw them," he muttered very quietly. "Yesterday. They weren't far from here. I tried to get help, but I couldn't find any. And then—"

"You—you saw them?" Paul said, standing up.

"I did. Their car was stuck in the snow. I—I helped them get it out. I didn't know it was them until it was too late."

"And they just let you go? After you saw their faces?"

"I ran. I ran here."

Paul looked at Michele, fear crawling across both their faces like hairy spiders. "We have to call someone. The police need to know. I'll be right back."

Michele sat down next to Vince, a comforting hand on his back. "Did they see where you went, honey? Did they follow you?"

"I—I don't think so."

"They're busy getting out of town," MJ said.

"In this?" Michele responded. "In this they're not going anywhere." Then, seeing her daughter's worried eyes, she changed her tone. "I mean, I'm sure they're going to keep a low profile. They don't want to arouse suspicion."

There was a noise behind them, and Michele jumped and screamed. Romeo, it turned out, had his entire head in a bowl of pancake mix, licking away as if he'd known he had only seconds to do so before being caught.

"Shoot!" Michele ran over and, after pulling the bowl away, led Romeo out of the room. When she returned, she made sure to put up a gate. Romeo of course was not happy with this and howled in disapproval.

"Oh, shush," she said.

Stepping over the gate, Paul returned to the kitchen. "I've called the police," he said. "I don't think they can do much, though. They said they'd get people out to patrol the area once the roads are cleared. Until then their hands are pretty much tied."

"That's just how they planned it," Michele said, licking some of the batter herself. "Makes me sick."

Paul pointed at the finger in her mouth. "That's what's going to make you sick."

"What? This?" she said, dipping her finger back in and sticking it in her husband's face as he backed away. "You wouldn't want me to be sick by myself, would you?" Then she began to chase him around the kitchen, much to MJ's embarrassment.

"Mom! Dad!" She buried her face in her hands and groaned. "They're the worst."

Vince just watched them. His parents once had acted the same way. Watching this couple circling each other around the kitchen table, shifting chairs to obstruct the other's path, he was thankful. These antics brought a wide assortment of pleasant memories rushing back into his head, like water freed from a dam. He saw his parents in love once again; he saw them tossing snowballs and sharing food from the same plate and getting competitive with board games and dancing to no music at all, and on and on and on. Everywhere he turned, the walls of this home fell down and were replaced by the walls of his childhood. All his furniture—the dining table, the couch, the lamps, the desk, the bookcases—returned, and he could hear his parents' voices in every room. He could watch as his mother and father picked him up or snuggled with him before the fire or exchanged presents on holidays. Seeing his mother dressed as a clown for Halloween, he laughed again and even harder when his father entered the room as a mermaid. Vince couldn't walk anywhere without being reminded of his past, and for him, that was wonderful. They were special memories, and he was afraid he had lost them for good. But here they were, as fresh as ever. It was some time before he stopped smiling.

From there the day just got better and better. Vince hadn't felt this good in a long time. There were plenty of laughs, and the flames from the fireplace warmed them all. Michele and Paul were unbelievably kind—their only rule was to not leave the house until the Byron Clan business was all cleared up—and MJ was turning out to be the perfect friend. They watched some TV together, played video games, ate a few highly stacked sandwiches for lunch, with some chips on the side, and shared numerous stories about themselves, Vince recounting many remembrances of his parents, including his belief that his father might still be alive and waiting for him in Dyerville.

"My father built this house," he told her. "Originally, I

mean. Before it burned down."

MJ moved in closer. "He did?"

"That's why I came here. I had to see it again, what was left. I had no idea it had been rebuilt."

"So you, like, lived in this house?"

"My bed was almost exactly where yours is." Grinning, he got up and ran to the window. "And look at this." He pointed out into the woods. "You can't really see it because of all the snow coming down, but back there my dad and I built a tree house. It was huge. So cool. We used to play in it all the time. Well, not all the time, but whenever he wasn't away. We'd have shoot-outs and adventure games, we'd make passwords to get in, and at night we'd tell scary stories. I loved that tree house so much."

"Oh, yeah. I remember now. I came across something back there once. It must have fallen down over the years because there were all these piles of wood scattered about. Although one tree still has boards nailed to it."

"The ladder!" With a hand against his head, overwhelmed by everything, Vince slumped down to the floor. "I didn't think it would feel like this, coming back here. I wasn't sure I'd feel anything."

MJ sat before him, crossing her legs as if she were about to meditate. "Give me your hand. The one you write with."

With an arched eye, Vince sat up and hesitantly extended his right hand. When it was close enough, MJ sprang forward and snatched it. She held his hand tightly, as if she didn't want him to pull back. Then, with her free hand, she reached behind her and pulled a book from off her shelf.

"I've been studying how to do this," she said.

"Do what?" Vince asked, curious.

"Read palms. My aunt got me started. She told me she always sensed I had spiritual abilities."

Was that true? Vince shifted uncomfortably. He was scared of what she might say.

"Don't be nervous," MJ said, as if sensing his fears. "Everything will be fine. You trust me, don't you?"

"I do."

"Besides, if I say anything you don't like, just dismiss it. You can chalk it up to my being a beginner."

Vince laughed. "Sure. I mean, it's not like this stuff is real anyway, right?"

"Who's to say? We won't know until it happens, now will we?"

Vince glanced over at his grandfather's book. He adjusted his posture and leaned in. "Okay. Tell me what I need to know."

"Great, let's see," she said, bowing her head, her eyes practically in his palm. "There has been much pain in your life."

Vince looked up at her. "Seriously? You're cheating. You

already know what happened to me and my family."

"I know that, but it's in your lines too. Right here." She traced her finger in an area near his thumb, creating a pleasant tingling sensation. "That says it all." Licking her lips, she shifted her focus up toward the top of his palm. "But you see this line? That means it will get better. And it will get better very soon too."

This sounded good to Vince.

"And this line here, this is your travel line. It's very long. This means you will be going someplace you've never been before, and it will be a very important trip for you. Life changing, in fact."

Vince wondered if by this last comment, she meant his trip to Dyerville. He wondered if she meant he would finally reunite with his father. That would certainly be life changing. He sat up even straighter, excitement coursing through his body.

"Your Mercury line is strong," she went on. "This means you are a great communicator." She paused. "I think. No. Yeah. Anyway, it's something you should continue." Blushing a little, she flipped some pages in her book and scanned a few paragraphs. Vince watched her lips open and close as she silently read the words.

"Okay, got it." She focused on his palm once again.

"This right here is your Saturn mount. It's pretty prominent. But don't worry, that's a good thing. It tells me you seek"—she glanced down at her book again for confirmation—"wisdom and understanding. You do, don't you?"

"So much."

"I think you'll definitely find it," she said with a nod and a smile, and Vince couldn't help smiling back, the two of them keeping their eyes on each other for some time.

MJ looked away first, awkwardly pulling her hair back behind her ears and forcing a cough. When her eyes returned to examine Vince's palm, it was clear she noticed something because she suddenly leaned back, her face twisted and scrunched in deep contemplation. "That's weird," she said, stretching the adjective. "I've never seen this before."

"What?" Vince asked.

"Look, your life line, it splits in two," she said, illustrating with her fingernail. "One is very short, but the other stretches really, really far. Look at that."

"My grandfather lived to be a hundred," Vincent said. Then he immediately recalled how his grandfather always told people he lived twice that. Was that possible? Why did it suddenly seem possible to him?

MJ let go of Vince's hand. "He sounds like such an amazing person. I want to hear more about him. I want to listen to you read his story."

"You do?"

"Yes. I mean, don't you find the story incredible?"

"It's the best story I've ever heard."

"What if it's true? What if parts of it were taken from real experiences he had?"

Vince didn't respond. He just watched as MJ got up and grabbed the book. When she returned, she handed it over to him.

"Read it to me. Just one more chapter."

Barlow Manor

Vincent was on the back of the horse, galloping along a dusty road, their shadows lost in the dense clouds of dirt violently kicked up behind them. The sun burned Vincent's golden skin without remorse, and his weight—he was nearly three times as heavy now, covered as he was in gold—had begun to drastically slow Orin. After riding for hours, they would need to rest soon. Luckily, they had drawn near to where Vincent had grown up. He knew exactly where to go.

"We have to stop soon!" he shouted into Orin's ear. "There's somewhere I wish to go. We'll have food, water, a place to sleep."

"Yes," Orin agreed, "I tire."

"Down this way," Vincent said, pointing west.

The trees he recognized appeared as old friends, branches waving. Every road told a different story he knew by heart. Even the sky appeared the same as when he had first set out those many months ago, not a cloud out of place. Nothing had changed.

Desperately, he wished to see his mother again. He wanted to calm her fears, tell her that he was okay. He wanted to be in her care once again. Safe, happy. And this time he wouldn't leave; with the gold book in his possession he would discover a way to end the curse once and for all. Oh, to be home; he wanted nothing more.

When they reached the house, Vincent dismounted Orin as if on a spring and, grinning with delight, ran straight inside.

"Mom? Mom?" he called, throwing open the front door so hard he nearly took it off its hinges. "Mother!" He waited for her to come running, hand on her heart, eyes filled with tears, but there was no response. *Is she out?* he wondered. He looked all over, searching every room, but couldn't find a trace of her. In fact, the house appeared to have been abandoned some time ago. The walls had begun to wither and crack; dust covered everything; bugs and critters roamed freely. The food had gone bad. *What is going on? Where is she?*

His nose twitched. What was that smell?

The answer became clear soon enough. Smoke. Smoke

and flames. As if Vincent were a lit match, the entire house caught fire. Everywhere he ran, flames followed and spread fast, consuming every corner of the home. Nothing could be saved.

Vincent ran outside, back toward the shed he'd built for her; that seemed to be another lifetime, another person completely. His heart pounding in his chest, he sprinted straight for it, passing his beloved garden, which had gone to seed. *What is going on? What is going on?* "Mom! Mom!" He ran harder, as if to crash right through the wood doors, the house behind him quickly burning away. Then, just yards from the shed, he was knocked aside by Orin. He landed punishingly on his face and chest, his breath knocked clear out of him. Gasping and grimacing, he gathered himself, looking up at the horse.

"Is she—is she in there?"

Orin shook his head. "No. You know that. And if you step inside that shed, it too will go up in flames, and yourself with it. It is the curse of the witch. You were never meant to return here. You were never meant to reunite with your mother or your past life. You belong to the witch now."

Vincent, overcome with grief, suddenly realized the full extent of the witch's power. His mother was gone, and he might never see her again. He didn't even know if she was still alive.

No, she is. I can feel it. I know it.

He tried to stand, but his legs gave way, and he collapsed, sobbing into his hands. "What did I do?" he cried. "I'm sorry, Mother. I'm so sorry. I should never have left. It's my fault. I'm the curse. I'm the curse."

Orin sat beside his friend, but neither of them had anything to say for quite a long while. Eventually Vincent found the strength to speak. "The witch did this," he told Orin, his tears still streaming, his hands grabbing at the dirt as the house continued to burn behind them. "Why did I leave? Why was I so foolish? I should have known what would happen. Instead of running, I should have waited for the witch and settled this myself."

Orin nodded in understanding. "Do not give up hope. Your mother may yet still live. Together we can find her and bring the witch to her end. By defeating her, we will return ourselves to our proper forms, no longer marked by her evil conjurings."

"But the giant made me gold; he turned you into a horse, not the witch."

"The giant was a thief, Vincent. He wasn't blinded because he innocently wandered into the witch's woods. He pursued her. He stole from her. Everything in that room, those magical needles and razors, the vial of water, the potion he used to transform me, everything on that shelf: they all came from the witch. That fountain was an ordinary fountain until the giant mixed the water with a concoction he pilfered from her home. And so, when she finally caught him, she blinded him. She marked him just as he has marked us, and she has done the same to hundreds of others. But we can kill the witch, and by killing her, we can reverse everything wrought with her magic. All will be set right."

"How do you know all this? How did you end up in the giant's cave?"

"What does it matter?"

"I want to know."

Orin was agitated. "You have to understand . . . I had no one. Nothing."

"You are an orphan?"

"It was an empty life, Vincent. I was like a ghost. No one saw me. No one cared. I walked into the giant's cave trying to change all that."

"You pursued the gold book?"

"A mistake. For which I am still paying."

"I see." Vincent glanced up at the blue sky. "And my mother, you think we can save her?" he asked hopefully.

Orin looked away. "There are no guarantees she is even alive. I'm saying it's possible."

They fell silent again. Vincent rested his head against the hard ground, a part of him wanting to sleep forever. But his thoughts would never let him, the fire inside his belly would never diminish, until everything was set right. When he spoke, he sounded different, on the verge of rage.

"That witch, my mother did nothing to her. It was me she wanted. I don't know why, but it was me. It didn't have to come to this. Yes, you are right. This all ends with the witch getting what she deserves. Tell me, Orin, how do we find her, how do we defeat her?"

"That I do not know. But I know of someone who does."

While Orin slept in the shade of the shed, Vincent watched his house burn to the ground. Slowly rocking back and forth with his arms wrapped around his knees, pulling them toward his chest, he had never felt so angry and so very devastated at the same time. Never had he felt the all-encompassing urge for revenge. Before he left home a second time, he swore upon the ashes of his house he would rid the world of the witch and her many evils and find his mother.

When he walked away, nothing was left standing but the shed he'd built with his own two hands, a monument to his mother.

Most of the following day was spent riding through the countryside. Vincent had no idea where they were going, but evidently Orin did. The horse rode with determination, with focus, stopping only when, in the distance, it saw a lone withered tree, stretching and twisting out over the road as if wishing to cross before dying. Standing beneath its dried branches, humming an ominous tune, was a bedraggled dwarf.

Orin slowly backed out of view, whispering to Vincent, "The dwarf up ahead sells items of a certain nature. There is a cloak in his collection. You must obtain it."

"A cloak? What for?"

"We are heading to the home of a man of great wealth. However, Mr. Barlow is also a man with the blackest of hearts. A greedy man. All he craves in life is more money, more power. He wasn't always like this, but now, if he were to see your gold body, you would be held captive all over again. And believe me, Mr. Barlow would see to it that you never escaped. Of course that is saying he doesn't chop your head off first, so that he could mount it above his bed. But we need him; he has great experience in tracking the witch. We need to earn his trust. And for that to work you will need a disguise."

"But we have no money to pay the dwarf."

"I know this. But such a thing must not deter us. You must obtain the cloak by any means necessary. Do you understand? We cannot leave without it."

Vincent and Orin made their way around the bend and over to the dwarf. This four-foot purveyor of random goods was broad-shouldered with a dark beard and beady eyes. He wore leather boots up to his knotty knees, the buckles of which were clearly made of fool's gold, as was his belt buckle. He was missing his left thumb. Beside him, beneath the tree, was a cart with various objects displayed upon it in a disorganized manner: brass plates and jeweled goblets, stained glass, assorted tools, and various odd trinkets. And there, hanging over the edge just above the cart's wheel, was a ragged cloak.

Upon seeing Vincent, the dwarf's eyes lit up brighter than Vincent's gold skin, glistening under the blazing sun. His whistling stopped abruptly, and his mouth hung open in disbelief, revealing several gold teeth—fake, of course.

"What have we here?" he said, hand stroking his disorderly beard.

"Good day, dwarf. I am interested in your wares," Vincent said in a failed attempt at sounding older than his years.

"Oh? Everything here has its price. Is there something in particular that catches your eye?"

Vincent, leaning over from atop the horse, pretended to browse the cart. "That cloak. I would like that cloak there."

"The cloak? Oh, that's a very special item. I'm not so sure I could part with it. Very valuable. Very valuable. It will cost you."

"I don't have money."

The dwarf laughed mightily at this. "You, a golden boy, no money?"

Vincent deepened his voice in yet another effort to come off more experienced than his years. "I'm willing to negotiate a suitable exchange. Perhaps there is something I can offer you. What is it you need?"

The dwarf eyed the sack strapped across Vincent's shoulder. "What do you have in there?"

Vincent placed his hand on the worn leather. He could feel the binding of the book bulging beneath it. It pulsated with life. Something would not let him part with it, not even a single page, no matter how badly they needed the cloak. He adjusted the sack so that it was farther away from the dwarf. "There is nothing of value in here."

"Don't lie to me. I can smell a liar."

"I told you, I have no money."

"You have money, boy. You're covered in it." The dwarf reached up and stroked Vincent's hand.

Quickly Vincent pulled it back. "I'm sorry, but this gold is a part of me. There's no more where it came from."

"Don't be sorry; if you want the cloak, I'll just take a part of you then." With this, the dwarf pulled free a large knife and began licking its stained serrated blade. "I don't need much."

Vincent recoiled. "I'm supposed to cut off a part of my body for you?"

The dwarf shook his head, a ravenous look in his eye. "Give me a part of your face. I want a part of that beautiful face."

"I will do no such thing."

The dwarf spit on the ground. "Then move on from

here. I have nothing for you."

"There has to be something else I can give you."

"There's nothing. I named my price," the dwarf said, turning his back to them. "Be gone if you can't pay."

With an incredulous glance Vincent looked down at Orin. But still, the horse nodded in the direction of the cloak.

Shaking his head and sighing, Vincent said, "Very well."

The dwarf spun around on his heels, grinning madly from ear to ear, knife extended.

Reluctantly Vincent grabbed the handle and brought the dull blade to his cheek. He dug the broken tip in. It took some effort to get past the top layer of gold, but soon enough, he was beneath it.

"Yes. Yes, go on," said the dwarf. "Get me a sizable piece."

The blade cut deeper, then deeper still. The pain was horrible. Vincent's eyes watered; his hand shook. Biting his lip, he slowly sliced away at his face. And that was how Vincent came to bear the scar he was to carry for the rest of his life.

Finished, he tossed the chunk of gold to the dwarf, who, upon catching it, danced around his cart, kissing his prize over and over.

"The cloak," Vincent demanded, a hand on his cheek, the blood issuing forth from that buried part of him that was still flesh.

"Of course, of course." The dwarf grabbed the cloak and threw it at him, never taking his eyes off the gold.

Thus the deal was made.

Vincent rode off, holding the cloak out before him. It was in tatters—holes, tears, stains, loose threads. It reeked. "I scarred myself for this?" he said to Orin, holding his nose. "What are we supposed to do with it?"

"You're going to use it to get a job at Mr. Barlow's home. You're going to work whatever position you can get. And you are going to excel. Over time, I hope, you will stand out for your achievements, endearing yourself to him. Then maybe, just maybe, he will reveal how to defeat the witch."

"Can't we just search her woods, track her down?"

"Many have tried before you, and all have failed. You see, there is something else to it that we are missing. Mr. Barlow has the key. He knows."

"You said I have to hide my body from him. Am I supposed to do that with these rags?" he asked, dangling the cloak before the horse, obstructing his view.

"Put it on," said Orin. "Then go have a look at yourself over there in the river."

Vincent slipped the cloak on over his gold body and, feeling no different, walked doubtfully to the river and peered into it. But immediately upon glancing at the water's surface, he snapped his head back to see if someone was standing over his shoulder. He stood, hands closed in fists, prepared to defend himself. But there was no one there. "Did you see anyone just now?" he asked Orin.

"There's only you."

Hesitantly, Vincent looked back at the water. The same man had returned. *It's me*, Vincent realized, touching his face. The reflection was of an old man, a beggar. Gone was the gold skin; gone were his youth and his handsome features. Amazed, he ripped the cloak off and peered back into the water. And there he was again: the golden boy.

"Come," said Orin, "we don't have much farther to go."

Vincent walked back to his steed, running his arm in and out of the cloak, watching it change from gold and taut to pale and wrinkled, and back again. "Astounding," he muttered.

"Let's just hope it gets us what we need."

A few miles later, far removed from any cities or towns, they approached a large iron and gold gate, the letter *B* prominently displayed in the center. "Quick," Orin said, "before anyone sees. Put the cloak on. Remember, you are an old man looking for work. Sell yourself. Get us inside."

With the cloak concealing the boy beneath, Vincent peered out from the hood, past the gates and in at the palatial estate beyond. It was a far grander home than he had ever seen before. There were too many windows to count, there were columns and arches and balconies and statues, there were separate quarters and several wings, there were stables and gardens and fountains, and that was just what he could see from the gate. The mansion must have sat on dozens and dozens of the most finely kept acres in all the country. There had to be some job he could do on such immense and immaculate grounds.

From down a long drive a finely dressed servant approached.

"Confidence," Orin whispered to Vincent. "He will succumb to confidence."

"Yes?" the servant asked when he reached the gate, blatantly scrutinizing the old man sitting upon the ragged horse.

"I've come seeking work," Vincent said, his voice naturally disguised by the cloak. It now rattled with age, a dying croak.

With a snide look the man said, "We have nothing for you," and began to walk away.

"Please," Vincent called out. "I work hard. You could hire no one better."

"I find that very hard to believe. Now, please disperse before I send for the dogs."

"Just give me a chance. I promise I will not let you down. I will complete the work of three men half my age."

The servant stopped and turned around. "You sound very sure of yourself. Have you gone senile? Has your mind withered like your body?"

"Please. Give me one day to prove myself. If I do not work to your liking, if I do not astound you with my abilities, you can let me go."

Curious, the man looked him over yet again, this time much longer. Finally he sighed. "You'll work at half the pay."

Vincent nodded. "Half the pay."

"Can you garden?"

"I can. I have had much experience in gardening. From the time I was young."

"That must have been some time ago."

Vincent smiled. "I remember it all like it was yesterday. In fact, I feel as if I haven't aged a day."

"Senility." The servant snickered. "Very well, come inside. By the end of the day I will let you know if you still have a job tomorrow."

He worked hard every hour, every minute of the day, forgoing breaks and meals, and was the very last one to set down his tools. And he did so only when the garden looked flawless and beautiful, and his entire body ached so badly that he could hardly lift his arms or move his legs. Late in the evening, when he finally had a chance to eat, he ate a small meal all alone under a tree, his hands trembling with exhaustion.

He kept his job that day. And he would each day after.

Months passed in this manner. Whenever Vincent had free time, he used it to read from the gold book that practically burned through the leather sack he never removed. The first time he wished to read it, the binding refused to give, as if all the pages had been glued together. A curious thought ran through Vincent's head: *Does the book find me unworthy? Does it believe I am not ready?* He glanced up at the sky and sighed. *I don't care what it thinks. If the answer to finding and helping my mother lies in here, I need to find it.* And just like that, the book opened up. The pages fluttered and flapped as if ruffled by a strong wind, and when they finally settled, Vincent was staring at a strange illustration. Encompassing the entire page was an intricately detailed drawing of a very old man, his arms like the branches of a tree, and, above him, illuminated by a great light, hundreds of birds carrying a sword and a bow. Not thinking much of it, he tried to turn back to the beginning, but the book wouldn't budge. He tried again. Nothing. "A sword and a bow," he muttered, running his fingers over the glistening weapons. With that, the book snapped closed on his fingers, and from then on he could open to whatever page he wished.

There seemed to be countless stories in the book, many written in foreign languages, and what little Vincent could translate didn't mean much of anything. It was riddle after riddle after riddle, all of them powerful and tantalizing. Other sections, however, were completely indecipherable, the sentences scrambled upon the page, random word following random word, sometimes not even arranged in a straight line, but jagged swirls and zigzags and clusters. It was as if the words were loose upon the page and shaken around into new forms every time the covers closed. There were illustrations throughout the book, and he tried to make sense of everything by analyzing these, although this too proved difficult. There was a lot of adventure, a lot of blood and death, anger and betrayal. But at parts there was peace, such unbelievable peace that Vincent wished to be absorbed into the pages. The book, he surmised, must have been hundreds of years old, and the stories—the ones he could read at least—even older than that.

When he couldn't read anymore without dozing, he would wander over to the stables so that he could say goodnight to Orin, who had grown quiet and testy since their arrival. The horse, unhappy with his current sleeping conditions, looked longingly at the mansion. Not that Vincent's were much better; he slept outside, under his favorite tree on the estate, the stars spread above him, the warm air surrounding him like a thick blanket.

Every morning Vincent repeated his routine, setting himself far apart from the other workers, who wanted nothing to do with him, likely because his work ethic consistently put theirs to shame.

And yet he was still unable to gain an audience with

the owner of the home, the ever-elusive Mr. Barlow. In fact, after several weeks he still had never even set eyes upon the man, although all the other workers acted as if he were standing over their shoulders. They spoke of him only in whispers, and not a word of it flattering. They spoke of a neglected son and a subjugated daughter. They spoke of a family tragedy. Vincent of course just kept his head down and toiled through it all, despite no indication that Mr. Barlow noticed.

There was one person, however, who couldn't help noticing him. And that was Stella, the young daughter of Mr. Barlow.

One day, in the middle of the hottest week of his life, with temperatures well over one hundred degrees, when all the workers were taking lunch in the servants' wing of the house, fans on full blast, as it was their ritual to do, and with Mr. Barlow reportedly away on business, Vincent decided to take a rare moment of being completely alone. It was his birthday, and he decided to have a quick dip in the pool.

With no one around, he slipped off his cloak, his youth and gold body immediately returning, and jumped head-first into the cool water. Being so heavy, he found it difficult to keep afloat. But the exercise was good for him, and he decided he would do this whenever he found himself alone.

As he was swimming, what he didn't realize was that Stella was on her balcony that very moment, watching his transformation take place. She couldn't take her eyes off him. Every day after, she hid out there from morning till night, waiting for the old man to remove the cloak one more time and reveal the golden boy beneath. And when he did, Stella just about swooned. She had to meet him.

And so, one afternoon, in the middle of his relentless gardening, while the other workers retreated inside, Vincent found himself face-to-face with Stella for the first time.

"Old man," she said, in a haughty voice, her hands on her hips, "why do you toil out here in the sun when everyone else is cool within their quarters? You never stop for lunch, never take a break. Surely, a man of your age needs to rest."

Vincent couldn't believe his eyes. The girl was like no one he had ever seen before. He wondered if she had come from a different time or place, pulled out of the gold book perhaps. She was enchanting, like the stories he read each night, fascinating in every way imaginable. Meeting her did something to Vincent, to his perception of reality. It was as if within seconds of his locking eyes with her, the world had tripled in size.

The girl kept her eyes fixed on his, as if she could see the real Vincent through the decay of age. She refused to look away, and suddenly Vincent found it very difficult to speak. He stammered and stuttered, completely captivated by this beautiful girl standing so self-assuredly before him.

"Well?" Stella said.

To speak, Vincent found that he had to look away. "I wish to leave an impression upon Mr. Barlow."

Stella laughed. "My father notices nothing. And why on earth would you ever wish to impress him in the first place? I'm sure you've heard how wicked he is."

"I also heard he is a wise man, that he knows many things. Including information that I need."

"In this entire world, is there no one else you can ask?"

"I'm afraid not."

Deep in contemplation, Stella brought a finger to her lips. Finally she asked, "What is your name?"

"Vincent."

"My name is—"

"Stella. I know. We all know. I've heard your name spoken many times. But why is it I have never seen you until now?"

"Oh, I suppose there are many reasons for that. Maybe I haven't wished to be seen until now—a girl must have her privacy, you know—and for some time there was certainly nothing of interest around here to pull me out of hiding. Until now. Or maybe after so long I just couldn't take being alone anymore, and I had to speak with someone, even an old man like you. Or maybe my father has forbidden my mingling with the help these many years and I sneaked out of the room, having decided to take a chance on you, test the waters, so to speak. But just maybe, since my brother's tragic incident my father has forbidden fun of any kind. He has locked me away. No friends my age. No venturing outside those gates. Total isolation from the outside world. And maybe in you I see escape."

"I'm sorry to hear such things, but you are mistaken. I can't help you."

Stella ignored this. "You're not from here, are you?"

"No," Vincent said, a hint of sadness in his voice. "I miss my home very much. I too feel like I've been locked away for so long. As beautiful as this place is, I long to see the mountains of my childhood again, the forests, the rivers. There are great wonders outside these gates."

"So I've heard. Thank you for pointing out what is kept from me."

"I didn't mean . . . look . . . I'm sorry, forget it."

Stella smiled at Vincent's awkwardness. She so badly wished to see his gold face blush. Stepping forward, she reached up for the hood. "Aren't you hot with that on? Why wear something so heavy on a day such as this?"

Vincent jumped back, his hands holding the hood firmly in place. "My skin, it's sensitive to the sun."

"Is it now?"

"It is."

"But I can hardly see your face. At least lower the hood for me."

"I cannot do that."

"And why not? Are you so hideous under there?"

"I am like nothing you have ever seen."

She paused, taking him in. "I'll bet you are." She nodded curtly, and Vincent watched as she walked away.

After this conversation, Stella was at Vincent's side every day. She sat with him while he worked, helping out wherever she could, getting her hands dirty for the first time in her life. She followed Vincent to the stable to see his horse, although Orin was always fast asleep. She even brought Vincent food when he refused to rest. Never once did she seem concerned about disobeying her father. Only when all the other servants went inside did Stella retreat to her balcony with some odd excuse. And with Vincent believing he was alone once again, he jumped into the pool. If he had not been underwater, he would have heard her sigh.

One day, while they were digging up soil so that they could plant some azaleas, Stella said, "I can help you, you know. I can get you an audience with my father."

Vincent stopped working and looked at her. "You can?"

"Yes, but I would need three things from you first."

"What are they? Anything."

"First, I want to know why you so desperately wish to speak with my father."

And so Vincent told her the truth, or a version of it. He

explained how he sought the witch, how he wanted to set all her evils right and avenge his mother. It bothered him to state that his mother was dead, but keeping in mind he appeared to be an old man, he thought this was necessary, as was making sure not to give away any further details about his travels, only suggesting it all happened a long time ago and he had been on this quest ever since.

"What is the second thing you ask of me?" he said when finished with this tale.

"I want you to lower your hood."

"I told you—"

"I know you did."

This time, when Stella reached for the hood, Vincent didn't pull away. Her small hands grasped each side and pulled it down, revealing Vincent's golden face.

"I've seen you from my balcony," Stella said in an awed whisper. "Why do you hide who you are?"

"I was told what would happen if your father were to see me. I couldn't take that chance."

"My father is very sick. He cannot even leave his bed."

"But I thought he traveled for business all the time. I heard he keeps close tabs on just about everything we do."

"Lies. My father has been sick for some time now, ever since he lost his son, my only brother. I'm sure you have heard that he is a hard man, and he was. All his life he wanted more and more. He was never satisfied, and he ran down anyone who got in his way. But my brother's vanishing, my father's illness: they have softened him. He keeps me in isolation only because he fears something happening to me. If I tell him you can cure him, he will see you."

"But I can't cure him."

"If you seek to destroy the witch, then you can."

"She struck him ill?"

"She did; ever since he has sought her dead for my brother's disappearance. Before that, he had been searching for her almost all his life, but to a different end. Back then he craved her power, her abilities. Like I said, he was covetous of all that wasn't his, and she had plenty. But now he believes it was she who took my brother, and he only wants her vanquished. Sadly, all efforts have failed. If you can change that, surely he will grant you whatever you wish. He can make you very wealthy."

"I do this for my mother and no one else. I seek no reward but her rescue."

"That is quite admirable, though you just told me you wished to avenge her death. Is that true, or do you believe she is still alive?"

"I do. I have to."

"You love her greatly."

Vincent, welling up, shifted the conversation back to her requests. "What is the third thing you ask of me?"

For once it was Stella's turn to blush and shyly turn

away. When she spoke, it was softly, with all her hardness and edge removed. "I don't want you to leave just yet. Stay with me. Like you are now." And she reached out and grasped his hand.

It wasn't supposed to be for very long, but the two of them spent the next three weeks together, every moment they could get. Now, when it came time for the other workers to go off for lunch, Stella did not retreat to her balcony. Instead, Vincent removed his cloak, and the two of them ran off to be with each other. They exchanged stories and gazed upon the stars; they got lost in the giant hedge maze; they swam in the pool; they played hide-and-seek. They danced.

It was a wonderful time they shared, the two of them growing closer every second. But with nightly visions of his mother, the possibility of her death or torture, Vincent soon felt the day had come for him to set out for the witch, and so Stella, as promised, arranged the meeting with her father.

Vincent, disguised, entered Mr. Barlow's impressive bedroom as the sun began to descend. He couldn't believe the opulence by which he was surrounded: priceless artwork and tapestries and statues, furniture of the finest wood, a gigantic fireplace, a sprawling crystal chandelier, a window overlooking the estate and everything beyond, precious metals everywhere; even the floor on which he walked was gold.

Mr. Barlow lay on a large oak four-poster bed that

practically consumed him. He was extremely pale and thin, his eyes sunken and bloodshot and racked with fear. His mouth, emitting strained wheezes, hung open as he struggled to breathe. He could barely look over at his guest.

"My daughter tells me that you can heal me. Is that right?" His frail voice echoed in the expansive room: vibrations of an impending death.

"I can try."

Mr. Barlow coughed into his hand, spitting up blood. "I don't need anyone to try. I need someone to succeed."

"I can defeat the witch. I promise you that."

If the old man was surprised that Vincent knew of the witch and her powers, he didn't show it. "Promise me? You think others haven't tried? Hundreds of men have tried. What is an old man like you going to do that they haven't?"

"Tell me how to defeat her. I may surprise you."

"That you may. My daughter certainly believes in you. She hasn't believed in much of anything for many years now." Mr. Barlow raised a trembling hand to his forehead. "The pain is unbearable. I should have died by now. I believe she is stretching it out, making me suffer."

"Tell me what to do," Vincent said. "I will end this."

"Men have believed that they killed the witch. They have come back to me swearing to it. Many have said they struck her down, burned her, drowned her, seen the life leave her eyes. And I'm sure they truly did. And yet still she lives.

After consulting forces beyond our realm, I have learned that there is a very specific reason for this. Because of her black arts, she has tied her soul to that of another creature roaming her forest. There is a wild boar in those demonic woods of hers, a boar of such immense size and strength that it has no fear of anyone or anything. It is very nearly indestructible. This is the source of her magic. Destroy the boar and only then will you be able to defeat the witch once and for all."

"Mr. Barlow, I will find a way to fell the beast."

"But there's more, my hasty friend. Both the witch and the boar have to be killed by a special weapon—the boar with a bow and arrow, the witch with a sword, unique weapons that have been created solely for this purpose many years ago. My men have scoured the land. Sadly, we have no way of knowing where they are."

Vincent's mind went immediately to the gold book, its illustrations. Yes, it was the first one he had seen, the very first page he had laid eyes on: the old man and the sword and the bow and the birds holding the weapons aloft. This was the key; he was sure of it. "I may know, sir."

"So you say. And I take it you won't tell me how you have come across such knowledge?"

"That is correct."

"I hope you succeed. If I live, I have much to amend. In these final days of my life I've come to realize the many failures of my past. I neglected my family. My focus was elsewhere. I sought the wrong things. I just want my son back. I want my daughter to be safe. I will give up all my gold, all my wealth, for this. If you find the witch, you just may find my poor son. Children: she takes them. For what, I do not know. I only hope it's not too late, for any of us."

That night Vincent fetched Orin from the stable. He hopped on and secured the book in the leather sack.

"You will come back, won't you?" Stella asked, emerging from the shadows.

Vincent eyed her even as Orin, eager to leave, tugged in the opposite direction. "I will, and your father will be cured, your brother at his side."

"And what about me?"

Vincent lowered his hood, his gold face gleaming in the moonlight. "When I see you again, I will carry you past those gates and into the world."

Stella smiled, her eyes brimming with tears. "I will be waiting."

And with that, Vincent and Orin set out for the witch.

CHAPTER 11

It was one of the very few stories Vince ever heard about his grandmother Stella, and he was deeply intrigued. Unfortunately, he'd never had the chance to meet her and knew even less about her than he did of his grandfather. She passed away when he was just six months old.

He wondered if this was how his grandparents had really met, on some massive estate, back when they both were just young teens. Was it really love at first sight? Then again, how could his grandmother not have been enthralled by a golden boy? It all seemed perfectly appropriate and romantic, especially for a couple who remained at each other's sides for the rest of their lives.

"But what about the weapons?" MJ asked him, breaking his train of thought. She had spent the morning rereading the tale, jotting down notes as she went along. "Did he ever find them? Did he get the witch?"

"I don't know."

"He never told you?"

"I—I was young. I don't remember. I don't think he told me any of these stories. Most of the memories I have of him are from when he was very old. I remember a lot of gibberish."

For the most part, this was true, but he had to admit he had the same questions MJ did. The book was taking hold of him, page by page, as if the words were floating free and wrapping themselves around his body like the giant's chain. It was almost as if his grandfather were alive again, as if Vince could reach out and touch him, like living history. He didn't believe his grandfather to be crazy, not like he used to anyway. Even in these tales of fantasy, every story within the book, every curious interaction, everything had meaning and logic, some kind of truth behind it. He saw his grandfather more fully now; he felt he was beginning to truly understand him. Somehow, they were closer now than ever before.

"Do you ever wonder about us?" MJ asked, closing the book and running her fingers across the cover, as Romeo curled up at her feet. "The story of our lives? What's happening to us right now?"

Vince thought about the tales he had told back at the orphanage. "All the time. I've just been trying to find the best version."

Right now he was enjoying where he found himself. How he loved being under this roof again. There were differences, of course, but for the most part, the house was reconstructed almost exactly as he remembered it. Maybe the same blueprints, the same foundation were used. Since his return he couldn't help wondering if his father's initials were still there, a permanent part of the home.

"I want to go outside and check something," he said to MJ.

"Oh, we can't. You heard my parents. They said we're not allowed. Not with the Byron Clan so nearby."

"I know, but I won't be long. I just want to see something real quick. I have to."

"Vince—"

"In and out. I promise."

After much coaxing, MJ finally gave in, and the two of them ran outside, with Romeo following. The snow had ceased falling, but it was piled well past their knees, yet that didn't stop the dog from hopping in and out of the piles like a bunny, its black eyes following Vince to the side of the house.

Riffling through his memory for just the right spot,

Vince crouched down and began brushing away at the snow.

"What are you doing?" MJ asked.

He was getting closer; he could feel it. The snow froze his fingers, but he didn't care, and when he saw bits of the cement, his hands worked even faster. He wiped away the last few inches of snow, and when it cleared, his face lit up with happiness. "See," he said, near tears. "I knew it would still be here." He pointed at the initials and was unable to shift his eyes from the crooked markings; they were just as he remembered them.

"You weren't lying," MJ said in surprise. "I thought maybe you were just telling a story."

"No. No, this is real. This is so very real." He ran his trembling fingers over the initials left by his father so many years ago. The feeling was haunting; it was like grazing his father's skin. "Back"—there was a catch in his throat— "back at the orphanage, I used to dream of him building this house, laying the foundation, nothing else around, the sun on his back, the taste of sweat in his mouth. I could just see it so clearly. He used to tell me how much he loved working with his hands, how it had a way of enticing the mind to wander, you know? He said it was the ritual of the thing: you're almost working mechanically and so your thoughts take over. Your mind and your actions, they're so far apart, he said, it's like they exist separately, in different worlds or something. Almost as if you're two people. I don't know . . .

I used to think of this, my father sitting here in this very spot . . . where did his thoughts go when his mind wandered? What was he thinking? I want to know. I want to know him." Choking back tears, he looked up at MJ.

MJ's eyes were watery as well. "I'll, um . . . If you need me, I'll be right over there." And she hurried off to play with Romeo in the front yard.

Vince sat with his back against the house, right beside the markings. He sat beneath the same sky as his father. He looked out at the same woods, smelled the same air, touched the same ground. He closed his eyes, trying to sync his mind with that of his father's.

"What did you think about, Dad? Who were you really?"

Vince wasn't sure. He never had a chance to ask his father. Not the real questions anyway, not the questions that truly mattered. Now his father was gone. He'd left— who knew why?—and now Vince would never have the answers to these questions. In his mind his father would always be incomplete.

He glanced to his left, out into the woods to where his tree house once stood. Dusting himself free of snow, he stood and headed straight toward it. As if not a day had gone by, he remembered exactly where it was erected. He knew the very spot at which to enter the woods; he knew the turns; he knew the trees. It was only another minute before he tripped over a pile of wood.

Bending down, he began sorting through the rotting boards, nearly cutting himself on a rusted nail. Dejected, he glanced up at the empty tree. The whole thing had come down. *How appropriate*, he thought. He stood and placed his hand against the thick tree. MJ was right. There were still parts of the ladder nailed into the trunk. He recalled hammering these planks in with his father, how much fun they both had had. It wasn't long after his father had helped him overcome his fear of heights by encouraging him to climb his first tree, where, at the top, looking over the town, Vince had yelled out, "Umbia Rah!" And then, not a week later, they had built this.

Wiping some snow off the boards, Vince noticed something carved into the third one from the bottom: numbers. They were hastily produced, not very deep, but he could still make them out: 60 135. He had no idea what these meant, but he was sure they hadn't been there when he still lived here. There was no doubt that he would have seen them. The numbers would have stared him right in the face every time he climbed up the tree. But what was it? Code? Coordinates? Once again, Vince's mind began to race. The night of the fire did his father escape and carve these numbers into the wood? Were they a message? Something told him his father was definitely trying to reach him. He knew Vince would go to the tree house to be alone. He knew he would read it. Yes, his father was still somewhere out there.

"Vince!"

It was MJ. She sounded frightened, Romeo was barking incessantly. Quickly Vince turned from the message and ran back to them, the snow he kicked falling upon the discarded boards of his tree house. When he turned the corner of the house, he found MJ, a hand over her agape mouth, pointing out into the woods with the other. Looking in this direction, a hundred yards from the house, he noticed an old woman standing upon a tree stump.

"Old Mother Byron," Vince said, slowly backing away. He grabbed MJ's hand and pulled her toward the house. "Hurry. We have to get inside."

With Romeo following, they ran as fast as they could through the dense feet of snow. Just before entering the house, Vince looked back into the woods a second time. They were empty.

Once inside, the two new friends hurried to the front window and nervously peered out.

"Is she still there?" MJ asked, her voice quivering. "Is she still there?"

Vince scanned the woods. Everything was still. Quiet.

"Maybe it wasn't her," he said, not believing this but hoping to calm down the girl to whom he owed his life.

MJ was trembling. "You saw her face. She'll be coming for you."

"No. They're going to want to lay low. They're in hiding."

There was a loud noise coming from outside. MJ jumped at the sound, clinging to Vince. "What is that? Vince, what is that?"

"Easy. It's just the plows. They're clearing the streets. Look." He pointed out the window, and sure enough, a plow came into view. "See. Just a plow. Everything's going to be okay. We'll be able to drive out of here if we need to." Only, instead of continuing down the street and onto the next, the plow stopped in front of the house, the engine shutting down. A moment later the door opened, and Vince's stomach dropped.

Out of the driver's seat stepped Lonnie, followed by his sister and, finally, his mother.

"It's them," he croaked. "Oh, no. It's them. They've found me."

MJ, close to hysterics, ran from the window. "Mom! Dad!"

Vince was frozen in place, as if he truly had been turned to ice. Looking out the window, he was reminded of that dreadful night from his past. Something horrifying was out there in the snow, coming to destroy him and everything he held dear.

From the street, Misty saw Vince crouching in the window. With a wicked grin, she waved to him.

"What? What's the matter?" Michele cried from the other room.

"They're here! The Byron Clan!"

Running over, Michele and Paul joined Vince and MJ at the window. "Michele," Paul said, clearly trying not to panic, "get on the phone now. Get somebody over here immediately. I don't care if they have to hop on snowmobiles or jump from helicopters. You tell them to get here now. MJ, help me make sure all the windows and doors are locked. Hurry."

Everyone scattered through the house. Paul, after securing the entrances, looked for a weapon of some kind. A golf club was the best he could do. At the window once again, he put his hand on Vince's shoulder. "They're not going to hurt you. Not with me around. I promise."

Lonnie and Misty stood staring at the house, their breaths spiraling to the sky like cyclones. Their mother was between them, a few yards back. With her cane she pointed toward Vince.

Lonnie and Misty started for the house.

"Back away," Paul said to Vince. He tossed everything off the dining room table and, with Vince's help, overturned it. Together they then shoved it in front of the large window. "I don't know if that will hold them," Paul said.

There was a loud bang at the front door. Then another. And another. Lonnie was trying to knock it down.

With Romeo barking over and over at every sound, Paul called out to his wife, "The police. What did they say?"

The banging continued, faster now, the new and urgent heartbeat of the house.

Michele was so terrified she was rambling. "I don't know. They said to hang on. They're trying to get here. The snow is so high. Twenty-eight inches or something. The streets are a mess. Roads are blocked; cars stranded. People stranded. It's too cold out."

"Michele. Michele! How long? How long did they say they were going to be?"

"They—they couldn't say."

The banging wouldn't stop. It sounded as if the wood would give at any moment. Once the door had weakened, Lonnie would certainly be able to rip the thing from its hinges. Vince looked out a side window, just above where his father's initials were, and saw Misty staring in. Then, just faintly, he heard her begin to sing. "Oh, I have the moon in me . . ."

"Dad!" MJ screamed, hearing the demented tune. "Over there!"

Misty took the heel of the knife and smashed the window with it. She stuck her hand through to open the latch, and that was when Paul came running and slammed the golf club down on her arm.

Misty recoiled in pain, squealing like a dying animal. It

215

looked like her arm was broken; it bent in a way that wasn't natural.

Somewhere in the middle of this, the banging stopped. The only sound came from Romeo's barking. Vince scanned the windows and saw a shadow move across the backyard. It was Lonnie. He was trying the back door.

Paul looked at Michele as the banging began anew. "That one's not going to hold. The guy's too big." Addressing his wife and the two children, he said, "Go in the kitchen, and grab yourselves some knives. We're going to have to make a stand. I'll go first. If they get through me, you guys do whatever you can."

But just as everyone was about to follow his direction, the banging ceased. Everything, even Romeo, went quiet.

"Where are they, Daddy?" MJ cried.

"I don't know. Get in the corner, away from the windows and doors. Hurry."

"They're back out front," Michele said. "What are they doing? What are they going to do?"

Looking out the window, Vince saw the Byron Clan gathered in the snow at the end of the property, a few feet from the snowplow. Lonnie reached into the truck and pulled out a can of gasoline. Their intentions were clear: they were going to burn the house down.

Vince began to shake uncontrollably. It was happening again. It all was happening again. Another fire. This house, his home. This beautiful family. It all was going to go up in smoke. He couldn't watch that happen. Not again. He reached down and, not realizing how much heavier it was than normal, picked up his backpack.

Determined, he ran to the front door, his footsteps reminding him of the sounds from that fateful night. *Whump, whump, whump.*

"No!" Paul screamed. "What are you doing? Vince, get back here!"

Whump, whump, whump.

With his bag over his shoulder, Vince threw open the door and ran outside with his hands up. "Stop this!" he cried. "Leave the house! Leave this family alone! Please! Just take me, and then we can leave."

Old Mother Byron smiled. She turned to Lonnie and waved her head in Vince's direction. "Put him in the truck. Don't hurt him too much. We could use a hostage."

Lonnie approached and seized Vince by the arm, his hand nearly wrapping all the way around it. The moment he pulled Vince away, Old Mother Byron turned to Misty. "Now get the others. They saw my face."

"Yummy."

"No!" Vince cried, struggling in Lonnie's grip. It was no use; the man was far too strong.

Vince was thrown into the truck as if he weighed next to nothing. "Now sit still," Lonnie said, setting down the gasoline and leaning far over his hostage and opening the glove compartment. Inside was a pair of rusted handcuffs.

He leaned over farther still, and Vince noticed something fall from his pocket onto the seat: his Zippo lighter.

Vince reached for it, and Lonnie did too, knocking over the gas can in the process, the brown liquid leaking forth. Holding the lighter, Vince slid over to the far door and opened it.

Frozen, the handcuffs dropping from his hands, Lonnie looked from the trail of gasoline to Vince. His mouth dropped.

Preparing to jump out of the truck, Vince summoned the flame. Lonnie reached for him, but it was too late. Just before he jumped from the front seat, Vince dropped the Zippo.

There was a massive explosion. Fire blew out the windows, spreading glass everywhere, and Lonnie could be heard inside the truck, screaming like something deeply inhuman.

Vince landed face-first in the snow, his hair singed but quickly cooling. Behind him, Old Mother Byron clutched her heart and Misty shrieked in wild agony as Lonnie, burning bright like a candle, stumbled out of the truck and dropped to the snow, snubbing the flames.

There was another noise too, but with his ears ringing, Vince didn't immediately notice. Yet, as it grew louder, it became undeniable. Sirens. A multitude of them.

Vince knew he had to get up quickly. If the cops found him, he would be back at the orphanage in no time; there would be no excuses. His journey couldn't end like this, not when he was so close to finding his father.

Trailing a league of snowplows, cops arrived at the house by the dozen. Just as they began to exit their cars, screaming for the Byron Clan to keep their hands up, Vince jumped to his feet and, clutching his backpack, ran for the woods. Glancing over his shoulder, he saw MJ watching him from the window, her face running with tears. He wouldn't have a chance to say good-bye. He hoped she and her parents would understand. They were a great family. He was sorry he brought this upon them. They deserved so much better.

CHAPTER 12

It was a brutal walk, both physically and emotionally. His legs throbbed with pain from moving them in and out of the deep snow, every inch of his body wet and frozen, his skin cracking, his hair matted with ice, but it was his heart that ached most of all. It was deeply upsetting to leave MJ and her family. He had been happy there with them. The pain of his past had dissolved beneath their roof.

And yet it didn't matter, he decided. It didn't matter because of the funeral. If his father was going to be there, then he had to be too.

Repeating this like a mantra, he continued walking through the woods, unsure of the exact direction he was heading. Eventually his backpack was beginning to hurt his shoulder, and he decided to stop and open it. He unzipped the main section and saw that it was filled with objects he'd never placed in there. There were gloves and a hat and some food and water and other provisions. He realized MJ must have stocked it for him without his knowing, and this made him want to cry even more. Ravenously, he devoured a sandwich and, with the dry hat and gloves and scarf warming him, pressed on through the woods with new determination.

Eventually he emerged on an isolated road. After passing a sign that said DYERVILLE, 6 MILES, he realized he was now actually closer to the town than he was to the train. But he wouldn't make it by nightfall. The sun was nearly over the horizon already. The wind was picking up again, and the temperature was dropping fast. Even with MJ's provisions, he had to find shelter soon.

There wasn't a sound to be heard on this last leg of his journey, as if the snow had muffled the land's mouth and pinned its creaking joints. The streetlamps on the side of the road were illuminated, giving off a magnificently haunted glow.

He staggered farther along, looking for anything that might help him survive the night. But there was nothing in sight. No homes, no stores, no cars, no people. Just white upon white. It could have been the Arctic. It could have been another planet.

Then, a little farther up the road, he spotted it: a bridge that went above a small river. It wasn't perfect, but it would have to do. He ducked down beneath it like a troll and, with a lighter packed by MJ, started a small fire to keep him warm, although it didn't do much. He couldn't sleep either, but he thought this might be a good thing. He might not wake up if he did. So, as he sat there by himself in the near dark, the moon a sickle in the sky, the hours went by like ice sheets across continents, while he shivered and tried to get what warmth he could from the fire.

What was he doing out here? he wondered. Should he have hidden in the woods until the police left? Should he have stayed with MJ for as long as he could?

The tears that fell from his eyes froze upon his coat. "No," he said again. "I have to know if my dad is there."

But even if his father was there at the funeral, that didn't mean he would welcome Vince with open arms. After all, he could have come back for him at any time. What would make him change his mind now?

Beneath his thin sweater, it felt as if his heart were slowing. What was he doing? Why was he out here?

He wanted so badly to pick up his backpack and return to MJ and Michele and Paul and Romeo and that wonderful house his father helped build and never leave. But he didn't. The funeral was near, Dyerville was near, and his father would be there and he would want his son back. He would have to.

And so, leaning close to the fire, he pulled out his grand-father's book to pass the last few hours until sunrise.

The Door on the Cliff

Vincent scoured the pages of the gold book, feverishly searching line by line, image by image, for some answer to how to locate the sword and the bow.

Sleep deprived, he read until his eyes ached, until his hands shuddered with exhaustion. However, the language of the book was difficult to understand, and the illustrations didn't offer much in the way of detail. All he could infer was that he had to find a very old man who might or might not live in the forest, an almost mythological being that the birds clearly trusted. And that was all. No information on how to find him, no information on how he could help. In the book there were no guarantees.

In the time he'd been working at Mr. Barlow's estate, things had changed. No longer was he solely on a quest to find his mother and destroy the witch for what she had done to him. Now Vincent also set out to save a family, as well as protect others who might come across the witch's path. To prevent these future sorrows, he knew he would have to push himself even harder. This was his purpose. He didn't want anyone else to lose a mother, or a son, or a sibling. No one should have to hide within his or her own home out of fear of this woman. Her spells should hold no threat over the world and the people in it. He vowed to make this so.

But the key to defeating her remained a mystery to him.

He combed through the first one hundred pages and then the next hundred, hoping to find the answer to locating the weapons somewhere along the way, maybe in a chapter in which he could actually translate the words. But he couldn't solve any of the puzzles, and days later, nearly eight hundred pages in, which was a little more than halfway through, he found himself imploring the book for help, communicating with it like an old friend.

With his palm flat against the illustration of the old man and the weapons, he said, "Please. There are so many counting on me. Help me find what it is I need. I beg you."

He had been frustrated and desperate and didn't expect a response, but then, as when he first opened the book, the pages flipped on their own, stopping toward the back, at one of the final entries in the book. Vincent read the first few paragraphs, and they seemed to concern some sort of doorway to a land of dreams. There was nothing to suggest he would find his answer here. "No," he said, turning back to the illustration with great frustration. "The bow and the sword: that is what I need." And again the pages flipped to this later tale. Vincent sighed. Perhaps the answer was in here after all. He decided to read further.

By the end it was, undeniably, the most beautiful part of the book, the most beautiful thing he had ever read in fact. The chapter spoke of a world in direct contrast with his own. A place where there was only peace, only happiness, only love. A place of no pain and no sadness, where people were never stricken ill and the only laws were of dreams and wishes and hopes and pure imagination. A place where one would want to live forever. And according to the book, it wasn't a fantasy. It was all real, all attainable, and very much within Vincent's reach.

The words consumed him, overtaking every thought. *Could it all be true?* he wondered, after feverishly reading the chapter a fourth time. *Maybe*, he thought, *if it is a place of dreams, then that is where I can find what I need to rescue my mother.* If so, he had to visit such a land. He at least had to try, to see if the entrance the story spoke of was real.

That night, while Orin was fast asleep, Vincent followed the book's map to a cliff not very far away. Here, in the darkness, the wind picked up something brutal, and the temperature grew quite cold, but none of this bothered him because there, illuminated in the moonlight, was exactly what the book foretold.

At the edge of the steep cliff, resting like an unguarded portal, was a door or at least the frame of one. The ancient wood was held in place by some bricks, as if the door had once belonged to some type of house or other building that had long since collapsed and fallen into the abyss, leaving only the entrance behind.

Vincent peered through the doorway where it went off the cliff. He walked around the side of the door and saw the drop to the dark river below. The winds rocked his body back and forth. He returned to the doorframe once again.

If I walk through that door, he thought, *and there's nothing there, it's a straight drop, hundreds of feet down to the icy waters.*

But the book did say there was something on the other side. The book revealed a certain word or phrase that was supposed to be uttered the exact moment the threshold was crossed. That, and only that, would open the door to the other world. But what if the book was wrong? What if it was just a story, something not to be taken seriously or literally? Vincent wasn't sure. Clearly, there was nothing on the other side of the door but cold air and a death plunge. Another world? It was a leap of faith.

He approached the door once more, the wind, active again, nearly pushing and bullying him through; the air was alive here. He braced himself against the frame, not ready to cross just yet.

Slowly he stuck his hand through the opening. *What are you thinking? It's impossible.* Frightened, he yanked his hand back, inspecting it. Did it feel warmer? *What if? Just what if?*

Having memorized the key to entering this presumed utopia, Vincent closed the book and placed it back in the leather sack resting across his shoulder. Then he took a step back and exhaled deeply, shaking the nerves from his hands. "I believe. I believe."

The wind picked up even faster now. Vincent could hardly hear himself speak over its incessant howling. *"IbelieveIbelieveIbelieveIbelieve."*

The door waited for him. What lay beyond it waited for him.

Would it really be there? Was there such a place? It was time to find out.

Vincent closed his eyes, spoke the phrase from the book

into the howling winds, and walked through the doorway.

He emerged in a field. All was quiet. There was no wind. He was alone. In the distance, up on a hill, was a dark house with a long dirt path leading up to it. In the silence he heard the front door open and close with a perfect click. A shadowy figure could be seen walking down the winding trail, making its way closer.

As he waited, Vincent took a look around. The doorframe was still behind him, but apart from that, there was nothing else in sight for miles; the cliff, and all below it, had vanished. It was neither hot nor cold, wet nor dry, and the air smelled sweet, as if perfumed. There were stars in the sky, but they seemed larger than they had ever appeared before, as if gravity had pulled them closer. The tall grass of the field swayed rhythmically. He had an urge to walk for hours. The book was right: he felt completely at peace.

Finally the shadow approached. To Vincent's utter surprise, he was staring at a large jackrabbit walking awkwardly on its hind legs. The overgrown hare, gone white in the face with age, was severely hunched over and hobbling with a cane. It grunted and snorted with each strenuous step it took. Its only piece of clothing was an overcoat, but it fitted him well.

"Hello, Vincent," the jackrabbit said in a soothing voice, its whiskers twitching with each syllable. He reached into his coat pocket and pulled out a handkerchief, which he coughed into rather harshly.

"You know me."

"I do. I am your guide here, and that," he said, pointing to the house on the hill, "is your home."

"Mine? I've never seen it before. My home was much smaller, it—"

"Everyone who visits here has a house specifically built for him. That one is yours."

"But how did you know I'd come? How did it get built so quickly?"

"Time, as you will discover, works a bit differently here from what you are familiar with. Wonderful things can be done when you have a proper grasp of what you call seconds and minutes and hours and days and months and years and decades and centuries and millennia and so on."

"What is this place?" Vincent asked, gazing far into the distance. The sun shone down in some spots—glorious beams of light—while the moon did so in others. "Does it have a name?"

"It has many names, but you needn't concern yourself with any of that just now. Enjoy it; that is all. Our homes are very special homes. We make sure to build them to your exact preferences, the exact specifications according to your dreams."

"Is that it? Am I dreaming?"

"Vincent, come now, does this feel like a dream?"

Vincent closed his eyes and took in the air. He could feel every particle travel throughout his body, mixing with his complex system. He could feel the rush of his blood, the snapping of his neurons, the noble efforts of his lungs to continue breathing. He felt everything. He opened his eyes, and that was when he noticed he also wasn't gold any longer "No, it doesn't," he said. "It feels better."

"Yes, better than a dream, because here your dreams can be realized. Whatever it is your mind can imagine, whatever it is you want or need, whatever it is you crave or ache or wish for, you will find once you open the front door of your new home."

"Anything?"

"Anything. Go ahead. Give it a try."

Vincent was quiet for some time, his mind going where it needed.

"I know what you're thinking," the jackrabbit said, his red eyes glowing. He turned and pointed to the house with his cane. Upstairs a light turned on. "She's in there now. If you hurry, you'll just catch her coming down the stairs."

Vincent dropped his leather sack with the gold book tucked safely within it and ran faster than he ever had before. He raced up the long, steep path, never once tiring or straining for breath. He reached the house in far less time than seemed possible, almost as if he had been carried along on a string. But this didn't matter; nothing else mattered apart from what he would find inside the house.

He threw open the front door and crossed the threshold. And sure enough, there she was at the bottom of the stairs.

"Mom!"

She looked just like he had remembered. Not a day older from the moment he left home, not a touch of the witch's sickness about her. He ran to her, straight into her arms, and they embraced long and hard. He couldn't believe it: she was solid; she was real. "I thought I lost you," he said, his voice choked with tears.

"I'm here," she told him. "I'm here."

And she really was.

She was there all day and the day after that and the day after that. She was there from the moment Vincent woke up until the moment he fell asleep. She was there to cook him his favorite meals and to join him in his favorite games. Together they talked for hours on end; they walked the mystical countryside so lightly they might have been floating. It was life as it ought to be.

They continued right where they'd left off, never once mentioning the witch or the curse. He didn't talk of the giant or the horse or his quest. But it wasn't as if he'd had to consciously make an effort to conceal such things. No, it was as if the thoughts never popped into his head to begin with, as if they couldn't possibly exist. Not even the weapons he was seeking came to mind. Here there was only room for happiness. Here he was home.

A week into his stay Vincent was outside lying in the grass, and it felt as if he had his own personal sun shining down on him. Above, the clouds took whatever form he desired. The grass tickled his skin, and the air cleansed his lungs. He was happy.

"Enjoying yourself? It's quite perfect, isn't it?" the jackrabbit asked, standing over him.

Vincent sat up, taking in his guide, whom he had not seen since his arrival. The hare, in such a short time, looked thinner, sicker than he had before.

"This isn't my dream," Vincent said. "This isn't even my imagination. It's better than anything I could ever create. I've never felt anything even close to this. I don't want to ever leave."

"Vincent, you are welcome to stay here forever, you know. All our guests are. You'll never have to experience another ounce of pain, another second of sadness. Never again. Your mother doesn't have to leave you."

"I think I will stay. I . . ." Vincent trailed off, his mind suddenly captured by another thought, one of great longing.

Reading his mind once again, the jackrabbit looked up at the house. "She is there too. As is your horse, Orin. They are waiting for you."

"That's what I was missing." Vincent jumped up, ready to run inside. But then he stopped and turned back to the jackrabbit. A look of concern crossed his face. It was an odd feeling that coursed through him, an unwelcome reunion with a bitter enemy.

"They're here," he said, his voice sounding like it came from far away, "but they shouldn't be. Just like I shouldn't be."

The jackrabbit coughed into its handkerchief. "Such thoughts . . . maybe I was wrong. Maybe you are not ready to be here after all."

"I—I hadn't thought anything like that since I came through that door. It's like I almost forgot what still has to be done."

"Yes, that is very interesting. I did not expect this."

"What I complete here won't be complete back there," he said, pointing to the door, "will it? Orin, Stella, what they experience here with me they won't experience back home."

"Does that really matter, Vincent? Reality is not black and white. There is no is and isn't."

"But I can't stay here yet, not if they're still suffering through that door. My friends, Stella's father, my mother, they're counting on me. The witch has to be stopped so that everything can be set right. I can't just wish for that."

"Here you can."

"But not there."

"Vincent, I have to inform you, once you leave, you cannot come back for a very long time, if ever. It isn't allowed."

"I have to help them. I've already been gone so long. I've abandoned them. What if it's too late?"

The jackrabbit laughed. "Nonsense. You haven't even been gone a minute."

"I've been here over a week now."

"I told you, time runs differently here. If you wish, you can stay for a lifetime and back home, as you call it, you won't have missed a thing."

"Is that true?" Vincent asked, his eyes filled with hope.

"I promise you, it is."

"I—I can be with my mother . . . just a little bit longer?"

"You are afraid that she won't be there for you when you walk back through the door. That the witch took her life and this is the last you will ever see of her."

Vincent couldn't even respond to this.

"Go to her now, then. Be with your mother, with your

236

friends, with whoever you want. Take as much time as you need, Vincent. Live the life you've been denied."

And together mother and son lived another lifetime, the lifetime they should have had if not for the witch. Vincent's mother had a chance to raise him into a man and see his love blossom with Stella, and he was given the opportunity to watch his mother grow old, to witness her as a grandmother. Decades of happiness. Decades of perfection and bliss.

And then . . .

"I don't want you to die," Vincent said to his mother, once again interrupted with troubling thoughts, when she was almost one hundred and twenty-five years old and he one hundred.

"Die?" his mother questioned, as if she had never heard the word before. "I won't. We'll both keep going and going here, and if you want to be young again, if you want me to be young again, then you just have to wish it. We can do it all over again. A million times over, a million different adventures."

"But I have to go back; there are things I must do. I can't risk forgetting. I came here for a reason. And I have to leave."

"I know you do, my son. I know you do."

"I wish I could see you back there. I've been looking for you, and I won't stop until I find you. I'm just scared that when I do, you'll be— The witch, she'll have—" He couldn't even bring himself to say the words. "If I lost you, I won't have gotten to say good-bye. Not on the other side of the door. I'll never have the chance to tell you how much I love you, how sorry I am about what happened. I feel like it's all my fault. I want to set it right."

"Never, ever blame yourself, Vincent. No matter what happens, once you walk through that door, just know that I am a proud mother. You have been a wonderful son, and so many others need you now. I'm so happy we had this time. It meant everything to me. This is our good-bye. A temporary one. Until we meet again."

"I love you, Mother."

"And you never had to tell me that. I felt that every second of our lives together. I love you more than you can ever imagine."

And with that Vincent left the house and found the jackrabbit at the bottom of the hill, just beside the door.

"It's time for me to go," he said.

"You will be one of the very few to ever leave," the jackrabbit told him. He reached into his overcoat and handed over Vincent's sack with the gold book. "This tome: we're quite familiar with it here. When you get back, I think you'll find it a bit easier to understand. My gift to you."

"Thank you," Vincent said, walking through the door.

But before the words were even out of his mouth, he found himself floating in the river at the bottom of the cliff, his gold skin pulling him down, his body in incredible pain, as if it had thrashed around in the rapids for hours.

With the sack over his shoulder, he struggled to shore, where he was pulled out of the river by Orin, nothing but a day having passed.

CHAPTER 13

The book made everything clear. Sitting before the embers of the dying fire, Vince no longer felt the cold that had ensnared him for so long, for he was now burning with clarity. He fully understood why his grandfather couldn't stay in that wonderful place, that land of perfection, for the rest of time. Back through that door on the cliff, he still had things to do, miles to go.

By the time the sun came up, he felt refreshed, even though he hadn't slept. The cold had little effect on his brittle body, and there was no sense of weariness or fatigue. Somehow, beneath his skin, he felt altered. Like a burden was lifted. His mind was lighter, and he began to feel like he had years ago, when he still hoped.

He picked up his bag, strapped it across his back, and set out for Dyerville, the snow finally starting to melt beneath his feet.

The streets were now cleared, having been continuously plowed throughout the night. Still, it took several hours before he was able to turn off the main road and down the series of side streets that led to Dyerville. They became narrower and narrower until finally he found himself on a deserted road, the snow filthy atop it. Mountains were in the distance; many trees, on either side. There was nothing else. No signs of civilization.

As he ventured forth, the road began to twist, and the forest closed in, thick trees reaching up and over, blocking out the sky like a canopy. Animals—deer and foxes and rabbits and assorted critters—could be seen darting through the woods, dodging trees, and bounding over ditches. It was a beautiful sight, and he could only imagine what the road looked like on a summer's day. Behind his eyes, he pictured all the snow melting away in a flash, the water draining into the ground, and the forest filling with leaves. He gazed into the woods, hearing the birds chirping their songs and the trees whispering their delight, and it was then that he noticed something that he ordinarily never would: there, along the edge of the forest, was an odd stump. *Could that be?* He leaned forward, mouth slightly ajar. It was his

241

grandfather's hometown after all. Could he have been born right alongside this very road, delivered by a witch?

An hour later, Dyerville finally began to emerge, springing out from the woods. It was a small town, it turned out: a few traffic lights and nothing more. On a nice day he supposed it would be bustling with quaint life, especially along Main Street, where all the shops and restaurants were located. Instead, there were only a few people here and there, milling about. Most were shoveling the walks, tossing handfuls of salt on the ground, clearing away the fire hydrants, and so on. Thick icicles hung precariously above them like bars of a half-lowered cage. The entire town had been locked into place by the freezing cold.

As Vince walked down the street, a lovely crunch under his feet, he noticed the bell tower of a church protruding from above the rooftops somewhere toward the center of town. It defiantly spiked the sky as if intending to pierce straight through it, puncturing the heavens and pulling it down to earth for all to embrace. Vince could make out the stained glass windows and the church's many spires through the drifting snow, the imposing cross, the ancient design, as if this building were far older than all the rest. It was here, he assumed, that his grandfather's funeral would be conducted the following morning; it was here that he would say his last good-bye.

With nowhere to stay until then, he headed for the

church; perhaps it would be able to put him up for the evening if he told the people there who he was. Maybe he could even get a warm meal and a place to dry his clothes.

As he trekked onward, his eyes focused on the cross in the sky above the other buildings, there was no way to avoid walking into the back of a man drinking a coffee as he leaned against a lamppost. "Excuse me," Vince said when the man turned around. The two locked eyes, and there was recognition on both ends. "M?"

"Vincent!" he hissed. "Run, kid. She's here for you."

Vince looked past M and saw Mrs. West conversing with some people on the sidewalk just ahead. He could hear her spitting orders at them as if they were standing a hundred yards away.

"He's somewhere in this town, I know it. Find him. Spread out. The place isn't that big. Knock on some doors. He's our responsibility. If anything were to happen to him, it's our heads. Got it?"

"No," Vince muttered as he stepped back in fear. "Not now. Not yet. I've come too far."

"Hide," M told him. "I never saw you. Hurry. Hide."

Mrs. West and her cronies began to disperse, and Vince quickly ducked through the first door on his left.

He found himself in a lobby of some kind of business. It was clean and beige with tacky artwork in green plastic frames hanging on the walls and nondescript music. Across from him was a woman seated at a desk, chewing anxiously on a pen. She promptly asked if she could be of any assistance.

"Um . . . yes . . . no . . . I'm not sure . . ." The words stumbled from his mouth, unable to clear the hurdles of deceit. What was his reasoning for being here? He had to think of something fast.

"Are you here visiting someone? A grandparent perhaps?"

Vince was startled by this question. How did she know? "Yes, my grandfather," he said. "Vincent Elgin."

"Oh," the woman gasped, a hand to her chest. "Oh, I . . . Let me . . . One moment—"

Clearly she was aware that his grandfather had passed away but wasn't sure Vince knew. As she walked away, he tried calling out to her to inform her that he did until he saw the sign behind the desk. This was an old-age home, the last place his grandfather ever lived. This realization hit him like a punch to his chest.

Moments later the front desk woman returned, escorting a hulking man with thick arms folded across a wide chest. She bent down before Vincent. "This man's name is Andrew Ennis. He can tell you everything you need to know about your grandfather."

That name: Vince recognized it immediately. It was the name on the letter he had received. And all at once he felt the great weight of disappointment. This man wasn't his father. Not even close. The phrase in the letter, the initials were all just some horrible coincidence. It was Andrew who had written down his grandfather's tales and sent them to him at the orphanage. His father had had nothing to do with it.

Andrew hovered over him at well over six feet and looked bothered by just about every inch of it, as if he would be hiding somewhere if not for so large a body. His face was covered in coarse stubble, and the hair hanging out from beneath his hat was long and thick and greasy. Each arm displayed deep bruises—clusters of color—while his hands were severely calloused. To Vince, his sloping nose appeared to have been broken several times over, and because of this, he could only breathe out of his mouth.

"Take a walk with me," Andrew said to him in a much quieter and more comforting voice than expected. "I'd like to talk with you."

Dejected, Vince followed, although he was relieved to be indoors and away from Mrs. West and her search group.

Walking the halls of this place, he felt his grandfather's presence. It was like he was alive and near.

Andrew took Vince into a large congregation area on the second floor. There were many elderly people milling about here, conversing, reading, playing board games, watching TV, enjoying a meal.

Andrew offered Vince a seat at a table, and the two of them sat down, the large man's knees popping like gun blasts, a dented and battered box of checkers left half opened between them.

"First, I'd like to tell you how sorry I am about your grandfather. He was a lovely man. I was honored to care for him."

"Thank you."

Silence. Vince sat there with his hands folded in his lap while Andrew took off his hat and wiped at his brow, then shoved the box of checkers aside.

"He could be difficult at times, your grandfather. Especially when he first arrived. Boy, did he give me a run for my money. But eventually we came to look fondly upon each other. There was respect there. Deep admiration on my part." He paused here, as if reflecting on it all. "I assume you received the book."

"I did."

"Have you read it?"

"I'm almost through."

"Just wonderful, isn't it? Every day we would sit over there by the window and he would tell me those amazing tales. His mind wasn't what it used to be, so he told me most of them over and over again, never realizing his mistake— not that I would ever complain or point it out. But you know what? As damaged as his mind became, those stories never changed. He could have told me them a million times over and they wouldn't have varied and I would have never bored of hearing them. Eventually I realized I just had to get them down before . . . well, you know."

Another moment of silence.

"There were others too. Other tales that aren't in the book. He didn't tell them as often, and I don't remember them well enough to have jotted them down. There were some about his treacherous voyage overseas, another one about a ghost he encountered on the side of a lonely cemetery road, another about the extraordinarily lucky necklace he came in possession of but subsequently lost. There were so many that eventually my head began to spin. I was swept away by it all, every word. *Who was this man?* I wondered. And my second thought was, *Could any of this be true, even in part?*"

Vince didn't wait for Andrew to answer the question. He did so himself. "There's truth to all of them."

Andrew smiled, his body finally relaxing. "I'm glad you said that. You know, everyone here has heard these stories at one point or another. They all have their opinions about them. But nothing got the people here more riled up than that story about the door on the cliff. Your grandfather loved telling everyone that it existed and that it wasn't very far from here. He would get up and point out that window right there and say that if you were to keep walking in that direction, a straight line from the church without ever diverging, eventually you'd find it. He said it was a steep cliff, steeper than any he had ever seen. And of course, all alone, just at the edge of the precipice, was the doorframe. No door, mind you, just the frame, leading nowhere. Been there for ages, he said. Go through it, and it's a straight drop, all the way down. Well, you could just imagine how people reacted to such a story. Many dismissed him right off the bat, and the others who held out hope for such a place begged him for the words to enter that world of dreams. Of course he never revealed them, and that got the rest of the believers to doubt the tale. 'If you know the words, then why aren't you climbing that hill now?' they asked. And your grandfather just sat there and smiled and said, 'I had my chance.'"

Vince almost asked if Andrew had gone through it but then realized that this man was alive and there was no way anyone would survive such a drop.

"As far as I know, your grandfather never told anyone the words, and he didn't put them in the book. Not directly anyway. I've had a couple of guesses as to what they were. But I don't think I'd ever be quite brave enough to try one of them out. Even if I felt ninety-nine percent sure. There is still that doubt. No, it takes a special person, one far stronger than I to walk through that door." He paused. "Or someone with absolutely nothing to lose."

"You've seen the door?"

Andrew chuckled. "No. I never even bothered to look. It's just something I fantasize about every now and then. In the end, though, I think it was just another one of your grandfather's stories. He had quite the imagination."

Vince sat back, his mind reeling. "But maybe there was something more to it than that. Maybe he really went through that door and left a clue behind. The words. They have to be somewhere, right? He wouldn't just erase such a thing. Maybe people have to seek them out. Maybe they have to really show they want them. Otherwise I don't get it. If the place was so special, why wouldn't he want to share it with everybody?"

"Vince, from what I knew of your grandfather, he was a very puzzling man, very mysterious. But he was old. His mind wasn't what I'm sure it once was. He always seemed to be one step removed, one step outside the ordinary. I'm sorry to say he was in this place for a reason. Maybe his mind was so fragile that he forgot those special words. Or maybe he never knew them. I think—I think maybe the door is just a metaphor. Do you remember anything? Anything he might have said to you when you were younger?"

Vince thought a moment and shook his head. He blamed himself for this. He, along with his parents, was one of the cynical doubters who believed his grandfather had lost his mind. He had forgotten the stories, the language they shared. The words, and any meaning that came with them, were now lost.

Andrew sat back in his chair. "I suppose it doesn't really matter. I suppose all that matters is what you take with you, what parts of your grandfather you take with you."

"That's why you sent me the book. So I could carry him with me."

"The tales seemed like they meant a lot to him."

"That's his life on those pages."

Vince said this and had to look away. He glanced around the room and noticed all eyes were locked on him.

Andrew, picking up on his guest's discomfort, turned around with a snort, and the others quickly diverted their eyes and returned to their activities.

"Don't mind them," he told Vince. "People in here have argued about that for some time now."

"Argued about what?"

"About the tales. Are those stories true or not? And you know what I say, Vince? Fact, fiction, what does it matter? Is anything really fact? There may come a time when one plus one doesn't equal two anymore. The world was flat; now it is round. The sun once rotated around us; now we rotate around the sun. The universe continues to grow as well as multiply; how far will it go? There are countless religions, various origin stories, alternate histories of every country and government. Fact?" He shrugged his shoulders. "What is a fact? We gather information; that is the best we can do. We gather as much as possible and lay it all before us. Then we decide what to believe."

"Then we grab the truths that speak to us."

Andrew leaned in, grinning. "You're a wise boy."

"But not until we hear the whole story, right?"

"Would you mind reading a tale to everyone gathered here right now? They all knew your grandfather and liked his stories, whether or not they believed them. I'm sure they'd love it."

Vince nodded and reached into his backpack. When he looked up again, everyone in the room was gathering around him. He felt like it was bedtime at the orphanage again, and he had everyone's rapt attention, every heart and mind yearning for somewhere to escape to. Once more the home for the elderly was filled with the voice of his grand-father.

The Trials

Everything was clear: every word, sentence, paragraph, and page. It all settled into proper form, not a single letter out of place. The book now explained to Vincent, in rich detail, how to reach the King of the Birds deep within the forest. It was this ancient man, it stated, who would tell him how to retrieve the sword and the bow he so desperately needed.

"It will be a long time before we come back out of these woods," Orin said to Vincent early one sunny morning, as they stood on the edge of the forest after a full day and night of travel. "If we make it out at all."

"We will emerge," Vincent said, his body still throbbing with pain from the thrashing it had taken in the river. He even felt feverish, cold. "But we will not do so without find-ing the witch first. It ends here."

"Yes, let us begin this final stage of our quest."

And so together the golden boy and the horse headed into the dark forest to meet their fates.

It swallowed them whole. This massive forest was alive in more than just the natural sense. The path vanished almost instantly, eaten up by the ever-thickening brush. All around them, the trees multiplied by thousands, seem-ingly springing up out of nowhere, more obstructions, more confusion at every turn. All directions appeared identical. It was as if they were lost to the world. The woods, in fact, seemed to be its own endless world. It had its own sounds, its own laws. It wasn't safe.

With the blotting out of the sun, temperatures dropped precipitously. Vincent could see the fog of breath emerg-ing from Orin's mouth and followed it up until it thinned and vanished in the darkness. With his eyes heavenward, he said, "I never felt so small. These trees, it's like they've been stacked one atop another. I can't see where they end. Do they end?"

"I have an uneasy feeling about these woods, Vincent. The longer we are here, the more likely we are to perish. We should make haste."

Vincent kept the gold book open before him, study-ing the text on how to properly navigate through such a merciless maze. "It says here that there should be a tree that is split in two, as if it were struck by lightning. We are to go in the direction of the left half."

"There!" Orin shouted, and sure enough, sixty feet ahead was a tree torn down the center, one half bending one way, the other in the complete opposite direction, the inside blackened and charred.

It felt good to be making progress. Vincent caressed the book like a beloved pet. He wanted to thank it for its help. But this was just the beginning.

From there the two had to follow certain slants of light, locate peculiarly twisted trees and curious clearings. Many times he deciphered the information incorrectly, and they had to retrace their steps for a mile or more, only to start over again. When the sun went down, not a thing could be seen, and they had to cease their travels and try to sleep. Although that was when the wilderness truly came alive.

Odd noises, the forest's wild midnight orchestra at play, surrounded them in the darkness. Creatures rustled the leaves, creaked the branches from which they leaped. There were shrieks and snarls, moans and cries, howls and bellows. Vincent and Orin heard the vile devouring of prey, the crunching of bones, the slurping of blood. Throughout the night, all around them was the sound of approaching footsteps—large beasts, no doubt. *The boar*, Vincent immediately thought. *It's watching us. And perhaps through it, the witch as well. But it is not yet time for our paths to cross.*

"When this is over," Vincent asked Orin before their crackling fire, "and you are human once again, what do you plan to do with the rest of your days?"

The horse neighed quietly and exhaled. "I'm not sure. A part of me fears that I have forgotten what it's like to be human. What if I don't fit in anymore? What if, no matter where I go, I'm not wanted?"

"Who wouldn't want you, Orin? I couldn't have asked for a better companion."

"We're an unlikely pair, the two of us. Perhaps something greater than ourselves brought us together. I have no doubt you will find your mother. After this is done, you will have everything you ever wanted."

Vincent stroked the horse's head. "I got this far because of you. I survived the giant and met Stella because of you. Whatever happens, you will never be forgotten. You will always have a place where you are wanted. Never question that."

A haunted howl cut through the woods, silencing their conversation. The two of them edged closer to the fire, their eyes scanning the dark and menacing surroundings. The night couldn't pass soon enough.

Over the remaining hours they slept poorly, and when morning arrived, they wearily set out once more, the days repeating with little difference and minimal progress. They found hardly a trifle to eat in the forest, and what they did consume usually made them sick. Their bodies grew heavy; their minds, fragile. Every muscle weakened, and all energy drained as if through a sieve. Vincent's fever rose dangerously high. At times the two friends believed they, like so many others before them, would embrace their deaths here in the woods.

But still, they were persistent, fighting through all illnesses and hunger, all fears and doubts, never wavering, and in the end such determination served them well. Nearly two weeks into their venture through the forest, they came to the tree they had been searching for.

"It matches the one in the book," Vincent said. "Exactly."

It was a thick tree, the thickest they had come across in all their travels. Nearly four hundred feet in height, the top was lost in the clouds, its own dank environment. At their feet, the roots must have plunged deep into the earth, ensuring the ancient tree would never topple or go hungry. The falling cones were as large as Vincent's head, and nearly every single branch supported a hundred birds all lined up and silently watching the pair's every move. It was as if every winged creature had sought this one tree, had been pulled to it. Indeed this was the home of the King of the Birds.

"He's inside there? How do we get in?" Orin asked, sidestepping another plummeting cone.

Vincent, gold book in hand, watched the pages flip.

When they settled, he read the unlocked words. "The book says to knock in a particular pattern." He hopped down from the horse. "Like on the door of a house." With his free hand, he reached out and rapped his knuckles against the trunk in the rhythm explained on the open page.

Almost instantly the trunk began to split open, kicking up dirt and sand into small clouds. The wood creaked so loudly it sounded as if it were being twisted and wrung dry. The thousands of birds scattered, and eventually a door took shape, revealing darkness within.

"We're one step closer," Vincent said, nudging Orin onward.

From the outside the tree was humongous. From the inside it was even bigger. There was an entire palace within, everything made of wood—tables, chairs, staircases, bowls, chalices, everything—all kept in place by their own roots. Like the forest itself, it was a living, breathing place. In the center of it all, high above them, Vincent found the old man from the gold book sitting on a throne of thick limbs. He almost looked like he was made of wood himself. His features were dark and gnarled and thick like bark. His arms appeared to be covered in dying moss, and his legs could have been trunks themselves. His beard, which straggled all the way down to his soiled feet, was littered with dried leaves and was crawling with insects. He wore a robe of tangled undergrowth. His nose was sharp; his eyes were bold and round and wildly unsettled. There were several birds lingering on his person, on his arms and shoulders, even his head. He fed them from a large bowl of writhing worms.

"I know why you've come," said the king, his voice so old it sprayed dust. "My birds have told me. They tell me all that goes on in the world, from every corner of it. There is nothing that escapes me. You seek the sword and the bow. Am I right?" He smiled, revealing a rotting set of wooden teeth.

"Yes. We've come a long way, my horse and I. Can you help us?"

"That I can. The fact that you have found me reveals your admirable determination and will, a will I will not crush by denying your request. I cannot give you the sword and the bow, I'm afraid, but I can tell you how to obtain them." As he spoke, he didn't budge, as if his body too were rooted in place.

"That is all we ask."

"To acquire the bow with which to kill the boar, you must first display great acts of stealth and cunning. To bring death to the witch, you have to first overcome Death yourself, for only Death can bring death. There are two" —he paused, carefully considering his next word—"creatures you seek. One has no name. Those who dare whisper about him simply call him the Tall Man. He sits beneath a tree deep in this forest. Whether it rains or snows, he never moves, never even stirs. Not unless something catches his eye, something special; then he hunts. He will find you, my golden friend, most alluring. His victims, you will discover, are displayed prominently all around him, like a warning. To retrieve the bow, you must not heed this warning. The Tall Man sits with the bow at his back, almost as a tease, a taunt; he wants you to come for it. You must snatch it without his turning around, without his spotting you. If he does, and you are not as cunning as he is, he will catch you, and your fate will be most horrendous. Do you understand?" Vincent nodded, and the King of the Birds went on. "The sword will be even more difficult to obtain, for you must face Death itself. Only such a being as Death can decide if you are worthy enough to carry such power in your hands, to deny Death a soul, for the sword itself is a soul killer. Death will not give it up easily. Beware Death's gaze; beware its touch." Silent, he stared down at Vincent, appraising what he saw. "Are you afraid of that which you must do?"

Vincent was very afraid, but he knew he couldn't allow such fear to penetrate deep inside him, for then he would most surely fail. "Afraid or not, I will succeed."

"I believe you just might. I suppose you would like to know how to find these two nightmares."

"Yes."

With a crunch, the King of the Birds pulled his arm free of the throne as if they were one and reached down beside him to pick up a small cage. In it were three birds: an owl, a raven, and a crow.

"To find the Tall Man, release the owl. It will take you to him, for it sees that which we cannot imagine. To find Death, set free the raven, for the two know each other well. Then, if you possess both the sword and the bow, release the crow, and it will lead you to the boar. Find and defeat the boar, and you will find the witch, for they are now linked for life."

"Thank you," Vincent said, stepping forward and taking hold of the cage.

"The birds of the forest will be watching. I will listen closely for your tale, my friend. Good luck. You will most certainly need it."

Outside the tree Vincent opened the cage. Without hesitation, the owl took flight off into the trees.

"Follow it," Vincent told Orin. "The Tall Man has our bow."

It was several hours of travel, but by the time the sun dropped to the horizon and twilight ensconced the woods, the owl had settled on a branch in the near distance, folded its wings, and tucked its head.

It was an eerie part of the forest. Everything was withered and dying. The trees were dry; their branches, brittle and bare. There was no greenery. It was as if a fire had burned here for many days.

"The Tall Man must be near," Vincent said, dismounting. His landing was awkward, the fever he still carried affecting his balance.

"What are you doing?" Orin said. "I'm coming with you."

"The King of the Birds said this task shall require great stealth."

"Stealth? You can hardly stand."

"I will be fine. And I'll be able to perform better alone. Wait here for me. Conserve your strength. You will need it when I return with the bow, for then we must flee and you must run faster than you ever have before."

"If he spots us, we will be doomed. The King of the Birds said so himself."

"Then let us hope it does not come to that."

Reluctantly Orin wished him luck, and Vincent trod carefully in the direction of the owl.

It wasn't long before he heard something familiar, a sort of creaking sound. The noise reminded him of walking the docks with his mother, boats all around waiting to be boarded. But surely there was no water or ships in the middle of the woods. What was it then?

Rope. Yes, it was the creaking of rope, not one but many. What exactly was out here in the forest with him? From behind a tree, Vincent peered out into the darkening distance, searching for what it might be. His eyes scanned

262

the trees, jumping from shadow to shadow to— His hand quickly covered his mouth as he choked back a scream. *Oh, no. Oh, no.*

From a single oak tree hung a score of men. They were tied to the branches by their legs, their arms dangling, nearly brushing the ground as they swayed. Their bodies were heavily decayed and scavenged. Not by carrion birds— that much was clear—but by what?

Then he spotted the Tall Man.

The creature sat cross-legged beneath the same tree from which his victims hung, his back to Vincent. Even sitting, he appeared to be taller than most men. In fact everything about him was stretched and pulled thin. He looked flattened, squeezed, and yanked into something inhuman. He was dressed in black rags, and an oversized hat hung limply atop his head. Whatever skin showed was so pale he was practically translucent.

More important to Vincent, however, was the bow with a small quiver of arrows tied to it, lying on the ground behind the Tall Man's back. It sat there waiting for him.

Should he create a diversion or just run and grab it? The Tall Man appeared to be in some meditative state. Maybe he was sleeping. Maybe it wouldn't be as difficult as he thought. *No, you must be careful. It won't be that simple.*

Vincent approached slowly. He moved slower than slow. Every step had to be sure. He couldn't make a sound;

he couldn't make one false step. He had to avoid all fallen branches, all piles of leaves. But whenever he looked up at the Tall Man, he nearly toppled over. Was it the fever? His mind played games with him. His thoughts didn't feel like his own. *What is he doing sitting there? Did his head just twitch? Is that noise coming from him? What is that? It sounds like a hiss.* Then, oddly: *His face, I want to see his face.* Vincent had to freeze. What had come over him?

When he felt he had regained his composure, he moved again, nearer and nearer to the tree. All around him the Tall Man's victims swayed back and forth in the wind, the ropes ominously creaking. Their reeking bodies brushed against Vincent's arms and legs. It was almost as if they were reaching for him, looking to keep him from moving forward. Their skin was rotting and discolored; large chunks had been ripped out, revealing bone; spiders made their homes throughout the remaining clothes, some even burrowing into the open wounds to lay eggs. It was a disturbing sight, but Vincent paid little attention. The closer he got, the more he was in awe of the Tall Man's size. One arm alone was nearly five feet long, if not longer. He could probably turn around and reach Vincent from here. *What would he look like if he stood up? Should I call out to him?*

Vincent was terrified now. It was as if his mind had been invaded, his thoughts maliciously toyed with. He felt close to passing out.

But he tried to brush such fears aside, for the bow was almost within his grasp. Just a few more steps.

He slunk closer. Closer still.

There it was. He just had to bend down and grab it.

Vincent reached over, expecting the Tall Man to turn around at any second. *Do it, I dare you. Turn around.* He stretched for the bow, his fingers writhing. He touched it with the tips of his fingers. Just another inch.

He grabbed it. And the Tall Man didn't even budge.

Just as carefully, Vincent began his walk back to the horse, a smile across his face. One down.

Turn back. Look at him.

Vincent froze.

His own voice repeated in his head, commanding him: *Look . . . at . . . him.*

As if compelled, Vincent glanced back over his shoulder. He just had to look back. And it was then that he saw the Tall Man's head begin to turn. It turned slowly, nearly spinning all the way around.

He has no face! He has no face!

Indeed it was a blur, his features smudged into nonexistence. And yet the Tall Man must have seen him clearly.

Vincent ran, nearly stumbling, and the Tall Man leaped to his feet. A towering phantom, he hunted his prey, his arms reaching out while his gangly legs moved far quicker than was possible. His limbs skittered across the ground like an arachnid's. Head to the sky, the Tall Man let out a haunted moan.

"Orin! Orin! Hurry!"

The horse came charging through the woods to Vincent. "Get on! Quickly!"

Vincent reached his horse, jumped on, and took off. Over his shoulder he watched as the Tall Man gained on them. Chased down, there was no doubt that they would be caught, and this time there was nothing to throw. It was too late.

Think, Vincent said to himself. *Think!*

The gold book bounced in its sack across his back. *The King of the Birds said the Tall Man stirs only for something special. He said he would want me especially. Why?* Vincent placed his hands on the book. *Gold.* Believing it was his only chance, he pulled it from the leather sack. "I'm sorry," he said. "You have helped me more than you will ever know." With a kiss to the cover, he tossed it to the ground.

The Tall Man spotted the gold pages immediately and engulfed it in his wobbly arms. He drew it close to his body, moaning an odd and grotesque song as he rocked back and forth, his arms wrapped completely around his wiry frame.

As he rode away, Vincent watched the Tall Man returning to his place beneath the tree, swatting at the hanging bodies, ripping off a chunk of rotting flesh, and throwing it into whatever mouth he possessed. Then he sat with the gold book resting in his lap. It was the last Vincent would ever see of them.

"Was that the Tall Man? What was he?" Orin shouted, his voice strained with horror.

"I don't know. I just know I don't want to ever see him again. He was in me, Orin. I felt him crawling around inside my head. He didn't want to leave."

"The book, its secrets—"

"I had to do it. It was our only chance."

Vincent was saddened at the loss of the book—the only comfort he possessed in this world—but he had what he had come for and knew he must now move on. In the clear, miles from the Tall Man's tree, they rested. At times he thought he could still hear the Tall Man slinking through his thoughts.

In the morning Vincent released the raven from the cage.

With the bow and quiver of arrows slung snugly over his shoulder and a poor night's sleep behind him, he followed the bird through the forest all day. By the time night fell, the raven's midnight body had been lost in the canopy of darkness.

"I can hardly see it," Orin said.

And as if it had understood, the raven screeched.

"Follow its cries; we can't be very far."

Ears perked, Orin did just that. And in the late hours of the fog-ridden night, the bird led them to a decimated part of the forest. Trees were toppled over and lying atop one another, while others seemed to be ripped straight from the ground, leaving massive holes in their wake. Others, looking like African baobabs, were thrust back into the earth upside down, roots sprawling in the misty air. There wasn't an animal about, and the ground was curiously soft. Ahead there was a clearing, as if the forest had been scalped, and here the moonlight shone down from the heavens, illuminating a circle of statues.

Orin slowed, trotting clockwise around the peculiar sculptures, each one so heavy it sat lopsided in the sodden ground, some deeper than others. Vincent noticed they were men, all frozen in various states, looks of torture and anguish etched upon their faces. They were uncanny in their detail, as if a volcano had erupted and real people had been caught in the ash, captured for all eternity.

After circling, Vincent and Orin hesitantly followed the raven into the center of the stone ring. The bird pecked at the ground. All around them the fog thickened.

Vincent waited for Death, a chill across his spine. What was this place? And if the raven stopped, if this was where they were supposed to be, then where was Death?

"I'm not ready to die," said Orin. "I can't die like this, not as a horse."

"When your time comes, my friend, I promise you, you will be a human again."

Clouds shifted before the moon, and a foul cry penetrated the forest. Spooked, the raven took flight. Something was coming.

Vincent descended from the horse and searched through the fog and into the distance. And then he saw it. Death.

The psychopomp emerged from the darkness. Before such a petrifying presence, the fog lifted, sucked back into the sky. Whatever grass had managed to grow quickly shriveled; the dried leaves crumbled. In its presence, nothing lived.

But Death was not quite the vision that Vincent had expected to see. There was no skeleton in rags, no hood or scythe, no hovering wraith. Instead, Death was wrapped in bright white cloth. It was bound so tightly that the sickness beneath—the wasting away, the rotten core that bled through—was clear. Its legs were wrapped together so that Death walked oddly, a limping and slumping gait. Even the face was concealed in an almost sheer sheet of white, only blood, rich red blood, seeped through and was splattered in various spots. Death's arm, free of any muscle, dragged a sword behind its emaciated figure. The sound of the blade scraping along the ground cut at Vincent's soul.

Death entered the circle of statues, and Vincent swore he could hear them scream from within their stone tombs.

"The golden boy." Death's voice was neither male nor

female, but a combination of the two. It was harsh, like glass continuously cut at the throat and severed the cords. "You've come for this." It dropped the sword on the ground between them.

Vincent found that he could not speak. He was cold, so cold.

"Your end, shall it come now, will not be like most. I will not bring you where you are supposed to go. There will be nothing better waiting for you. No, if I choose you should die, I will keep you for myself." It pointed to the statues surrounding them. "Like I did the rest who sought the sword. They are my special collection, my trapped souls. Are you sure this is the path you choose?"

Vincent nodded.

"You sacrifice much in this decision. If you walk away with the sword, there are worlds beyond death that you may never see. It is the rule."

"I will not waver."

"You won't. But what of your friend?"

Death pulled away the white sheet covering its face. Its mouth was a deep dark hole that widened as it wailed in Orin's direction.

Immediately the horse crumbled to his knees, and Vincent could see his friend's soul being ripped from his body. Death was consuming him.

"It's me!" Vincent screamed. "I challenged you, not him! Me!"

Death turned its gaze on him. "Then look into my eyes."

With Orin moaning and writhing in pain, Vincent stared Death in the face. There were no eyes at which to glare, only eye sockets. They nearly engulfed the entire face. The nose was a hole to match, same as the mouth, which continued to feast on the soul of his friend. Nothing but black holes on a hollowed face of oozing flesh.

Vincent tried to look away but couldn't. Something, an unnatural force far stronger than anything of this world, restrained him. He stared into Death's eyes, and it was like he was absorbed by them. He felt his consciousness ripped from his skull and pulled into the darkness, falling into a never-ending pit of despair. There he saw the most horrific images he would ever see. Things that would keep him up nights for the rest of his life. He saw sickness, torture, darkest hate, insanity, brutality. He saw plagues and famine, war and disease. He saw Stella alone and broken. He saw Orin descending closer and closer to death. He saw his mother, struck by the witch in the doorway of his home. He saw the sadness in her eyes, the fear; he felt the pain coursing through her. He saw her life as not her own.

He wasn't prepared for this. He wanted to curl up and weep, sink into the earth like the statues and vanish. His knees weakened; his pulse raced. His throat tightened, and his eyes began to roll. He was dying.

Meanwhile Death's eyes penetrated Vincent's. Death wandered past them casually, touring Vincent's past. It was judging him. It saw his flight from home and his capture by the giant and his escape from him. It saw the encounters with the gnome and the dwarf and Mr. Barlow. It saw his walk through the doorway on the cliff. It saw the Tall Man. It saw Vincent, at this very moment, staring into Death's eyes.

Vincent felt a rush of air, an explosion in his head, and he collapsed in a heap. Beside him, Orin's soul rushed back into his body, bowling him over.

Slowly Death replaced the white covering. "You are worthy," it said, standing above Vincent. "My touch cannot take you just yet." As if to demonstrate, it reached down with a single finger and touched Vincent's face. The skin burned, but he didn't die. And that was how Vincent came to bear the scar he was to carry for the rest of his life.

"The sword is yours to take, as is the witch's soul. However, when we meet again, my touch will not be so forgiving." And with that, Death left, heading back into the dark of the wilderness.

Vincent didn't speak for some time. Nor did Orin. They couldn't. In the center of the circle, they huddled close and slept for two full days.

When they finally woke, they felt healed. They felt new and strong. Vincent especially. Having faced Death and survived, he vibrated with life. It was a new day.

With both the sword and the bow in his possession, he released the crow. It was time he faced the witch.

CHAPTER 14

Deeply engrossed in the story, Vince had nearly forgotten he even had an audience until the second he closed the book. With the story finished, some people simply stood and walked away, while a few others stayed and asked him to keep reading.

But Andrew waved them quiet, stating, "No, no, no. That's quite enough. You all know the story."

After some grumbling and groaning, everyone acquiesced. It sounded good to Vincent too. He wanted to read the final tale on his own, when he could really take it all in. His grandfather was so close now to finding the witch. How would it end?

"Come with me," Andrew said in his weary voice when everyone finally backed away from Vince and spread out across the room. "I have something to show you."

As Vince followed him out the door, the inhabitants were consumed by their own conversations, some of which he couldn't help overhearing.

"I'm telling you, the cave collapsed," he heard a man say. "I've seen it. No way anyone can dig through now. You would have to blow it up with dynamite."

"I swam in the lake a handful of times in my youth. Definitely salty. Wait a minute, I just realized: could that be the blood?"

"You're as crazy as he was!"

"I talked to the dwarf's son some years ago. Showed me the cart. Not for sale. That guy doesn't sell a thing. Nothing like his father."

As Vince trailed Andrew up another flight of stairs, he couldn't help smiling. The stories might have been fiction, but their effect was real enough.

He walked down a dimly lit hall with several identical doors on either side. When they reached the third door on the right, Andrew pulled a key from his pocket and unlocked it. But he didn't turn the knob.

"This is your grandfather's room—was your grandfather's room. I haven't gone through it yet. I was hoping you would come first. Figured you'd want to poke around. He didn't have much, but you can take anything you'd like. I'll be back in a bit." He paused, scratching his scruffy chin. "Wait a second. Do you have a place to stay until the funeral tomorrow?"

Vince shook his head and cast his eyes to the grimy carpet. "I was thinking of maybe sleeping in the church."

"What? On the steps? In the freezing cold? Look, I work late tonight, but I'm going to make a phone call and make sure you're taken care of, okay? I have some good friends in this town. Practically family."

Vince thanked Andrew for his kindness and watched as the large man vanished down the hall. He was glad his grandfather had been in such good hands.

Standing in the doorway now, he hesitated before going inside. What would he find in there? Was he supposed to be the one going through his grandfather's things? It felt like something an adult should be doing.

A full minute later, when he finally had the strength to open the door and turn on the light, he found himself looking in at a small and tidy room. There didn't seem to be much to his grandfather's name, not even a picture frame. Had someone else already cleaned it out?

Lingering in the air was a sweet scent that carried Vince years back in time the moment he inhaled. It was undeniable; it was his grandfather. After all these years Vince had almost forgotten. His breathing sped up; his eyes watered;

his hands trembled. It was almost as if his grandfather were still alive, still in this very room. They had just missed each other by a matter of days.

The moment he stepped through the door, the light flickered out overhead, casting the room in near darkness. Vince flipped the switch back and forth. No luck. The only illumination now came from the gray skies outside a small window on the far side of the room.

As he ventured deeper into the lengthy shadows, he saw something sitting on an end table. It was the only object that didn't have its place in some drawer or closet. Or maybe this was its place. It was a small box, its lid half opened. Inside, something glistened.

He crept closer, his eyes adjusting to the shadows with each step. When he reached the table, he dropped slowly to his knees so that he was at eye level with the gleaming object. He picked up the box and brought it close to his face. Inside, he saw a gold ring.

He gently removed it and rolled the band over and over in his palm. *Is it—?* He wasn't sure. It had been so long since he had seen his father's ring. And it was dark in here, too dark. But for some reason that he could not explain, he didn't want to bring it out into the light; he didn't want to ask Andrew about it.

The ring was warm in his hand, like it just came from the fire. He slipped it on a finger on his left hand. It felt right, like it was meant for him. It had to be his father's.

But how did it get here?

His father was in Dyerville, he realized. He had been in this very room: a final good-bye. And when it was time for him to go, he had left the ring behind; after all, it had originally belonged to Vince's grandfather.

All Vince had to do now was just make sure he arrived at the funeral the next day without being spotted by Mrs. West. That was it. As long as she didn't see him, he would be reunited with his father in less than twenty-four hours, these past few years nothing but a long and unfortunate detour. But she would be looking for him no doubt, especially at the funeral.

He would need a disguise.

Hanging on a hook on the back of his grandfather's door was a ragged coat, not unlike what he pictured his grandfather purchasing from the dwarf in the story. Was this the same cloak? He grabbed it and left the room as quickly as he had entered.

Downstairs he ran into Andrew, who was standing in the lobby with a boy a few years older than Vince. He had glassy eyes and a sweaty brow, a somewhat mature yet nervous teen.

"Done already?" Andrew asked. "Then again I suppose there wasn't much to collect."

"I have what I need," Vince said.

"Good. I'm glad. If I come across anything else, I'll make sure to send it to you. Now, this guy right here," he said, clasping the teen on his shoulder, "is Christopher. You'll be staying with him and his family tonight. Chris's mother will take good care of you. Many years ago she took me in when I was lost. You'll be in good hands."

Vince thanked Andrew again, and the two boys made their way out of the building and into the icy streets. Vince huddled beneath the ragged coat, throwing its hood over his head.

"That thing is filthy," Christopher said. "You look like a beggar or something."

One of Mrs. West's search party approached a few minutes later. Vince thought it might have been the guard at the front gate, but he couldn't tell for sure because he thought it best to keep his head down and the hood over his eyes. *Let's see if this works.*

"Have you seen this kid?" the man said, stopping the two of them in their tracks.

Vince peeked out and saw that the man was holding a picture of him standing with his arm around Anthony's shoulders back at the orphanage. It seemed like ages ago.

"Well?" the man pressed, moving the picture back and forth in front of the two boys' faces.

Vince shook his head and muttered a no. The man turned to Christopher.

"What about you? Might be a little something in it for you if you have any information. A nice juicy reward."

Christopher's eyes lit up at the comment. He began to move side to side, little steps of excitement.

Vince meanwhile felt completely exposed. This was never going to work.

"The chubby one?" Christopher asked.

"No, not the chubby one," the man said, his scrutinizing eyes still locked on Vince. "The other one."

"The chubby one looks like one of my brothers."

"I'm asking about the other one, kid." Slowly the man reached out for Vince's hood, his fingers eagerly twitching away.

Vince wondered if he should make a run for it. The man's fingers were getting even closer now. His identity would be revealed at any second.

"Wait, let me see again," Christopher said, swiping the picture from the man's hand and turning his back on him.

The man quickly spun away from Vince and charged after Christopher. "Hey, give that back. I have to show other people, you know."

"Oh, sorry. Here you go." Christopher handed the picture back all crumpled up.

"What'd you do?" the man said, flattening it out. "You ruined it. You can't even make out his face anymore!"

"Well, I got a good look in. We haven't seen him," Christopher said.

The man walked away shaking his head, and Christopher turned to Vince, nodding his head once. "That might buy you some time."

Vince lowered the hood. "You could have given me up."

"To some random guy? You're here for your grandfather's funeral. What's the problem with that? Why are they looking for you anyway?"

"I ran away from my orphanage to get here. I must have upset a lot of people."

"And they never stopped to wonder just how upset you might be?"

The walk was a long one, and the coat didn't do much for the cold. He might as well have been wearing a net. He was more than thankful when, almost an hour later, Christopher finally pointed out the house, tufts of smoke coming from the chimney.

"Home sweet home."

Warmth. He felt the warmth of the fire the moment he walked in, like an abrupt shift in seasons. He could hear the flames crackling. The fireplace was oversize, almost encompassing the entirety of the far wall. Pictures hung everywhere in simple frames: all portraits, many of them children.

Christopher guided him across the wood floors, each beam creaking beneath the pair's feet, and into the kitchen. Exhausted and shivering, each pulled up a chair at the table and sat down. Vince sneezed.

"Did you go out without your coat?" somebody called out. The voice, filled with both concern and agitation, came from upstairs, as did plenty of other noises, which Vince, because of his experiences at the orphanage, quickly recognized as boys roughhousing.

"Yeah, I went out naked," Christopher shouted back, concealing his laughter.

"Don't you get wise with me, I'll—"

"Ma," he yelled, stopping her, "we have a guest."

"What do you me—" A woman was in the doorway now, hands on hips. Upon seeing Vince, her eyes revealed that Christopher was lucky to get away with one, and it looked like her son knew it too. "You're Andrew's Vincent?" she asked.

"Vincent Elgin, ma'am."

"Right, right," she said, ambling over. "It was your grandfather who just passed away earlier this week. I'm so sorry about your loss, dear, dear boy." She placed a compassionate hand on the side of Vince's face and rubbed his cheek with her thumb.

"Thank you," he said.

The woman had wavy hair, cut above the ear, hair that

wanted desperately to curl but came up just short. Her skin was dark and smooth; she looked like she should have had wrinkles, but there weren't any at all. However, it was her eyes and smile that truly gave everything away. In them she carried more warmth than the fireplace.

"My name is Marie," she said. She looked at Vince's ragged coat and turned to her son. "Christopher, what are you doing? You make him sit here in damp clothes? Take his coat." As Vince handed it over, she turned back to him. "I'm sorry, you give these kids life, you sacrifice day and night for them, but when you try to instill some civility in these brutes, they're found wanting. Vincent, can I get you anything? Something to eat, drink?"

"I'll have some water, please, if it's not too much trouble."

She hustled across the kitchen and was about to pour Vince a drink when she reached back and grabbed his hand. Her face shifted to one of concern. "My dear, you're ice cold," she said. "Look at your cheeks. Look at your lips. They're purple. I'll tell you what. I'll make you tea, how about that? It's mostly water, so this way we both win."

"That sounds good."

"Can I have hot chocolate?" Christopher asked.

"If I make it for you, I have to make it for everybody."

"So?"

With a great sigh, Marie went and put up a pot of water. When she came back, she rested her elbow on the table and her chin in her hand while looking into Vince's eyes. Shaking her head, she appeared to be on the verge of tears. "What are you doing here all by yourself at such a difficult time?" she asked. "Where is your mother?"

"I don't have a mother."

If Marie was embarrassed for asking, she didn't show it, and Vince was grateful for that. "I'm so sorry. Is your father here with you?"

Vince shook his head.

"No siblings either?"

"No."

"Well, who's looking after you?"

"No one. I ran away to get here."

"There are people looking for him," Christopher interjected.

"What? What people?"

"From the orphanage. I wasn't allowed to come here. I snuck out of the orphanage and hopped a train."

Marie looked a little shaken, but she paused, calming herself. "Don't you worry about a thing. You'll be safe here."

"That's very kind of you. Thank you."

"Don't you worry about it. I've taken in many a child in my day." She waved her arm around the room, gesturing at the portraits. "I take in the sick, the poor, you name it. It's the least I can do." The teakettle went off. "Water's boiled." She shuffled over and prepared his tea.

"Now, drink up," she said, setting it before him. "Get warm."

Vince sipped the tea, nearly burning his tongue.

"How is it?" she asked.

"It's perfect."

Vince spent the rest of the evening talking with Marie and her five boys around the kitchen table, drinking tea and eating cookies. They were a rambunctious lot, but they were funny and pleasant—a real family—and it kept his mind free from the anxiety that had been building for the funeral.

When it was time for bed, Vince followed Marie to the second level, down a hall, and into a dark spare bedroom.

"Bah!" two of the five boys screamed while jumping out at them from behind the door. Marie, nearly toppling over, began swatting at her sons as they squeezed by and took off down the stairs, laughing all the way.

"Don't do that to me!" she yelled down at them. "You know I hate that! Nearly gave me a heart attack." With a hand on her heart in an attempt to calm herself, she turned to Vince. "Don't mind them. They tend to get a bit wild and silly, especially around bedtime. I shouldn't have given them the hot chocolate."

She moved to a closet, grabbed a heavy coat, and raised it up to Vince's frame. "This should do. Here," she said, passing it to him, "try it on. No one should be walking around in such a skimpy coat. Not in these temperatures."

Vince threw his arms through the sleeves and adjusted the collar. A perfect fit.

"I knew it. Much better than that raggedy thing you came in with." Marie also handed him some gloves and a hat—everything in pristine condition and of very high quality. Then she gave him another look-over, inspecting him closely. After a few moments she spoke softly, a frown on her face. "You know, I have an extra suit in here too, Vincent. For tomorrow."

Vince looked beneath the fine coat at the clothes he had collected from the orphanage. It was already a sorry assemblage, and now after all his travel it looked even worse—especially under a coat of such value—enough to make him feel ashamed that he had even thought he could pass it off as acceptable. He would be a disgrace entering that church.

"You don't have to take it if you don't want," Marie added. "You look handsome as is."

But he did want them. He wanted to do his grandfather proud. "If you wouldn't mind. I promise I won't get it dirty."

"Don't you worry about that. Keep it. Tomorrow you will be a fine-dressed gentleman. Your grandfather will watch you from above and smile."

Vince's eyes began to water. He had to look down and bite his lip.

"Now"—Marie went on—"don't get upset. You're here

for him. He would be happy to know it."

Vince liked the sound of that. Marie reminded him of his mother, and he felt himself tearing up again. "Thank you. For everything."

Marie smiled. "I'll be there tomorrow too. With my boys. You don't have to know a person to be at his funeral. I make sure we pay our respects to everyone who passes away in this town. It's the least we can do. Now get some sleep." She bent over and turned on a night-light. "My boys are scared of the dark, the little babies."

"I used to be," Vince said. "Not anymore."

When she left, before undressing, he looked out the window. Everything was still, quiet, and the light from a lamppost outside cast a warm glow in his room.

He climbed into bed, thinking about tomorrow, when he would finally meet his father. Then, fully prepared for what was to come, he slipped *The Dyerville Tales* out of his pack and opened to the final chapter.

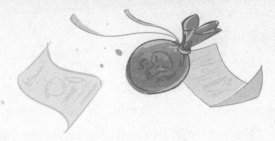

The Witch of the Woods

The crow flew for days. Occasionally it descended, and believing they were close, Vincent felt his breath catch in his throat. As his eyes darted about the bleak landscape—a path of trees snapped in half as if knocked over by outsize forces—his hand tensed around the grooved handle of the sword. His breathing intensified; his pulse quickened. He wasn't sure he was ready for what was to come.

But then, after circling an area of the forest several times over, the crow would let out a cry and suddenly fly higher than it had before. Another false alarm. The witch, it appeared, was on the move yet again.

"The boar is following in the path of its master," Orin pointed out. "It feels the pull, the link between the two."

"The witch will have to set her home down at some point," Vincent said, his voice dry and scratchy, all adrenaline rapidly draining from his body. As he wiped the sweat from his hands on his legs, he wasn't sure if he was relieved or not. "We have to remain ready."

"I have waited so long for this," Orin said, "a few days more mean nothing to me."

And it was a few days more before the crow finally settled.

At first, Vincent couldn't believe it; he had just about given up hope of ever finding the witch and her wandering abode. He imagined himself trekking through the forest until he was a very old man, no longer in need of the aging cloak to appear withered and brittle. But now, on a damp morning just before dawn, in the distance, through the thickness of the trees, he saw a hut. It blended in well with its surroundings, as if a spell were concealing it from adventurous travelers. Had the crow not been staring directly at it, Vincent most likely would have wandered right past, never knowing how close he had actually come.

The nearer they approached, the more rank the air became; it was a truly putrid and foul smell, one that lingered like a fog, infiltrating the nose and clinging to the skin. Gagging, he felt his stomach roll over. "What is that?" he asked, trying hard not to vomit.

Orin gazed ahead, his eyes alert. "It is evil. Pure evil."

The crow, out of anxiousness or recklessness they didn't know, flew even closer to the cottage, urging them to follow, which they did.

When Vincent and Orin were close enough, they hid behind some brush and peered through it. They spotted the crow perched upon a skull. It pecked at something inside the hollowed nose and came up swallowing. The skull, cracked and eerily small, bottom jaw missing, sat tilted on a wooden post—a grim warning to all. There were many skulls atop many posts surrounding the cottage, although some remained empty, as if the witch were expecting more victims. With a hand rubbing at his throat, Vincent wondered if he was next.

There was debris and bones and trash scattered all around, dirty water in rusted buckets, rats the size of cats eating rotten food. It seemed that wherever the home traveled, its deplorable surroundings came with it, as if it had ripped up the earth on which it sat. All the trees, all the bushes and plants and flowers sitting within range of the cottage must have died upon its arrival. Only weeds, dried grass, and withered vines remained.

How did the house move, though? Looking for an answer, Vincent believed he could make out long, thin legs that were tucked under the floor of the house: black magic.

Dark smoke escaped from the chimney, the source of the rancid smell. Vincent pointed to this as he hopped down from the horse. "The witch is inside. I'm going to have a look."

"Don't be crazy. What if she sees you? We don't want to confront her until we have struck down the boar."

"I have to see if my mother is in that awful place. I'll be careful. I promise."

Vincent crawled ever so slowly across the ground, the rats not intimidated in the least by his presence. They skittered beside him, smelling his gold skin. One tried to take a bite out of his leg, and he had to smack it away with the back of his hand. He passed a skull that had fallen from a post, one that had become home to a red and black snake. Vincent swore to whoever it belonged he would avenge him for what the witch had done.

When he reached the house, he ducked below a small, solitary window on the far side. It was opened just a crack, and he could hear noises coming from inside. Something told him not to look in, but he pulled himself up and did so anyway.

It was a strange sight. Apart from the fact that the hut's interior was an absolute mess, the first thing he noticed was the several people, some men and women, some children, casually walking about inside. They weren't chained up;

they weren't helpless or screaming or crying; no one was trying to escape. They were simply working. They cooked, mixed potions, captured rodents and insects and reptiles, tended to the cast-iron oven burning oh so brightly in the center of the room. But why would they do such things? They looked like good, kind people.

Then he noticed they all bore the same blank expression, as if their souls had been sucked out of their eyes and left them hollowed. *They have no choice*, he realized. They were being controlled, forced into servitude, not by whips or chains but by the witch's spells. Suddenly Vincent was hit with a bleak realization. These people must have once been children, bartered away by their parents, kidnapped right from their homes. One of these might even be Stella's brother. Had Vincent not run away, he could have been here as well.

But where was his mother? Did she too share this fate?

Just then a skull rolled out from under the house and settled at Vincent's feet. He looked down at it, rage surging through his body. *If the witch had killed her . . .* And for what? What was the curse all about? This? So the witch could have one more able body to perform her incantations? *Where is she?* he thought, his hand tightening on the sword once again. *I want her. I want her now.*

And as if hearing his thoughts, the witch emerged from deeper in the room. She sat down at a table in the middle, set down a large plate of food before her, and began to eat. Bits of meat soon hung from her face, thick juices running down her chin and hands. Licking her lips with a long, fat tongue, she picked up another slab and shoved it deep into her mouth. She ate ravenously, as if she hadn't eaten in weeks. Each bite was savored. She squirmed in her seat, sucking her fingers dry. "More," she called.

A servant removed another heaping portion from the oven and set it before her, and Vincent turned away in disgust. Her meal didn't look like any animal meat he had ever seen. The revolting smell of the food wafted out the open window, watering his eyes. He had to take deep breaths, calm himself. When he glanced back, the oven door was still open, and he saw what was cooking inside. There were body parts. Human body parts: hands, feet, arms, legs. On the witch's empty plate sat the remaining bones, scraped clean.

Vincent, his mind reeling, backed away from the window and returned to Orin to fill his friend in on what he had seen.

"That vile hag"—Orin spit, once he'd heard enough—"she must be stopped."

"I agree. The time has come."

"And your mother . . ."

"No sign of her. If that witch—"

"Vincent, we must concentrate. Don't let your anger overwhelm you. We must be careful not to take the lives of her servants," Orin said. "If they defend her, wound them at most, for when the witch is finished, they will return to their true selves, as will I."

"Are you ready?"

"I am. The boar must be somewhere close by."

"Then let's—"

There was a noise behind them, the sharp snapping of a twig. Vincent turned around, only to find one of the servants staring blankly at him from within the woods. She stood frozen, her arms full of firewood.

Vincent slowly raised a finger to his lips. "Miss, we're here to help you. Don't—"

The logs tumbled from the woman's arms as she let out a horrible, piercing scream. It could be heard for miles.

The door to the hut was thrown open; the servants spewed forth. They ran right for Vincent, their mouths wide open, teeth bared. There was life in them yet.

Orin quickly jumped in front of his friend, kicking two of the attackers aside with his back legs. "Get on."

Vincent, however, didn't move. He was horrified by what he saw. These were innocent people turned into monsters.

"Get on," Orin screamed.

Another servant was sprinting in their direction; she had a knife in her hand. She raised it over her head, the sunlight gleaming off the blade and directly into Vincent's eyes.

His trance was broken, and he pulled himself onto the horse and grabbed his bow. But no sooner had he done this than the woman lunged forward and stabbed Orin.

The horse bucked wildly, kicking the woman and sending her flying backward into a tree.

As yet another servant approached, Vincent shot an arrow into his leg. Then he fired another clear through the man's arm.

"Vincent, remember," Orin yelled to him, "you must save the arrows for—"

The boar. From out of nowhere it slammed into Orin's side, sending Vincent flying. As he crashed to the earth, he fell on his sword, severely cutting his leg. The pain was horrible; he couldn't get up.

With a grotesque squeal, the boar rammed Orin again, slamming its tusks deep into his side. Blood spurted forth in a bold stream. Orin stood on wobbly legs, trying desperately to kick the massive beast, but he missed. He connected on the second try, but it was a feeble blow; the boar wasn't even fazed. It just lowered its head and proceeded to crush Orin's ribs. The bones cracked audibly.

Orin collapsed to the hard ground. "Help me!"

Hearing his friend's frantic cry, Vincent gathered himself, blood gushing from his wound. He picked up his bow and grabbed an arrow from the quiver. Grimacing through the pain, he aimed for the boar. He pulled the arrow back.

He steadied. He had the boar in his sights.

As Vincent fired, a slave, a small boy, lunged for him and clawed at his arms, sending the arrow wide. It sailed just past the boar's head.

The slave was incredibly strong, knocking Vincent down and proceeding to scratch and snap at him like a rabid dog. The boy was hungry for him, groaning and grunting all through the vicious attack, but his eyes, deep within them, showed fear, as if he hadn't wanted to do this, as if he'd had no control.

Vincent reached to his side and picked up a rock. "I'm sorry," he said. Then he slammed it over the servant's head and knocked him cold.

On his knees, Vincent looked to his right. Orin was being pummeled. The boar was relentless in its attack. After each slam into the horse, it backed up and charged again, an amazing burst of speed and awesome display of strength.

Vincent picked up his bow and steadied it in the animal's direction once again. His friend, his poor friend . . . He had to end this. But as he pulled the arrow back this time, he heard a strange sound coming from behind him. The earth quaked, as if something were erupting from beneath it. He turned and saw the cottage begin to rise from the ground. Holding it aloft were four gaunt legs with claws as feet. They extended fully, dirt falling back into place. Then the hut was on the move. The witch knew the boar was threatened and that she was in danger. She was escaping, and possibly Vincent's mother with her.

Vincent was going to miss his chance. He had to go after her. But the boar, Orin. The poor horse was howling in pain.

Vincent aimed again, and this time he got the shot off cleanly, a direct hit in the boar's side. But the crazed beast didn't even seem to notice. It just kept attacking.

"Again!" Orin yelled. "Aim for the heart!"

The witch was getting away. Her cottage was knocking down every tree in its path, the servants giving chase so as to not be left behind. Soon it would have enough room to run.

Orin meanwhile was bleeding badly. There were deep gashes all across his body; blood pooled around him. Vincent had to act now or Orin wouldn't make it. He aimed for the heart of the boar, the sound of falling trees filling his ears. He fired.

Hit, the boar stumbled back, the arrow mere inches from its heart. It cried in pain, recklessly slamming its body into trees. The protruding arrow snapped in half.

Grunting and snorting, the boar gazed at Vincent, its new target found. It squared with him and charged.

Even wounded, it ran incredibly fast. Vincent couldn't believe how big it was, as large as Orin. It was like a bear coming for him. If he missed with his next shot, the boar almost certainly wouldn't. Vincent would be pulverized, his body crushed, his bones dust. If he hit the ground, he knew he would never get back up.

He aimed again, its heart in his sights.

The boar was very close now, the ground trembling beneath its feet, thick clouds of dust kicked up behind it. It lowered its head, tusks stained with blood.

Vincent had only seconds to spare. The bow shook in his hands. His aim had to be true.

The boar was practically on top of him.

He cleared his head of all thoughts, all distractions. It had to be now.

Eyes closed, he fired.

The boar never reached him. The arrow pierced its heart, and the beast crashed to the ground, just feet away from Vincent. It was dead. The witch's soul was now complete again. The sword could play its part.

Vincent turned, but the hut was no longer in sight. He would have to hurry if he were to catch her.

"The witch," Vincent said to Orin. "Come on."

But the horse didn't move.

"Orin, I need you. I can't make it without you."

"I can't," Orin said, spitting up blood. "The boar, it—"

Vincent knelt beside his friend. One of Orin's legs was broken, snapped cleanly in two. Another bone poked through his skin. The bloodied horse was breathing deeply; they were strained and garbled breaths. "Rest," Vincent said, laying his hands on him. "I'm going to finish this. I'm going to set you free. Then we'll get you the help you need."

"You're going . . . going to do it, Vincent." Orin said, struggling with each word. "I know . . . I know you will. Ever since I saw you in the giant's cave . . . Go, bring peace . . . bring peace to this land."

"I'll be back for you. Just hold on. I'll be back."

Vincent ran for the hut, following the path of devastation. He ran with a severe limp, sword drawn. Each step was agonizing pain. He tried to fight through it, but he was losing far too much blood, far too much ground. His pace slowed to that of a fast walk. The witch had gotten away. He didn't think he would ever catch her. He had failed. He had failed everyone.

The crow was flying just above his head, screeching, coaxing him on. But he couldn't go any farther. His vision blurred. He was at the point of collapse.

The crow called out to him again, and when Vincent looked this time, he saw three more birds. Then he saw a dozen. Then, soon after, he saw hundreds, all different variations, flying together. The forest was filled with birds.

Vincent fell to his knees and leaned against his sword. "Help me," he said.

In unison, the birds swooped down and grabbed hold of his weary body. Vincent watched as his feet slowly left the ground.

They carried him through the forest at tremendous speed, dodging trees and branches with ease. The freedom of flight was incredible. He felt life rush back into him.

Just minutes later Vincent saw the hut in the distance. It was bounding forward, kicking over whatever got in its way. But they were gaining. This time, the witch couldn't hide.

The birds placed him gently at the side window. They hovered silently before him for a few seconds, perhaps making sure he was well enough to continue on. Then, as he waved to them, they scattered.

Left alone, Vincent took a deep breath. It all came down to this.

When he was ready, he raised the window and tumbled inside, practically thrown by the wandering home. But the witch was nowhere to be seen. The room was empty, not even a servant about. As the hut rhythmically tilted back and forth in its rampage, everything was crashing down and rolling across the floor. Cabinets clattered open and closed, their contents spewing forth like vomit. Chairs slid from one wall to another. It was madness.

Barely able to keep on his feet, Vincent began searching the home, flashbacks of when he had returned home in search of his mother. But no, not quite. There was no warmth, no love in this place. The smell was horrible, tightening Vincent's stomach with each breath. He kicked the oven door closed.

"Show yourself!" he yelled, sword raised. "Where are you?"

No sign of her.

Then, just above him, something creaked. Vincent glanced up, and there was the witch, crawling like a spider across the ceiling.

She jumped for him, landing hard on his back. Vincent, breath knocked clean out of him, crumbled, his nose smashing into the floorboards. The crunch was audible. The witch, mouth wide open, hideous yellow teeth snapping, lurched for his face. She bit down, dug in, and gnawed away like one of her many rats. And that was how Vincent came to bear the scar he was to carry for the rest of his life.

He screamed and tossed her off. She flew onto the table, crushing it, but she sprang back up as if nothing had happened. She wasn't anything like his mother had described. She was no longer old, haggard. There was youth in her, strength. She walked toward Vincent again, and as she did, the hut's lurching movement smoothed. It was still running quickly, but it was no longer nearly as rough a ride.

"My mother, where is she?" Vincent said, blinking away his pain, blood running down from his broken nose and into his mouth.

"The golden boy," she cackled. "The sad, pathetic golden boy. You want your mommy, do you? What is left of her?

Then, by all means . . ." The witch snapped her fingers, and seconds later a trapdoor in the floor flew open. Two battered hands bound by chains reached out, scratching against the wood beams. The figure pulled itself up, emerging from the darkness of the subterranean, and Vincent saw the face of his mother.

She looked as if she had aged a half century. Her hair had grayed and thinned, her face sagged, and her mouth was missing teeth. There were open sores, bruises, and deep gashes across her yellowed skin. She was dressed in tattered pieces of cloth that reeked, and there was a metal collar around her neck from which hung a long chain. But worst of all were her eyes. They had dimmed of all life.

She was one of them now.

Vincent glared at the witch. "You—you took her as a slave."

"Oh, not just any slave, boy. She is my most prized possession. She is my pet. My beautiful pet. You see, unlike the others, I didn't steal her as a child, and so my spell isn't quite as strong. I have to control her in other ways." She tugged on the chain. "She's not so obedient, this one. She's more like a stubborn dog I have to beat to keep in line. She is a fighter, but I like that."

Vincent stepped closer to the woman in chains. "Mother, it's me, Vincent. I've come for you. I've come to take you home." He reached out his hand for hers, and his mother recoiled and hissed.

"You have no mother, boy. You lost her the moment you ran away. This is your fault. You did this to her."

"I did no such thing."

"She cries at night, my pet does. She whimpers. Sometimes, if I'm feeling generous, I will throw her a bone. I'm sure you've noticed I have an abundance of them around my abode. It calms her. You should see how she clutches it, how it helps her sleep."

"Witch, hear me now," Vincent said, his chest rising and falling. "I have found the bow. I have found the sword. Your boar is dead, and that leaves you vulnerable. You return my mother to her rightful state this very minute, and I will see that your death is quick."

He raised the sword, ready to strike.

The witch, however, just laughed at this, raising her hand. Her palm glowed blue, and suddenly the sword flew out of his hands and across the room as if pulled by a string.

"You thought by following those rules you would finish me, did you? If someone else were to try, then yes, I would be in danger. But you see, I've been expecting this. I've seen this day long before you were even born. I saw it all, my death included. I knew it would eventually come, it had to, and I knew you would be the one to kill me. I couldn't allow that. And so I found a loophole. I found a way to escape such a fate. This is how a witch survives—at whatever cost.

Once it was to separate my soul and meld it with that of the boar, but with you, all I had to do was make sure you were cursed at birth. You are under my spell, Vincent. Thanks to your mother, you always have been. And by being under my spell you cannot kill me, not even with the sword. Fates can be changed."

"If that is so, then what makes you think you are safe now? Fate was changed once; it will be changed again. You are meant to die, and so you will."

The witch threw her arm back, and the sword hovered to her glowing blue hand. She extended the weapon to Vincent. "Here, my confident friend. Try. Just try."

Hesitantly Vincent took the sword from her. Feeling its weight in his hands, he pulled it back. *For my mother*, he thought, and with all his strength he slung the steel forward. But just as the blade was about to strike, his arms stopped dead. He found he couldn't bring the sword any closer, as if there were a shield protecting her. He brought the weapon over his head and tried again, but to no avail. She was right. He couldn't kill her. It was hopeless. Fear shadowed his face, and the witch guffawed at his terror.

"I will have you for myself, Vincent, like I was always supposed to."

Vincent backed against the wall, nowhere to go. "I will never be your slave."

"Oh, I don't want you for a slave," she said, creeping

closer. "Why would I want you for a slave when I am utterly convinced you will taste so very delicious?"

The witch leaped for him, but he knocked her away with a solid blow from his forearm. Suddenly she was all over the house. She jumped from wall to wall, crawled across the ceiling, hissing and spitting. Vincent had no idea where she would be next. With her hand, she levitated knives that zipped just past him, digging deep into the wood behind him.

The hut meanwhile continued its run through the forest, and it was again wild and lurching, as if picking up speed. Everything shook, more objects falling from cabinets, human bones sliding back and forth, and Vincent was tossed violently to the floor, the sword skittering far across the room. Seeing her chance, the witch jumped atop him, her hands suddenly burning red. She laid them upon his gold body. Vincent could feel his skin bubbling. The pain was excruciating.

"Why don't you die?" the witch howled. She strained even more, her hands glowing like the brightest of fires.

Vincent pulled his knees back, then shot them forward, kicking her clear across the room.

"The gold," the witch said, rising to her feet, "it protects you from my spells. I should have known. No matter. If I can't kill you with magic, you will die by my hands."

As she flew toward him, Vincent dived beneath her and

lunged for the sword. He didn't know why he grabbed it, he saw how useless it was, but he felt stronger with it in his hands.

The witch, however, merely extended her hand once again. It glowed blue, and the blade was yanked from his grip and flew against the far wall as if magnetized. It hung there as if on display.

The witch turned to Vincent's mother. "Anna, my dear, my lovely pet. Finish him."

Vincent's mother didn't budge. She just stared out blankly, as if she were sleepwalking. The witch bent down and grabbed at the chain connected to her collar, yanking hard. "Kill! Kill!"

Anna was nearly jerked to her knees. Her eyes blinked as she turned to the witch.

"Kill the golden boy!"

Slowly she focused on her target. Then, with a hiss, she staggered forth.

"Mother, no!"

Anna attacked her son, her jaws snapping, as the witch looked on, her cackle filling the room like a lunatic's cry.

Vincent backed away madly, hid behind tables, shoved chairs in her direction, but she kept coming. "Mother, please. It's me."

But there was no reaching her, no stopping her. Hurdling like a beast, she jumped on the table and then soared through the air at her son. The two clashed in the center of the room. Vincent found his mother to be far stronger than she appeared. She had the strength of at least three men. She gripped his arms, digging her nails in, and tossed him four feet backward.

"I see you in there. I know you're still fighting. The witch isn't in control of you, Mother. You fight her. You fight!"

Anna screamed and charged. She struck her son in the chest with her shoulder, cracking a rib and pinning him against the wall. Vincent saw the sword dangling just beside his head. He could almost grab it, but to do what? He couldn't strike his mother.

"Yes! Yes! Now hold him," the witch said, gliding closer. "The golden boy is going to burn. I want him in my oven."

The witch was binding his hands with magic. He could see nothing when he looked at them, but somehow, they couldn't move.

"I'm hungry, boy. Time to eat." And she pulled him off the wall and shoved him closer to the oven. He tried to resist, but she overmatched him at every step. He was being pushed closer and closer to the flames, closer and closer to a fiery death.

Her fingers writhed for his eyes, to gouge them. Vincent pulled his head back. His world was upside down. He saw his mother leaning against the wall behind him.

"Mother," he called out. "Please! Help me!"

But with his attention diverted, the witch kicked him in the stomach, and he doubled over. Then she quickly dug her sharp nails deep into the gash in his leg. Vincent crumbled.

Laughing, the witch grabbed his head and began to shove it closer to the oven. The heat burned his face. As if assisting its master, the hut tipped him closer to the flames and slammed his body against the warm iron. A human bone, a femur, came tumbling out, falling at his feet.

Vincent couldn't fight anymore. She was too much. He had to do something.

With the last of his strength, writhing in her grip, Vincent reached for the bone. Fingers extended as far as they could go, he was just inches short.

His face neared the threshold of the oven. Soon she would throw his entire body in.

"I'm going to eat you up, Vincent! Every bit of you!"

The hut rocked yet again, and the bone nearly rolled toward him. *Come on, come on.* With both bound hands, he stretched as far as possible, but it still wasn't enough.

"Don't worry," the witch shrieked, "I won't cook you long. I like my meat rare."

The heat from the oven was unbearable. His body sizzled; his hair was singed.

"Perhaps your mother too would like a taste. Maybe the heart!"

The hut rocked again, knocking over a tree. But this time it did so in Vincent's favor. The bone rolled to his outstretched hands. Grabbing it tightly, he amassed whatever strength he had left. With two hands he swung the bone at the witch, striking her right across the face, shattering her teeth.

The witch, dumbstruck, stumbled back, and Vincent pounced. With her dazed, he tackled her hard to the ground. But she was so quick and powerful she was on top of him in no time, the broken bone at his throat like a razor.

"Give up," the witch said, spitting green blood. "You can't kill me. I won. I won the day you were born." She dug the bone into his neck, piercing the skin. "It was your mother, Vincent. You have her to thank."

"Yes. Yes, you're right," Vincent said, gazing past the witch, tears in his eyes, the bone cutting even deeper now. "Thank you."

The witch's eyes narrowed. There was an odd sound, like a giant snail being ripped from its shell. When the witch looked down, she saw the sword sticking straight through her chest. "I—" With a painful moan, she fell to the floor beside Vincent, the sword sliding back through her body. Looking up, she croaked, "My—my pet—"

Vincent's mother stood over the witch, the blade dropping to her feet.

The witch's hands grasped desperately at her wound, attempting some dark magic to heal it. "No," she kept saying, "no," over and over again.

Vincent knelt beside her and whispered into her ear. "You were right," he said. "Maybe I couldn't kill you. But fates can always be changed."

She turned her head to him. Never had he seen such fear and hate in one's eyes. With her last breath, the witch cried out something horrid and her body shriveled into nothingness. In a matter of seconds she was gone.

Vincent looked at the dark rags on the floor and the green blood puddled all around them. Then he looked at his hands. They were unbound and changing color. The gold was receding. He had done it.

The hut crashed back to the earth, the legs beneath it vanishing. It had settled for the last time.

Everything around him was still. Still and quiet. It felt something like peace.

And then he saw his mother. He saw her as he remembered her, as he always loved her. As she dropped to her knees, her youth and beauty returned, the shackles came undone. But best of all, the life in her eyes came shining back like the brightest of stars.

"Mother!" he cried, running into her arms.

"Vincent! Oh, my Vincent! I never thought I'd see you again!"

Together they embraced and wept, the curse lifted. Vincent's long journey was over.

Before they left the hut, Vincent pushed over the oven, and the flames spread quickly. The witch's home burned to the ground in no time.

Outside, standing with his mother, watching the flames, Vincent realized who was missing. "Orin," he said, "my dear friend. We have to go back for him."

They moved as quickly as possible, but it was miles from where he had left Orin, and Vincent was too badly hurt. He couldn't make it through the forest in this condition. Not for days.

And that was when the birds returned. They came from all around, filling the forest with life and color and song, and they lifted both Vincent and his mother and flew them back through the forest. They soared past the towering trees and through the clearings and over the many animals emerging from their hiding. In minutes they dropped their passengers right where Vincent had last seen the horse and now found a boy, a boy not much older than he was.

"Orin," Vincent said, collapsing beside him. "The witch is dead. I have my mother. It's over. Look. Look at yourself. You're back."

Orin slowly opened his eyes and looked down at his body. A small smile crept across his face. "So I am. It's—it's amazing. How about that? I'm—I'm human again. I'm Orin Barlow again."

Vincent cocked his head. "Barlow? You? You're the missing son?"

Orin nodded, grimacing in pain. "I am."

"But we were there, why didn't you say anything?"

"No. I—I would not be reunited with my family as I was."

"Well, you can be reunited with them now. Come on. I'll take you back."

Orin shook his head, his eyes fading. "No, Vincent. I'm—I'm not going to make it."

"Yes, you are. You'll be okay. We'll get you help. Come on."

"You've already helped me more than you could ever, ever imagine. I'm back, Vincent. I'm human again. You . . . promised me that. You said when I died, I'd be human. And you were right."

"You're not dying, Orin." Vincent's lips trembled. His words were stopped by his tears. "You're my only friend; you're not dying."

"But I am."

"Orin—"

"Thank you, Vincent."

"Orin . . ."

And there, in the middle of the forest, leaning against a fallen tree, Orin passed away. Vincent could do nothing but weep beside his friend, the best he'd ever had.

When he finally picked his head up sometime later, all the witch's slaves were around him. They too were returned to normal, no longer bound by her evil spells. Along with his mother, they helped Vincent to his feet and tended to his wounds.

Two men bent down to pick up Orin, but Vincent told them not to. "I'll carry him home," he said.

And he did. For days, alongside his mother, he rejected the help of the birds and carried Orin out of the forest and along every single arduous mile all the way back to Mr. Barlow's estate.

When he arrived, Mr. Barlow's body was healed, but his heart wasn't. He mourned his son deeply. There was a great funeral, and Orin was buried properly, for which Mr. Barlow was very grateful.

Afterward he allowed Vincent and his mother to live with him there in the mansion. He soon fell in love with Anna and asked for her hand in marriage. For the rest of his days he cared for Vincent like the son he had lost. And with the witch gone, Stella of course was given her freedom. She and Vincent used it well too. They saw everything in the world there was to see, and for the rest of their lives the two never left each other's side. They had one child, a son. And that son had a son too. That boy, more than anything else, is their legacy.

CHAPTER 15

The end.

Vince glanced up from the book, a conflicted look upon his face.

It was the ending he wanted to read, but he was sad that there wasn't another chapter, that it couldn't keep going and going and going until the end of time, like in that land beyond the door. It was over.

He had trouble falling asleep after this. He kept thinking about the ring he found in his grandfather's room, what it meant. Morning would arrive soon enough, and with it, his grandfather's funeral. After everything he had gone through to get here, after every story in *The Dyerville Tales*, every story that he would have once dismissed as the crazed ramblings of his late grandfather, he was now more convinced than ever that his father was still alive and that they would be reunited when the sun came up. The tales that he abandoned years ago in the orphanage returned, and with them, hope.

Tomorrow, he thought. *Tomorrow.*

That night Vince went to bed with his fingers crossed.

Morning arrived, and the mood in the house was much more somber than the night previous, the five rambunctious boys eerily subdued. Everyone was dressed in a dark suit or dress, Vince in the fine clothes that Marie had kindly provided. She even cut and styled his hair.

"Look at you," she said, stepping back to take him in. "You look like a new man. It's as if you had gone to sleep as one person and woken up as another." Indeed, Vince felt that way.

Downstairs Marie cooked them an enormous and delicious breakfast, and he sat down to eat with the boys. For Vince, as delectable as the food was, it didn't go down easily. He found himself much too nervous to eat; his stomach felt tightly bound with anticipation, closing itself off from anything he might swallow. All he could do was think of the various ways in which he would run into his father at the church, the different things each might say to the other. And when he went home, it would be in a different direction. Home would be someplace else. *I'm not going back to the orphanage*, he thought. *Never again.*

To be polite, he finished as much of the meal as he could and helped Marie clean up, which warranted a kiss on the forehead from her.

"Your grandfather will be with you today and always," she said. "I'm sure he is so very proud of you."

When it came time to leave, Vince made his way to the church with Marie and the boys, walking the cold streets, the sky once again threatening snow, apparently unsatisfied that everything was buried feet deep in white powder.

It was a short walk, and when they arrived at the church square, there was only a small handful of people lingering outside, hesitant to venture indoors. Vincent eyed this half dozen or so closely, searching for the one face he so desperately needed to see. It was an uneasy feeling, like being at the orphanage again, eyeing each new visitor to the premises in the hope of finding his father.

He began to wander past the mourners, lost in each person's eyes. *He has to be here somewhere.* Circling, he wondered if he would even recognize his father anymore. *Of course I would.* Then, carrying on the conversation with himself: *But what if he went through some sort of physical change? What if he had to have some type of surgery to alter his appearance so that any enemies might not notice him? Maybe I've run into him already and didn't even know it. He could be watching me right now. He probably was all this time.*

But no. These were all elderly people, most likely from the home his grandfather had been in. There was nobody Vince recognized. The only person who stood out was Mrs. West. She was across the street, making her way toward the church with her three accomplices, scanning the area for their lost boy.

Marie, who was walking beside Vince, must have felt him tense up. "Is that her?" she asked, as if gearing up for a fight. "The one who is looking for you?"

Vince nodded, and Marie turned to her five sons, bent over, and put a finger just before each face. "She is not to be let in. Do you understand? Not under any circumstances. This is a trying time for Vincent. He doesn't need this. You boys stand outside this church and block her entrance. The boy has a right to see his grandfather one last time. If they want to talk with him, they can do so afterward."

The church bells went off, and everyone started moving slowly inside. Vince, thankful for Marie's support, as well as that of her sons, began to walk into the church. He even brushed right by Mrs. West, who looked straight past him as if he were wearing a mask. Clearly, she wasn't expecting such a clean-cut and handsome boy, not after years of seeing him in various states of rags and filth. No, his cover wasn't blown until he was climbing the steps and a man from within the crowd desperately called out his name.

"Vincent. Vince! There you are. I've been looking everywhere for you."

Vince's breath rushed from his lungs as if he had been punched in the gut, and his skin went so pale he could have been lost in the snow. Fueled by rampant adrenaline, nerves surged across his body in powerful waves, quaking his arms and legs so that he appeared to be shivering, stuck out in the cold for days. A radiant smile exploded across his face. *Father.*

Vince spun around so quickly he went dizzy; the church square becoming a carousel on which he was caught. But when his eyes finally settled, he indeed found a man standing before him. But it wasn't his father. It was Andrew.

Not that Mrs. West cared. With grim determination, she proceeded to follow Vince into the church. But that was when Marie's five sons stood in her way.

"You're not going anywhere," Christopher said, folding his arms across his chest.

Mrs. West's head jerked back in disgusted disbelief as she eyed each of the boys. "I beg your pardon?"

"This is a closed mass. You can wait outside until it's over."

"Is that right?"

"Yes. Because we're not moving." And the boys folded

their arms across their chests in unison.

Just inside the church doors Andrew had pulled Vince aside. "I came with the group from the home. They all wanted to be here so badly." It was clear the setting made him uncomfortable. His large body shifted back and forth on its heels. "Listen, let me get to the point. Before you go inside, I have something for you. I went through your grandfather's room last night after you left. I found this in one of his drawers." He dug into his coat pocket and pulled out a thin envelope. "I have no idea what's in it. It's addressed to you, so I made sure to keep it sealed. Whatever it is, I hope you find solace in it."

Receiving the envelope, Vince thanked him.

"We should find our seats. The service will be starting shortly."

The church was gorgeous, sunlight sprinkling through the stained glass windows, emitting a terrific warmth. Statues of saints and angels, their hands up in blessing, lined the interior, and the pews shone with a holy gloss.

Making his way down the aisle, Vince looked at the small scattering of people occupying the pews on either side. The nerves he was so badly attempting to keep at bay had now completely consumed him. They were so severe he could hardly even stand. It was almost as if he were feeling his father's presence. *He is somewhere in this church,* he thought.

Anxiously he scanned every face on both sides of the aisle. He didn't care if he was staring or rude or obvious. He had to look.

But no, his father wasn't there. Maybe in the front pew, the one usually reserved for family. Vince sat down but appeared to be among strangers. Still, he didn't give up hope. He had come too far for that. That was the point of the tales, right? To believe again, to hope. The miraculous was possible. He was convinced now more than ever. His father would be here.

Maybe he was late. *Unless,* Vince thought, *he is so overcome with grief he decided to remain in the back of the church.* He stood up to look, but the priest had reached the pulpit, and the congregation quieted. The service had begun.

It was a beautiful and touching service, filled with heartfelt readings and stories by those who knew him only through his last days. There was singing and prayers and shared kisses throughout. There were tears and laughs and remembrances. A two-story organ brought it all together with each enchanting note. It was a serene and graceful closure for all involved.

At one point, toward the very end, every person in the church was asked to walk down the aisle and touch the coffin, saying his or her last words, beginning with Vince. The coffin was clear, made entirely of glass, and one's fingerprints would remain on the surface for all time.

Vince approached. It was the first time he had seen his grandfather in years. It was almost as if he had forgotten what he looked like. He saw him differently now, as if with new eyes. They did look alike, he noticed immediately. Vince could almost believe he was at his own funeral, nearly a century from now. Except for that scar. There it was high on his grandfather's cheek like the mark of a branding iron. Looking at it now, Vince thought it could have been caused by any one of the many situations mentioned in *The Dyerville Tales*. Not that it really mattered. What mattered was that it was there. Regardless, his grandfather was now at peace. That much was clear. He almost had a thin smile on his aged face, one more wrinkle among so many deep creases. His silver hair was neatly combed; his waxen hands were dramatically folded across his chest. There was even a shine to his skin. A nice golden shine. He looked beautiful. He looked like a man full of life and stories. A tale for every day of his life. This was a man who had lived and would continue to do so.

Bowing his head, Vince reached out and touched the glass with two fingers, just above his grandfather's face, his lips. *I wish I could see you again. I wish I could hug you and tell you I love you. I wish I could tell you I believe.*

But returning to his seat, he wondered if that was true. Did he believe? Last night, just this morning even, he had thought he did. But then, where was his father?

Vince watched each person in the church approach the coffin. He watched every one of them very carefully, for if his father were to appear, it would be now.

Person after person knelt before his grandfather, saying a prayer and touching the glass. A few nodded to Vincent, extended their hands to him, along with kind words. But not one of them was his father.

All of those in the church paid their respects, and in the end, there was no one left. The service was over. His father never came.

Tears filled Vince's eyes. He wept openly, and everyone believed this was for his grandfather.

And Vince realized he *was* crying for him. He was crying for his grandfather and his father and his mother all at once. He was crying because he felt so alone. He was crying because of how badly everything hurt. But most of all, he cried because of how foolish he was. Why did his father have to be missing from the fire? Why couldn't they have just found a trace of him somewhere within the ashes? If they had, Vince wouldn't have had to keep up with the stories. There would have been no hope. He could have moved on. Instead, he had kept his father alive with his own tales for years. He invented a new past. It was the same thing his grandfather had done with *The Dyerville Tales*. But that wasn't meant to be taken literally, was it? Like his own stories about his father, they were just elaborate fantasies and nothing more. In reality, Vince's father was gone long ago. In that fire or out in the world. Telling tales are just that, he realized. Wishes and dreams.

The church empty, he sat alone in the front pew, his face buried in his hands, stifling his unceasing sobs. *What now? What now?* He rocked back and forth, trying to calm himself, trying to convince himself that everything was going to be okay, even though he knew it wouldn't. He felt like disappearing. A vanishing act. He pulled his extremities close to his body, hoping to collapse into nothingness.

But as he did this, something crunched within his coat. Paper.

Knees to his chest, Vince froze, recalling what Andrew had given him just before the service. With a trembling hand, he dived into his pocket and pulled out the envelope. It weighed close to nothing. As he wiped his eyes on his sleeve, he noticed his name was scrawled across the envelope in handwriting very similar to his own. He waited a moment, then ripped it open.

Inside was a single page, folded neatly in three. Vince placed the torn envelope beside him on the pew and gently unfolded the letter. Blank. He turned it over. Here he found his message.

In the center of the page, scribbled in dark ink, there was nothing but two small words, "Umbia Rah."

Vince just stared at it. He didn't know what to think.

Umbia Rah? Umbia Rah? This was what his grandfather left him? This was his final wish, his final words? This was what Vince meant to him? A joke?

He crumpled the paper into a tight ball and wept even harder.

I believed, he cried. *I believed, I believed, I believed. I just wanted to see my dad again. I didn't want to be alone anymore. I just thought that if I wished hard enough, he'd come back to me. You found what you were looking for, why didn't I? Your tales were supposed to guide me, Grandpa. I needed them to guide me.*

After another five minutes, the paper still crumpled in his fist, Vince rose out of his seat and sluggishly ambled down the aisle and out of the empty church, nothing left behind but the echoes of his footsteps.

Outside, the light assaulted his eyes; the cold, his skin. Hand shielding the sun, heart slamming hard within his chest, he looked about the square. It was empty except for an idling car melting the snow upon which it sat. It was waiting there to take him back to the orphanage. Mrs. West stood outside it, M holding the door open.

"You won, Vincent," Mrs. West called out to him, her tone full of bitterness. "You got what you wanted. And I get to take you back in one piece. Mission accomplished. Time to go home now."

But this was not the home he was looking for. As the snow began to fall yet again, Vince gazed across the square and noticed another car pull up to the church, its doors opening at once.

Emerging from the vehicle were MJ and her parents. They rushed Vince, embracing him as one.

"We were so worried about you," Michele said, hugging him tight. "You didn't need to run. We would have seen that you got here."

"I'm so glad you're okay," MJ cried.

Mrs. West hustled over, brusquely interrupting the reunion. "What is going on here? Vincent, who are these people?"

Paul turned and glared at her. "Are you from the orphanage? Are you the one who wouldn't allow him to come say good-bye to his grandfather?"

"It's okay," Vince said in a weak voice. "It's over now. It's time for me to go back."

"Yes. Right this minute too," Mrs. West said. "He's been gone long enough."

"Mom!" MJ shouted, and Michele bent down in front of Vince, a hand on either shoulder.

"You don't have to go, Vince. Not if you don't want to. You—you can stay with us. You can come home with us right now. For good. We'll give you the best life we possibly can."

Vince, eyes filled with tears, didn't know what to say. It was what he'd wanted for so long.